A FOOL'S JOURNEY

A FOOL'S JOURNEY

JUDY PENZ SHELUK

W★RLDWIDE

TORONTO • NEW YORK • LONDON
AMSTERDAM • PARIS • SYDNEY • HAMBURG
STOCKHOLM • ATHENS • TOKYO • MILAN
MADRID • WARSAW • BUDAPEST • AUCKLAND

WORLDWIDE™

ISBN-13: 978-1-335-58912-5

A Fool's Journey

First published in 2019 by Superior Shores Press.
This edition published in 2022.

For questions and comments about the quality of this book, please contact us at CustomerService@Harlequin.com.

Harlequin Enterprises ULC
22 Adelaide St. West, 41st Floor
Toronto, Ontario M5H 4E3, Canada
www.ReaderService.com

Printed in U.S.A.

In memory of Nestor "Sam" Sametz

ONE

I STARED AT Leith Hampton, déjà vu enveloping me. It had been fifteen months since the first time I'd sat in the law office of Hampton & Associates. An unexpected connection had brought me back to learn of another inheritance. And once again, there were strings attached. What can I say? In my life, nothing is ever as simple as it seems on the surface.

This time, I'd inherited $365,000 from my great-grandmother, Olivia Marie Rosemount Osgoode. I'd met her for the first time a few weeks earlier while attempting to sift through the life and times of Anneliese Prei.

I liked Olivia, though I'm not sure I knew her long enough or well enough to claim the emotion I felt for her was love. It was hard to forgive someone who, along with her son, Corbin, and his wife, Yvette—I prefer not to think of them as my grandparents—had disowned my seventeen-year-old mother when she became pregnant with me. My father went to his grave despising anyone who bore the Osgoode name, and a lot of his bitterness had been passed on to me. I wondered what he'd think, now that I was the primary beneficiary of her last will and testament. I suspect his personal code of ethics might have led him to refuse the money. I'm not quite as principled.

"You said there was a condition," I said, and waited for one of Leith's well-practiced courtroom sighs.

He nodded, the theatrical sigh coming on the heels of the nod. "Olivia was fascinated by Past & Present Investigations. Fascinated and proud. She began to worry that a significant sum of money might decrease your need, and ultimately your desire, to find another case."

"So she found one for me?"

Leith nodded again. "I'll admit I wasn't completely on board with the idea, but Olivia was a stubborn woman, and no amount of discussion was going to dissuade her."

Stubborn I could understand. I'd inherited the same trait from my father, apparently burrowed deep into my DNA. I turned my attention back to Leith, who was still talking.

"Of course, you're free to decline, in which case your inheritance will revert to Corbin Osgoode."

I thought about my grandfather's fury at the reading of the will and suppressed a smile. "I wouldn't dream of declining, and not just because of the money. Tell me about the case."

THE CASE, Leith informed me, was the story of Brandon Colbeck, a twenty-year-old college student who left home in March 2000 to "find himself." He was never heard from again.

"The family is, understandably, still looking for answers," Leith said. "Did Brandon come into harm's way? Or did he simply decide to disappear and start a new life? His mother, a woman by the name of Lorna Colbeck-Westlake, admits, albeit reluctantly, that there had been some harsh words spoken by her husband, Michael Westlake, after Brandon dropped out of college. However, both insist that they never wanted Brandon to leave home. Rather, he'd been given some 'tough love' choices in the hope that it would provide motivation. It was a popular strategy, back in the day. It may still be, in some circles."

He slid a thin leather briefcase across the mahogany boardroom table. "The little that Olivia accumulated is in here. I will warn you, there's not much to go on. A couple of newspaper clippings, one that is dated four years ago, another quite recent. Barely enough to bother with, and yet…" Leith spread his arms out, palms upward, and shrugged.

I was getting used to going on not much. What I wasn't used to was having my great-grandmother getting involved, especially from the grave. "I'll admit I don't know a lot about our family, but the name Brandon Colbeck means nothing to me. Are we related?"

"Brandon's great-grandmother is Eleanor Colbeck, a friend of Olivia's at the Cedar County Retirement Residence. A year ago, Eleanor was diagnosed with Mild Cognitive Impairment or MCI. I'm told it's a condition that doesn't get better, only worse, and the decline can be rapid. Eleanor was close to her grandson and six weeks ago, she received a telephone call from a man claiming to be Brandon Colbeck. He said he missed her and wanted to come home, but didn't have the funds available to travel."

"Let me guess, he asked her for money."

"Not in so many words, though he did mention a friend in a similar situation whose father had used a wire service like Western Union. The family reported the call to the police, who determined it was a scam, one of many that targets the elderly. Nonetheless, Eleanor remains convinced that the call came from her grand-son, based on the fact that he'd called her Nana Ellie."

Eleanor Colbeck. Now *that* name rang a bell, though I wasn't sure why. "The name sounds familiar."

"Eleanor contributed to several community-based charitable initiatives, long before you moved to Market-ville. Cedar County Retirement is far from inexpensive and Eleanor has been living there for the past decade. As her condition worsens, medical expenses increase."

"Where I know her name from probably isn't im-portant," I said, knowing that I'd keep digging until I remembered or discovered the truth. I tapped my fin-gers against the briefcase. "You say there's not much in here. Am I expected to find out where Brandon went and what happened to him? Or am I to determine the call was a fake? Does the family approve of my getting involved? What's the bottom line?"

Leith leaned back and smiled for the first time. "Olivia may have been old, but when it came to legali-ties, she was on top of her game. The family is willing to assist you in whatever way possible. I have signed affi-davits from Lorna Colbeck-Westlake, her husband, Mi-chael Westlake, Brandon's stepsister, Jeanine Westlake, as well as Eleanor Colbeck, granting Past & Present In-vestigations carte blanche to do whatever is necessary to find Brandon. They are also willing to sit down with you at any time, though from what I gather, they know little, if anything, beyond what's already been reported."

"What about written permission to post relevant ma-terial on the Past & Present website or on social media sites like Facebook and Instagram?"

"Inside the briefcase you'll find a notarized doc-ument to cover exactly that concern, signed by each member of the family. As for the bottom line, in order to inherit you must make a reasonable investigative effort over the next three months. After that, you're free to walk away without further obligation."

Three months. I wanted to solve it in two.

TWO

I left Hampton & Associates with a briefcase firmly tucked under my arm. I hustled my way down Bay Street to Union Station, hoping to catch the noon GO train leaving for Marketville. I had planned to spend a few hours in Toronto, checking out the Royal Ontario Museum and the tony shops of Yorkville before grabbing dinner at one of the many restaurants on the way to the GO. Now all I could think about was getting home. I needed to develop a plan.

I managed to reach Union with three minutes to spare and sprinted up the stairs to Platform Twelve, breathless by the time I reached the top tiered "Quiet Zone" of the train, and grateful for the silence it afforded. I found an empty seat, sat down, and got to work. The trip to Marketville would take just over an hour, and I didn't intend to waste a minute of it.

Leith had warned me that there wasn't much to go on and there wasn't. The manila folder, neatly labeled "BRANDON COLBECK," contained two carefully clipped articles from the *Marketville Post*, and some handwritten notes by Olivia Osgoode. Still, I couldn't help but smile at the thought of my great-grandmother investigating a cold case at the age of ninety-one. Maybe we shared more than stubbornness in our DNA.

I unfolded the first clipping, smoothing out the creases. It was dated Thursday, March 19, 2015.

"Brandon Colbeck Still Missing 15 Years after Disappearance" the headline stated. A color photograph of a young man in his late teens or early twenties took up a quarter of the page. He appeared to be standing on a dock, ripples of blue water behind him, though the photo had been cropped close to focus on Brandon's smiling face. It was a nice face, free of guile, with full lips, warm brown eyes, and a well-proportioned nose. His hair was blowing in the breeze, wavy copper with glints of gold. He looked happy. I set about reading the story for the first time, knowing it would have piqued my interest had I lived in Marketville at the time it was published. The byline, "Jenny Lynn Simcoe, with files from G.G. Pietrangelo," piqued my curiosity all the more. I'd met Gloria Grace during my investigation into my mother's disappearance. She'd left the *Marketville Post* a dozen years ago to start her own photographic studio. How much did she remember about this cold case? I made a mental note to find out and turned my attention back to the article.

The family of Brandon Colbeck is still hoping to be reunited with him nearly fifteen years after his disappearance. Brandon was twenty on March 9, 2000 when he left a note for his parents that said he was leaving home. "I was completely blindsided," said Lorna Colbeck-Westlake, Brandon's mother. "Brandon borrowed my car that morning to go job hunting. He dropped me off at my office and was upbeat about the prospect of finding work."

When Brandon didn't pick up his mother at the prearranged time, a co-worker drove her home.

"I remember being embarrassed and more than a little annoyed," said Lorna. "At the time I just assumed it was Brandon being unreliable."

Annoyance turned to shock when Lorna found a note from Brandon on the kitchen counter. "He wrote he was going to 'find himself,' and told us where he'd left the car. I ran to his bedroom," said his mother. "He'd taken his laptop, toiletries, and most of his clothes, but no identification, not even his health card or driver's license. I called Michael in a panic."

Michael Westlake is Lorna's husband and Brandon's stepfather. The couple found Lorna's unlocked vehicle in the parking lot of a neighborhood strip mall. The keys were underneath the driver's floor mat. There was no trace of Brandon.

Although it's been fifteen years, the family has not given up hope. "We believe Brandon wanted a fresh start, which is why he didn't take his ID," said Westlake, reiterating a statement from an earlier interview. "He'd dropped out of college in his second year, moved back home without a plan, and didn't seem motivated to find gainful employment."

"There was tension in the house," admitted Jeanine Westlake, Brandon's stepsister, who was twelve at the time of his disappearance. "My dad was a firm believer in tough love, and that only intensified after my brother quit school. Brandon didn't respond well to that approach."

Brandon Colbeck's profile has now been added to the Ontario Registry of Missing and Unidentified Adults, along with two age-progressed sketches supplied by the Cedar County Police Department's Forensic Identification Unit. His grandmother, Eleanor Colbeck, best known for her widespread community philanthropy, was recently interviewed at her retirement residence in Marketville. She believes the pictures are an accurate representation of what Brandon may now look like at age thirty-five.

"I have never stopped believing that my grandson is alive and well," said Eleanor, her eyes glistening with tears. "I'm waiting for the day when the telephone rings and Brandon says, 'Nana Ellie, I've missed you. I'm ready to come home.'"

Nana Ellie. There it was for any scammer to read. The term of endearment that had convinced Eleanor Colbeck that her grandson was still alive. Add the implication of Eleanor's advanced age and wealth, and I could understand why the police had dismissed the telephone call as a scam.

But there were questions the article didn't answer, and Olivia had written them down. I smiled. They were the same questions I would have asked.

- Who is Brandon's biological father? Where is he now? Did he play any part in Brandon's upbringing?
- How old was Brandon when Mike and Lorna met and got married?
- Who were Brandon's friends?
- How close were Brandon and Jeanine? Did he confide in his sister about his plans to leave?
- Why did Brandon drop out of college?

I wondered if Eleanor Colbeck had the answer to any of those questions, or if they were locked inside her mind, no longer accessible. I reread the article, thought for a moment and then added one final point.

- Find Michael Westlake's earlier interview (and G.G. Pietrangelo)

I moved on to the second clipping. It was dated 2018, nearly three years to the day after the first, the headline announcing, "Phone Call Scammers Target Grandparents." Once again the byline was that of Jenny Lynn Simcoe, this time without a nod to G.G. Pietrangelo.

There have been numerous reports of unsuspecting seniors receiving phone calls from callers claiming to be a grandchild in need of money. Referred to by police as the 'grandparent scam,' these calls play directly on the emotions of the elderly. For example, a scammer will call an older person and pretend to be their grandchild. In one scenario, the caller will ask if they know who is calling. When the grandparent guesses the name of one of their grandchildren, the scammer pretends to be that grandchild, then tells the grandparent that they are in a financial bind. Typically, they will also ask the grandparent not to tell anyone else about their situation because they are ashamed or embarrassed.

In another scenario, the caller knows the name of the grandchild along with one or two key facts, information culled from social media posts or newspaper articles, and assumes their identity.

While not all scams targeting seniors involve grandchildren, they inevitably include requests for money, usually by Western Union wire transfer. "There are as many variations of the grandparent scam as there are grandparents," said Detective Aaron Beecham, who heads the Cedar County Police Department's recently formed Fraud Investigation unit. "If you have a senior in your life, please take the time to educate them about scams targeting the elderly."

For a list of the latest scams, visit the Cedar County Police Department's website and click on the Fraud tab. To file a report, call 555-835-5763, ext. 35.

Detective Aaron Beecham. That name also sounded vaguely familiar, but I couldn't place it, not that it mattered. It angered me to think there were unscrupulous people whose sole purpose in life was to swindle seniors.

What about the real Brandon Colbeck? Was he long dead and buried in an unknown grave? Or was he still alive, living somewhere under a different name, perhaps with kids of his own? If so, what sort of person left his family in limbo for nearly twenty years, and why?

I was still mulling things over when the train pulled into the Marketville station.

THREE

I CALLED CHANTELLE as soon as I got home, anxious to get her on the case. "Do you have any plans for dinner?"

She laughed. "I wish. Sadly, Prince Charming has yet to come my way. Not even a frog, which at this point, I might actually consider. Then I think about Lance the Loser and I come back to my senses."

Lance was Chantelle's ex-husband, and I knew that despite her cavalier attitude about him she was still hurting, especially since he'd left her for an adolescent—her words, not mine, though she wasn't far off the mark. "You'll meet the right guy when the time is right," I said.

"I'm not holding my breath. How did your meeting go with Leith Hampton?"

"It was…interesting. Olivia left me some money in her will. More than some, actually. Enough to pay off my mortgage."

"Wow, well done, you. I assume Corbin was less than impressed."

"You could say that. He accused me of undue influence. I gather he was the sole beneficiary until a few months ago. Leith assured him that Olivia had revised her will long before I reentered her life."

"She knew about you, even though you didn't know about her? I expect that infuriated him all the more."

"He was livid," I said, thinking back to the scene in

Leith's office, the way my grandfather had spat out the words that would hurt me forever, my grandmother sitting stone-faced and silent beside him. *You were a mistake, Calamity. No amount of money will ever change that.*

"He threatened to contest the will. Leith doesn't believe Corbin stands a chance, since he also inherited a sizable sum, but who knows? I'm not counting on the money until probate is granted, which, as I understand it, can take about a year. Of course, if Corbin does contest the will, the timeline will almost certainly be prolonged. In the meantime, there is a slight catch."

"What sort of catch?"

"In order to inherit, Past & Present has to attempt to solve a cold case."

"Attempt, meaning we don't have to solve it, we just have to try?"

"According to Leith, it's the effort during the next three months that counts, not the end result." I bit my lip. "The thing is, Chantelle, I'm not sure I could accept the money if we didn't find out the truth."

"Then we'll have to find out the truth, won't we?"

"Exactly. Can you come over tonight? I can fill you in on the details over pizza and wine."

"I thought you'd never ask."

CURIOSITY GOT THE better of me and I decided to check out the online Ontario Registry of Missing and Unidentified Adults while I waited for Chantelle. The web page was attractive and easy to navigate, with three blocks at the top of the home page: *Search Unidentified Adults, Search Missing Adults*, and *Publications*. Beneath these were the dated bullet points: *Recent News* and *Updates*.

I'm not sure why I started by clicking on Unidentified Adults, since I was looking for a missing adult, but that's what I did. I was taken to a page where I could enter a number of parameters: Gender, Race, Date of Discovery, Location of Discovery, Province of Discovery, Hair Color, Eye Color, Age (Low) and (High), and Weight (Low) and (High) and Keywords. I left all fields blank and hit Submit, surprised and saddened to find eight pages with twenty-five cases per page, most with the caption "no image available." Two hundred unidentified men and women, their bodies, or in most cases, their remains, discovered as far back as the 1960s, and no one had come forward to claim them. Did they not have families, or in the absence of family, at least someone who cared? Or was there an assumption that the person had left voluntarily and didn't want to be found? Whatever the situation, it was heartbreaking to think that their death didn't matter.

I spent the next three hours reading each entry, looking for signs of Brandon in the case files, all the while fully aware that the police and members of Brandon's family would have scoured the records many times over. I'm not sure if I was actually expecting to find something they missed—*Calamity Barnstable solves the case in a matter of hours,* the headlines screamed—but the only results of my search were a stiff neck, a sore back, and a pervading feeling of doom and gloom.

I got up, stretched, made a cup of cinnamon rooibos tea, and settled back to the task at hand, this time clicking on the Missing Adults page. The news here was even bleaker, with eighteen pages of twenty-five missing adults in the database, one going as far back as 1935. *Four hundred and fifty missing adults,* I thought, doing the mental math. I entered Brandon Colbeck's name in the appropriate Search fields, and was directed to the data about his case.

SUMMARY
Date of Disappearance: March 9, 2000
Location of Disappearance: Marketville, Ontario
Age at Disappearance: 20 years
Height (estimate): 5'9"
Weight (estimate): 150 lbs.
Hair: reddish brown, wavy
Eye Color: Dark brown
Gender: Male
Race: Caucasian
Aliases: None known

DETAILS
Dental Information: Teeth-described as good
Medical Information: Unknown
Clothing/Jewelry: Sheepskin-lined jean jacket
Other Personal Items: Dell Laptop Computer
Notable Identifiers: Upper left arm: A black outline of the bottom quarter of the sun emanating multiple rays, shining on the face of a wavy-haired boy. At the time of Brandon's disappearance, this tattoo was recent. It may since have been colorized or enlarged.
Additional Information: After failing during his second year at Cedar County College in Lakeside, Brandon returned to live with his parents in Marketville in late January. He had been studying Computer Science.

Until a few months before his disappearance, Brandon had been a straight-A student, described as having an inquisitive mind and quick wit. His behavior started to change in his second year at Cedar County College, although the family is unsure of the reason. As his grades dropped, he began to withdraw from family and friends until there was virtually no contact.

The rest of the entry recapped what had been in the news articles, noting he had not tried to contact family or friends.

There were two Source Links, the first leading to the *Marketville Post* article dated March 19, 2015. There were no prior newspaper reports, not that I was surprised. The "earlier interview" mentioned would almost certainly have been within a few months of Brandon's disappearance, predating online coverage. I hoped Gloria Grace still had her files, and that she'd be willing to share what she knew with us.

The second link led to a "Find Brandon Colbeck" Facebook page listing Jeanine Westlake as the administrator. She'd posted the same photo and sketches as those on the Ontario Registry for Missing and Unidentified Adults website, but despite multiple shares and eighty-nine friends, there was nothing in the way of helpful comments, and all activity ground to a halt in early 2016. I made a note: *why 2016?* Too many dead ends?

Under Related Photos, there were four thumbnails that could be enlarged to full size by clicking on each individual photo. The top photo was the now familiar *Marketville Post* photograph of Brandon. Beneath it there were two full-page, age-progressed artist sketches, one depicting Brandon with short hair, parted on the right, the other with shoulder-length hair, parted in the center, and a slightly scruffy beard, lips closed, with a hint of a smile. He had a narrow face with high cheekbones and a perfectly proportioned nose. He was a good-looking man, even scruffed up. Both sketches were signed and dated March 1, 2015. How much more would he have aged in another four years? Would the reddish-brown hair now be tinged with gray?

The fourth thumbnail was a rough sketch of the tattoo. It looked incomplete, a black outline of something more to come, and yet there was something oddly familiar about it. I stared at it for several minutes, enlarging it on my screen, zoning in and out, frustrated that nothing came to me. I knew I'd seen this somewhere.

I went back to the images, saving each one to a "Brandon Colbeck" folder on my computer, then printed all three sketches. One thing I've learned from my past investigations is that being organized makes everything easier going forward.

I just wished I could shake the feeling that nothing else about this case was going to be easy.

FOUR

CHANTELLE ARRIVED A little after five, her tablet in one hand, a bottle of white wine in the other. I handed her the manila folder in exchange for the wine, and updated her on everything Leith had told me.

"The main article raises more questions than it answers," I said. "I jotted down what came to me and would like you to do the same."

Chantelle nodded, sat down at the long mission oak dining room table that doubled as a desk, and began reading.

"With files from G.G. Pietrangelo," she said, looking up.

"Gloria Grace is definitely on my to-contact list."

She nodded again, turning her attention back to the article. I ordered the pizza—extra sauce with hot peppers—poured us each a glass of wine, forced myself not to pace, and dabbed on some cocoa butter lip balm. The lip balm helped a little. The wine helped a little more.

"There's a fair bit to read between the lines, isn't there?" Chantelle said, after she'd finished.

"Does the name Detective Aaron Beecham mean anything to you?"

Chantelle wrinkled her brow in concentration, then shook her head. "No, should it?"

"Probably not." I handed her the two age-progressed

sketches of Brandon Colbeck. "These are on the Ontario Registry of Missing and Unidentified Adults mentioned in the newspaper article."

"Interesting," Chantelle said, her fingers tracing the outline of Brandon's jawline. "In the one with the short hair, he looks like any number of clean-cut, thirty-something men. The one with the long hair and slightly scruffy beard lends him an appearance of someone who's been living on the street."

"Really? I didn't interpret it that way, I just thought of a free spirit, maybe someone who worked in a field where being clean-cut isn't an expectation. But, yeah, you could be right."

Chantelle bit her lip. "You know, as detailed as these sketches are, they don't look like the young man in the photograph. At least, not to me."

"I thought that too, at first, but these are black-and-white sketches versus a color photograph and the sketches were done fifteen years *after* he disappeared. People change a lot between twenty and thirty-five. I know I did. Plus, according to the newspaper, Eleanor Colbeck believes these are accurate representations of what Brandon might look like now. Maybe she saw a resemblance between this older version of Brandon and his mother or biological father. Even the stepsister, Jeanine, could bear a likeness from the mother's side. I've learned that age-progression is a combination of science and art, similar to facial reconstruction. Not an exact likeness, but someone who knows the person should see enough of a resemblance to recognize them."

"Valid points," Chantelle conceded. "What else have you got?"

I handed her the rough sketch of the tattoo. "According to the Registry, this tattoo is on his left upper arm. I know it's incomplete, but does it remind you of anything? I keep thinking I've seen this before."

"Hmmm. Not really. But I'm not an expert on tattoos."

"Probably just my imagination then," I said, but I knew it would niggle.

"We could always take this to a tattoo parlor and see what they have to say."

It was a good idea, one I'd add to my growing to-do list. "There's one more thing, a journal that belonged to Olivia. I thumbed through it before you got here. Her handwriting isn't easy to decipher, and it's not much more than a list of questions, versus answers. I'm not sure whether that's because she ran out of time, or because Eleanor's cognitive issues had advanced to the point where her memories were no longer reliable. Overall, it's not much help."

"It's a starting point." Chantelle logged into her tablet and began typing. That's one of the differences between us. I tend to be more of a pen and paper thinker. The other difference is that even with her blonde hair tied in a ponytail and her face devoid of makeup, Chantelle was drop-dead gorgeous, with charcoal gray eyes that seemed to smolder and a killer body developed from years of working as a personal trainer and fitness class instructor. I'm not unattractive—black-rimmed hazel eyes being my best feature, though I could live without my unruly chestnut curls—and as a runner I'm in decent physical shape, but I'll never be in her league. Then again, despite Chantelle's obvious attempts at flirtation, I'd been the one Royce Ashford had asked out.

The thought of Royce momentarily distracted me.

We'd left things in limbo, neither one of us quite sure where our relationship was headed, or if we even wanted a relationship. I pushed him out of my mind and gave Chantelle my undivided attention.

"Now that you've seen everything I have, does anything stand out? Beyond the files from G.G. Pietrangelo?"

"My gut feeling is that Michael Westlake and Brandon Colbeck were at loggerheads, and it didn't start with Brandon dropping out of college. The whole 'tough love' business that Jeanine alludes to, for example."

"What else?"

"I'd want to know who Brandon's biological father is, what role he might have played in his son's upbringing, if he played one at all. His name is noticeably absent from the report. I also wonder when Michael Westlake entered Brandon's life."

"Great minds think alike. What are your thoughts about Jeanine? She'd be thirty-one now, if my math is correct, eight years younger than Brandon. I'm an only child, completely out of my element on this one. You, on the other hand, had five siblings. Would you have confided to one of them if you were going to leave? Would any one or all of them have confided in you?"

"I honestly don't know," Chantelle said. "It would depend on how much we wanted to leave, and why. I come from a close family, and I don't think that's just because we were related by blood. My parents tried to treat us all equally, albeit differently based on our individual personality traits. Was that the case in the Colbeck-Westlake household? It's something we need to find out, though whether anyone will tell us the complete truth remains to be seen. I definitely think Jeanine knows more than was reported in the article."

"My thoughts exactly. Lorna may also be hiding something. She claimed to be blindsided by Brandon's disappearance, but we only have her word for that. Maybe she's trying to protect her husband. Or Jeanine? From what or who is the question."

"We need to interview Lorna, Michael, Jeanine, and Eleanor, but we may only get one kick at the can," Chantelle said, "and that's if they agree to see us."

"The family has signed affidavits giving Past & Present carte blanche, and Leith assured me that they are willing to cooperate in any way. The questions we ask will be as important as the answers we hope to get. We'll have to do some prep work before approaching anyone."

"Agreed. I'm also curious about Brandon's friends, before, during, and after college. Hopefully someone in the family will be able to provide that information."

Who were Brandon's friends? "There's a 'Find Brandon Colbeck Facebook' page on the Registry, with Jeanine Westlake as administrator. It's been inactive since 2016, but the group has eighty-nine friends." I shuddered at the thought of tracing all eighty-nine, sure that both Jeanine and the police would have already done that, but knew it might have to be done. "I'm not sure how easy any of this is going to be."

"If it was easy, the police would have solved the case long ago," Chantelle said with a smile. "Let's consider ways the team can help us."

In addition to Chantelle and me, the Past & Present "team" consisted of Shirley Harrington, a retired research librarian, Misty Rivers, a self-proclaimed psychic who posted tarot messages on our website and social media channels—surprisingly well-received despite my initial skepticism—and, on an "as needed" basis whenever antiques and collectibles came into the mix, Arabella Carpenter. Shirley's skillset in digging through newspaper archives would definitely come into play, but I couldn't imagine how Arabella or Misty would be of assistance in this particular case. Arabella wouldn't expect to be consulted, but Misty would, and she'd definitely want to be involved, though how tarot would figure in was anyone's guess.

Chantelle read my mind. "We can skip Arabella for this one, but we should hold a team meeting with Shirley and Misty."

"Agreed. When are you available?"

"My shift at the gym doesn't start until three o'clock Monday afternoon, so Monday morning would work for me."

"I'll try to set something up tomorrow."

Chantelle was already tapping away on her phone. "Just sent them both a text. Now where's that pizza delivery guy?"

The doorbell rang in that moment. "He must have heard you," I said, grinning. "Get the napkins and plates. I'll get the pizza. First we eat, then we brainstorm."

FIVE

CHANTELLE CHECKED HER phone as soon as we'd finished eating. "Good news. Both Shirley and Misty texted back they're good for nine o'clock Monday morning. We should make photocopies of the newspaper clippings and the age-progressed sketches of Brandon. That way each of us will have the same information going forward."

It was a good idea, though copying the oversized newspaper articles on our compact black-and-white printer would pose a challenge. Plus, the photo of Brandon would serve us better if it were reproduced in color. "I'll go to the Copy Center tomorrow."

"Sounds like a plan. Now, enough shop talk for a Saturday night. Tell me what's happening with you and Royce."

"I wish I knew. There's definitely a physical attraction beyond our friendship." I blushed, remembering our one evening together. Only a week ago, and yet it seemed like forever since I'd seen him last. "We had plans for today, which I had to cancel because of the meeting with Leith. To be honest, I was relieved, and I got the impression that Royce was, too."

"What sort of plans?"

"Royce's sister Porsche is in a play in Muskoka. *Pygmalion*. She's Eliza Doolittle."

"Sounds like fun. Why were you relieved?"

"His mom, dad, and aunt were going to be there. There's no love lost between us and I don't think that will change. There's too much history there with my mother and neither side is willing to forgive and forget."

"Could be a problem if you wanted to get serious, but it's not like you'd be marrying his family, and Porsche is good people."

I laughed. "Who said anything about getting married? We haven't even spent a weekend together."

Chantelle grinned. "Ah, but the way you're blushing tells me that you've spent a night together."

"I didn't say that."

"You didn't have to. Look, why not just go with the flow for a while, see where it takes you?"

"We did discuss spending a couple of days in Niagara Falls."

"There you go. Start with that."

"Maybe once this case is done."

Chantelle studied me through narrowed eyes. "There's more, isn't there? Beyond the issues with his family?"

"I don't know. It's ridiculous, actually. Royce is a great guy. On paper he ticks every box. But…maybe he's too nice. I've gotten used to two-timing triathletes and getting dumped on Valentine's Day."

"I get it, you've been hurt before, and more than once. You don't want to risk getting hurt again. I'm in the same leaky boat. The thing is, we're both going to have to start paddling again."

I knew Chantelle was right, but it was more than that. I should have been filled with longing to see Royce again, or at least anxious to call him and find out how Porsche's play went. And yet I lacked the desire to do either. The only thing I could think about was finding out what happened to Brandon Colbeck.

It didn't bode well for a future with Royce. I just hoped this case was worth it.

I MET MY Sunday running group at the gym at eight a.m. sharp, logged in a hard-fought ten miles on the town's paved trail system, grabbed a quick shower and change of clothes, and headed to the local coffee shop for my post-run reward: a large coffee with real cream, toasted sesame seed bagel with peanut butter, and a smattering of run club chatter as the group traded quips and tips about sore muscles and what to do about them. The thought of sleeping in on a Sunday never occurred to any of us, regardless of weather. "We can sleep when we're dead," was our motto, and thinking of that reminded me of Brandon. Was he dead, or only sleeping?

Brandon firmly in mind, my next stop was the Copy Center, where I spent the next thirty minutes making copies for the team. I wound my way home, baked carrot date muffins for the next morning, gave the house a thorough cleaning, right down to dusting the baseboards and purging my clothes closet of anything I hadn't worn in the past twelve months.

What can I say? My best thinking is done when I'm not actively trying to think.

Except this time it didn't work, though I did have baked goods and a nice tidy house and clothes closet to show for my efforts. I checked my phone and saw two missed calls, both from Royce. I knew I should call him back.

I didn't. Instead I turned on the TV, flicked until I found a marathon of *Gilmore Girls* reruns, and reread the newspaper clipping of Brandon's disappearance, looking for any clue I might have missed. Convinced I hadn't missed a thing, I googled "tattoo with a boy's head and sunshine." At some point I must have fallen asleep, because the next thing I knew, my neck was stiff and my back ached.

It was also too late to call Royce.

SIX

THE PAST & PRESENT team of Chantelle Marchand, Misty Rivers, and Shirley Harrington joined me at nine o'clock Monday morning, taking seats around my long mission oak table that doubled as a desk, printer stand, conference center, and anything else requiring a large flat surface. I served coffee and tea, along with the carrot date muffins, and handed each of them a file folder containing the two newspaper articles, a printout of Brandon Colbeck's Registry of Missing and Unidentified Adults case page, the age-progressed sketches of Brandon and his tattoo, as well as a notepad and pen.

"This is Past & Present's latest case," I began. "I'm going to suggest that you read the articles first, then study the photos. Please make note of anything or anyone that might strike a chord with you. No detail is too small, so don't be shy to share or offer suggestions. We might not know what you know, even if you think it's common knowledge."

"What about questions?" Shirley asked. "Do we hold off on those, or ask anything that pops into our mind?"

"Chantelle and I have already compiled a list of questions, but you might put forward something we haven't considered. In other words, ask away, and if we can't answer it, we'll add it to our list."

I tried not to hover while the group went to work. I'd

read the clippings and Registry page so many times I could probably recite them verbatim, had studied the sketches until they were permanently imprinted on my brain.

Chantelle finished first, which made sense since she'd examined everything the day before. She waited quietly next to me, checking her phone and texting someone—Lance?—while Shirley and Misty dutifully read, reviewed, and made notes. By the time they both looked up, ready to discuss, they'd spent the better part of an hour scrutinizing the documents. For a moment we all just sat there, looking at one another. I decided to start with a simple question, albeit one that hadn't been on my list.

"The name Eleanor Colbeck seems familiar to me, but I can't put a finger on it. Leith Hampton said she was once known for supporting local charitable initiatives, but that ended a decade ago when she moved into the Cedar County Retirement Residence. I've surfed the net for her name and come up empty, which isn't unusual. A lot of octogenarians aren't active on social media."

"Hey, I almost resemble that remark," Shirley said, her reading glasses perched on the top of her head, and we all grinned. Shirley might be gray-haired and newly retired, but she was a young and vibrant sixty-five, and having spent years as a research librarian, she was as adept at finding her way around the internet as the rest of us. Maybe more so.

"All kidding aside," Shirley was saying, "I believe I know why the name Eleanor Colbeck sounds familiar to you, Callie. She went on to support the food bank initiative that your mother started before she…" She blushed.

"There was a small snippet in the *Marketville Post* at the time. It's in the paperwork I gave you, and it stuck with me because Eleanor also served on the Library Board in the 1980s, and I'd met her a handful of times."

Any talk of my mother made me want to put my hands over my ears and sing, *"la, la, la, la, la, I'm not listening,"* but I had to at least pretend to be an adult. Besides, everyone here in this room knew that the food bank initiative Shirley was referring to was in 1985, when my mother was still married to my father, when they were still supposed to be in love. For all her faults, my mother had some redeeming qualities; her charitable initiatives had proven that. And while the last thing I wanted to do was revisit anything that had to do with my investigation into her disappearance, it did provide another "in" with Eleanor beyond my connection to Olivia and her request—no, make that *demand*—that I search for Eleanor's grandson, Brandon.

"That's probably it, but I'll double check to be certain," I said, and quickly changed the subject. "Maybe one of you can help me with something else that's been bothering me. Brandon's tattoo. It reminds me of something. I tried googling 'tattoo with a boy's head and sunshine' but nothing came close."

Nothing came close was an understatement. Despite scrolling through online images until I'd mercifully fallen asleep, the only thing I'd come up with were tattoos with the words, "You are my sunshine," and dozens of suns in various shapes and sizes, and occasionally, with a boy's face inside them.

"That's because it's not finished yet," Misty said, her face flushed with excitement. "It's The Fool."

"Who's the fool?" Shirley asked.

"Not who, what," Misty said. "The Fool is number zero in tarot, and the first card in the Major Arcana." She riffled through her rainbow-hued handbag and pulled out a deck. "I never leave home without them. You can never be sure when a reading will be needed."

The moment Misty had said "The Fool" I knew Brandon's tattoo had been derived from the tarot card of the same name. Despite my skepticism of all things remotely occult, I should have connected the dots earlier. I glanced at Chantelle and could tell by the expression on her face that she was thinking the same thing. How had we both missed it, especially since Misty had updated the Past & Present website with images of every Major and Minor Arcana card in tarot? Her "Misty's Messages" had resonated enough to help Past & Present solve its first case. Despite my reluctance to believe in tarot, I felt the first stirrings of hope. This might well be our first real clue. And as unlikely as it seemed, Misty was the one to unveil it.

Misty laid the card on the table in front of us. "The design on the tattoo is from the Rider-Waite deck, which, as you know, is the one I use. The Fool is even on the front of the box. That's why it probably looked so familiar to you, Callie. Had it been one of the lesser known cards in the Minor Arcana, it may not have triggered any memory at all."

The Fool depicted a young man standing on the edge of a mountain cliff, his face tilted with reverence toward the sun. There was a small white dog by his right foot, leaping up with apparent joy. Perched atop the boy's wavy golden hair was a small cap with a scarlet feather. He wore a flowered tunic in jewel-toned colors of yellow, blue, green, and red over a white long-sleeved shirt, and bright yellow calf-length boots. In his right hand he held a single white rose, in his left, placed across his left shoulder, a long stick with a small brown bag tied to the end of it. The entire image evoked a mix of innocence, joy, and youthful exuberance.

"There's so much symbolism in this card," Misty said, her voice filled with admiration. "I like to think that the purple feather stands for freedom, the white rose for purity, and the dog for adventure. Note the bag at the end of his stick he's carrying, like an old-time hobo. Some believe the bag contains all his worldly possessions, others his memories of past lives. I like to think it's filled with life experiences to date, ready to be expanded as he travels. A.E. Waite, the designer of the card, wrote that the boy 'is a prince of the other world on his travels through this one.'"

"He's very close to the edge of the cliff," Shirley said. "Does that have any meaning?"

Misty beamed. "A very good question. We are left to wonder if the boy will fall off the cliff, though he looks unconcerned, ready for every adventure as he embraces the beauty of his surroundings. Perhaps he believes his tunic will open like a parachute and save him from a rapid descent. Whatever you might derive from this card, it's widely accepted that The Fool represents new beginnings, and the number zero a chance to start over. You probably don't know Eden Gray, but she wrote widely about the tarot and their use in fortune telling, and coined the term 'Fool's Journey' in her book, *A Complete Guide to the Tarot*. Many advocates of tarot, including myself, believe that The Fool travels through each card in the Major Arcana."

"It definitely fits with a young man going off into the world to find himself," Chantelle said. "I wonder why the Registry didn't mention that it was The Fool? Surely the police would have figured it out."

"Maybe they did, but they hold back some details to authenticate tips," I said, with the assurance of someone who had binge-watched the first four seasons of *Bosch*.

Chantelle nodded. "That makes sense. I guess the bigger question is what we do with this information, now that we have it."

"Do we have permission to recreate this on our website?" Misty asked.

I nodded.

"In that case, I'd be happy to create a post for the website and Facebook page."

"I'm not sure how that will reach Brandon Colbeck," Chantelle said, "but it's worth a try."

"It doesn't have to reach Brandon," I said. "All it has to do is resonate with someone who's seen that tattoo on a man that resembles one of the sketches."

"Exactly," Misty said. "First, I'll set up a separate 'Find Brandon Colbeck' page and add the sketches and photograph of Brandon. I'll also include a photo and description of The Fool. Then I'll share the link on our Facebook page and Twitter, and post pix on Instagram and Pinterest."

I stared at Misty, open-mouthed. A day ago I couldn't imagine what help Misty would be. Now she was all but leading the investigation.

"What can I do?" Shirley asked.

"I thought you'd never ask. In the 2015 newspaper article, there's reference to an earlier interview. I suspect it's in the *Marketville Post*, but it's not in their online archives, which don't start until 2010. While it's almost certainly written by G.G. Pietrangelo, who I hope to interview, it will be better if I know what the article says before I meet with her. Other papers may have picked up Brandon's story as well, and not just in our local area. Do what you do, and get digging. And by that I mean, don't just dig into Brandon. I need you to find out anything and everything you can about Eleanor Colbeck, Lorna Colbeck-Westlake, Michael Westlake, and Jeanine Westlake. If they were mentioned attending a store opening, we need to know about it."

Shirley clapped her hands, the wide grin on her face threatening to split it apart. "I'll start first thing tomorrow."

"Where do I fit in?" Chantelle asked, her face crestfallen.

"You're going to put your genealogy skills to good use and see if anyone has started a Colbeck family tree. Call Lorna and see if she'll reveal the name of Brandon's biological father, along with any other known relatives. Tell her that Brandon may well have done the same thing in an effort to 'find himself' and that he may have contacted a family member, even if he did so surreptitiously."

"I'm on it," Chantelle said, "but what about the Westlake side of things? I'm not sure it's necessary, given that Michael Westlake isn't a blood relative of Brandon's, but I'm willing to check the records you think there's an angle there."

I thought about it for a moment. "Can you just do a search on Michael? That should be sufficient."

"I can do that." Chantelle's gray eyes sparkled. "We

can do this, Callie. We can find out what happened to Brandon Colbeck."

I just hoped Chantelle was right. Because even though I'd given everyone else an assignment, I still wasn't sure what I was going to do. I just knew I needed to do something.

SEVEN

AFTER A NIGHT of tossing, turning, and endless deliberation, I decided my first step would be to meet with Eleanor Colbeck. I flipped through the newspaper clippings I'd accumulated during the investigation into my mother's disappearance, scanning them until I came up with a small column dated Thursday, May 15, 1986 in the *Marketville Post*, byline G.G. Pietrangelo.

Town Philanthropist Feeds Food Bank

Well-known local philanthropist Eleanor Colbeck has put her money where the town's mouth is with a $10,000 donation to purchase food for the Marketville Food Bank. The food bank, started by Marketville resident Abigail Barnstable last summer, has been struggling since Ms. Barnstable's unexplained disappearance earlier this year. Volunteers and donations of food and cash are desperately needed.

The address, phone number, and hours were listed at the end of the article.

I pulled out the contact list provided by Leith, rang the Cedar County Retirement Residence, and cringed when I heard the voice that answered. Without question, it was the icy platinum blonde gatekeeper who'd made every effort to keep me from seeing my great-grand-mother. I thought about affecting an accent of some sort, but they were bound to have caller ID.

"Room 312, East Wing, please," I said without pre-amble.

"Mrs. Colbeck is not to be disturbed," Platinum Blonde said, her tone acerbic.

Says who, I wanted to ask, but bit my tongue. Nothing would be gained by antagonizing the woman. "It's rather important, I'm afraid. I have her, and her family's, permission to visit." Not entirely true, but not a complete falsehood. I *was* promised carte blanche, and I did have the signed affidavits.

There was a disdainful sniff at the other end of the line and then a reluctant, "Very well. She's resting now, but she'll be up and about shortly and would likely enjoy a companion at her midday meal. We haven't reassigned seating since…of course we plan to, it just hasn't… Mrs. Colbeck will be in the dining room at one o'clock, table seven. I suggest you arrive five minutes early so you can pay for your lunch. The charge for guests is ten dollars. Today's special is macaroni and cheese with tea or coffee, and rice pudding for dessert."

I envisioned mushy mac and cheese and mushier rice pudding, both flavorless. I thanked Platinum Blonde and hung up before she could change her mind.

I killed some time checking out tarot tattoos on Pin-terest, unsurprised to find hundreds of variations inked onto virtually every part of the body, along with multiple sketches and drawings. There were also symbols for the cards in the Major Arcana, The Fool represented by a round circle with a diagonal line cutting through the top left-hand corner.

Tarot appeared to be a popular subject for tattoos. But were tattoos popular in 2000 when Brandon got his?

I ARRIVED AT the Cedar County Retirement Residence with ten minutes to spare, passed muster with Platinum Blonde, who offered a robotic "I'm sorry for your loss," before accepting my lunch money and directing me to the dining room. Table seven was set for two, with cutlery, white china cups, and cloth napkins. A glass vase sported a single red carnation, and for a moment I got misty-eyed thinking that this had been my great-grandmother's seat. True, in the brief time since we'd met, I hadn't gotten to know her well, but I had liked her, and I was sure I could have come to love her, given half a chance.

Eleanor Colbeck was wheeled to the table at two minutes before one o'clock. There was an oxygen tank strapped to the back of her wheelchair, the plastic tubing inserted in her nose, and I realized she had more than Mild Cognitive Impairment.

The personal support worker, a slender amber-eyed, brown-skinned woman in her early thirties, transferred Eleanor from wheelchair to dining chair with expert efficiency. Eleanor stared at me with rheumy eyes, her pale face flushed and breathing labored from the effort. I recognized the symptoms of Chronic Obstructive Pulmonary Disease—COPD—from volunteer work at a nursing home in Toronto. Cigarette smoking had been fashionable back in the day, and there were plenty of seniors now suffering the consequences.

"Do I know you?" she asked. Her voice had the reedy timbre of someone permanently on oxygen, but there was also a trace of uncertainty in it, as if she should know me and didn't.

"No. No, you don't. My name is Callie Barnstable. My great-grandmother was Olivia Osgoode. I understand you were good friends."

"Olivia died."

"I know."

"I miss her. She was my friend."

"I miss her, too."

"Is that why you're here? Because of Olivia?"

"In a way. Do you remember signing a paper?"

Eleanor frowned. "I don't think so. What sort of paper?"

"A paper saying that you would help me find out what happened to your grandson."

"Brandon. His name is Brandon. He disappeared a long time ago."

"Yes, Brandon. I'm an investigator."

"An investigator." Eleanor chewed at her bottom lip and I waited as she processed the information.

"Does that mean that you investigate things?"

"Yes."

Her face brightened. "He phoned me. Brandon did. The police said it wasn't him, that it was a lie. Do you think it was?"

"I don't know."

"I forget things now, so no one believes me. But he called me Nana Ellie, just like he used to. I'm sure it was Brandon."

"Can you remember other things about Brandon? Besides that he called you Nana Ellie? Things that might help me find out what happened to him?"

"I'd really like to try," Eleanor said, and began to cry.

I looked around, unsure of what to do or who to call. Fortunately, lunch was delivered to our table, distracting Eleanor. The mac and cheese looked mushy as expected, the cheese sauce runny and an odd shade of orange. The rice pudding had been liberally sprinkled with cinnamon, as if the addition could make up for an otherwise bland dessert. Each tray also contained a container of white milk. Not much for ten dollars.

"They'll come with tea or coffee after we eat," Eleanor said, spooning the mac and cheese into her mouth. "I don't like their tea, though. Tastes like dishwater."

I grinned, once again reminded of my great-grandmother and her exacting standards for making the perfect cup of tea, which involved rinsing a teapot with boiling water and letting the tea steep for exactly four minutes, not three, and not five. "Do you have tea in your room? If so, I could come up with you and make you a cup. Would you like that?"

Eleanor nodded, and I breathed a silent sigh of relief. It would be easier to talk about Brandon outside of this very public dining room.

"Okay then, as soon as we're done with lunch, and don't worry. Olivia taught me how to make a proper cup of tea."

"Olivia," Eleanor said, tears staining her weathered cheeks. "She died, you know."

She was still crying when I wheeled her into her room.

EIGHT

I GOT ELEANOR seated on a brown leather sofa, plumped the multi-colored pillows surrounding her, and made a pot of Earl Grey tea. A quick search of the cupboard next to a small refrigerator led me to a box of digestive biscuits, six brown earthenware mugs, a couple with chips on the rim, and a collection of mismatched dollar store paper plates and napkins. I placed napkins, a plate of cookies, and two mugs on the coffee table, got the tea, and poured.

"Sugar or milk?" I asked, not sure if Eleanor had either.

She shook her head and I took a seat in one of two chairs upholstered in a nubby taupe fabric, dragging it into position to face her. I knew it was best to wait until she spoke again and settled in for the duration. Brandon had been missing for nearly twenty years. Another ten minutes wasn't going to change anything.

I was on my second cup of tea and third biscuit when Eleanor spoke. The tea had served to both calm and revive her, the tears subsided, a flush of color back in her cheeks. "You're here about Brandon. What sort of things do you want me to tell you?"

"Anything that might help us to iden…locate Brandon." I studied Eleanor, hopeful that she hadn't noticed the almost slip of "identify" versus locate. Identify conjured up images of dead bodies. Locate was far more optimistic. The vague expression on her face assured me she'd missed it, but the faux pas served as a reminder to choose my words wisely. I continued on, my voice soft, a gentle exploration into this woman's past. "A place he might have loved as a child, for example. A favorite activity of his, perhaps one you both enjoyed together. Do you remember anything like that?"

"The past is something I do remember, or at least most parts of it," she said with a sad smile. "Just don't ask me what I did yesterday, or how to work the microwave. Where should I start?"

"Wherever you'd like."

"You said a place Brandon might have loved. My husband, Tom, and I used to own a two-bedroom cabin in Lakeside, direct waterfront on Lake Miakoda. For over thirty years, we spent every weekend there from Victoria Day in May to Thanksgiving in October, plus the entire month of July. I sold it after Tom died, too much work and too many memories." Eleanor grimaced. "The couple who bought it tore it down and built a monstrosity of a house to live in year-round."

My grandparents owned one of the McMansions that Eleanor was referring to, a medieval fairy tale castle with a fieldstone façade, turrets, and two-story towers. The only thing missing was a moat. "I take it Brandon loved the cabin?"

Her face was wreathed in a smile. "That boy was made for the outdoors. On nice days, he'd be outside every waking minute, swimming, exploring, bike riding, fishing off the dock, catching frogs, begging Tom to take him for a boat ride. On rainy days, we'd play board games and cards, or work on paint-by-numbers and jigsaw puzzles. Sometimes we'd bake chocolate chip cookies or brownies. He loved my brownies, always liked to lick the batter from the bowl."

"Did Brandon come to the cabin very often?"

This netted me a disdainful sniff. "He did—at least before Lorna met Michael. After that…"

Her voice trailed off, but judging from the tone, there was no love lost between Eleanor Colbeck and Michael Westlake. I felt my pulse quicken. It wasn't much, but it confirmed my earlier suspicion that Brandon and his stepfather didn't get along. "What changed when Lorna met Michael?"

"Michael thought that Tom and I spoiled Brandon." Eleanor sniffed again. "Well, of course we did. That's what grandparents are supposed to do, am I right?"

I've never experienced any such spoiling from my own grandparents, but I nodded anyway. It was enough to get Eleanor talking again. I leaned forward in an "all ears" stance and hoped it would encourage her to go on. It did.

"We may have spoiled the boy," she said, "but we were never careless with his safety. We always made him wear a life vest in the boat and Tom taught him to swim, for pity's sake. None of that mattered to Michael."

"Why do you think that was?"

"Easy. If Brandon was with us, he wasn't under Michael's thumb."

Eleanor's bitterness was palpable. It also provided the perfect opening to ask one of my questions. "How old was Brandon when Lorna met Michael?"

Eleanor frowned in concentration, and I hoped I hadn't pushed too hard.

"Dates can be fuzzy for me," she said, still frowning. "Let me think."

I waited silently as she touched her fingers one at a time, as if counting numbers. After a few minutes, she nodded, a wide smile crossing her face.

"I remember that Jeanine was born a few months after Lorna met Michael." Eleanor's voice dropped to a whisper. "A *very* few months if you get my meaning."

So Lorna was already pregnant when she married Michael. I wondered if the pregnancy was planned, or if it had been the reason for the nuptials. I also knew Jeanine was eight years younger than Brandon, which meant he'd been seven, coming on eight, when Michael Westlake had entered his life. Since Brandon's last name was Colbeck, he hadn't been adopted. Or had he? Better not to assume, and ask.

"Did Michael adopt Brandon?"

"No." Lips pressed closed, posture rigid.

I was surprised by Eleanor's body language and her abrupt response. Until now, Eleanor had been very forthcoming. I was deliberating on how best to pursue the topic when she spoke again.

"I'm not trying to be, um, unhelpful, is that the right word? I'm not sure that it is, but you know what I mean. Anyway, I can't tell you why Michael didn't adopt Brandon because I don't know the reason. Lorna never discussed the matter, and it wasn't my place to ask. It was a topic relegated to 'need to know' status and apparently I didn't need to know. I'm sorry I can't be more help."

I felt an irrational tug of disappointment. Had I really expected this oxygen-dependent, wheelchair-bound woman with memory problems to answer all of my questions? "You've been a great help, Eleanor. All of the things you've told me, like the jigsaw puzzles, paint-by-numbers, and brownies, will go a long way to vetting anyone who might come forward."

Her watery blue eyes assessed me, and I caught a glimpse of the intelligent woman she used to be, before old age and illness had beset her. "Thank you for being so kind," she said after a few moments. "I'm embarrassed that I didn't think to ask Brandon any of those questions when he telephoned. The minute I heard the words 'Nana Ellie' my heart melted. I haven't been called that in many, many years. It had to be Brandon, don't you think? Who else would know that?"

Anyone who'd read the article in the Marketville Post, I thought. "I don't know," I said truthfully, "but I'm going to do everything I can to find out."

NINE

I MADE MY way to a stone bench on the perimeter of the Cedar County Retirement Residence and checked my phone. There was a text from Chantelle with a cryptic message: "No go from Lorna. Call me."

I did as instructed. "What's up?"

"Nothing's up. I called Lorna Colbeck-Westlake as you suggested, and she told me she would only speak to you, even after I explained that we were partners. She was having none of it. Apparently that's the way Leith set things up."

"No worries, I'll call her now. Hang tight." I hung up, found Lorna's number, and dialed.

Lorna answered on the first ring. I introduced myself as Calamity Barnstable, co-owner of Past & Present Investigations, the firm appointed to investigate Brandon Colbeck's disappearance.

"I recognized the name on my call display," Lorna said, her voice so quiet I had to strain to hear. "I've already heard from your partner, a Chantelle Marchand? Your lawyer made it clear we were to deal with you directly. We promised to cooperate, but I'm not sure what you expect to accomplish."

Hardly the words of a mother desperate to find her son. What had changed since that newspaper article three years ago? Or had it all been for show? "I thought the mandate was clear. We've been hired by the estate of

Olivia Osgoode, on behalf of Eleanor Colbeck, to find Brandon, or at least what became of him."

"I understand that part. What I don't understand is why a total stranger would care all these years later."

"Olivia was your mother's friend. She was also my great-grandmother. Regardless of the personal motivation, I'm trying to fulfill the terms of the contract." I fought to keep the annoyance out of my voice. "I need your help. Right now, all we have to go on are some sketches and a three-year-old newspaper article, which may or may not be accurate."

There was a long silence. "You must find me tedious. It's just that I don't know how many more times I can go down this road. Every time I try, it chips off another piece of my soul. My husband, Michael, and I had agreed, after the report in the *Post* didn't yield a single result, that it was time to let it go. Especially after that scam phone call to my mother. What kind of person does that?" She didn't wait for an answer. "You may find our daughter, Jeanine, holds more optimism, though you'd have to ask her. I assume you have her number?"

The strain in Lorna's voice spoke volumes. Clearly her son's disappearance had fractured the family. "Yes, I have her number, thanks so much for asking. I'd also like to meet with Michael. Even the smallest detail or bit of history can help move an investigation forward. The police tend to be clinical in their approach. Our approach is more…organic."

That netted something that may have been a choked sob or a dry chuckle. Without seeing her, I couldn't be sure. "In that case, I'll sit down with you, though I suggest that you and I meet without Michael, at least

initially. I'll ask him to give you a call after you and
I have met." There was a lengthy pause, as if she was
waiting for a rebuttal. When none came she continued.
"Let's just say Michael has a tendency to be every bit
as clinical as the police."

Interviewing each family member separately during
the first sit-down was my ideal scenario, though Lorna
making the suggestion spoke volumes about her relationship with Michael. "I'm happy to do that. When and
where do you want to meet?"

"Do you have an office?"

"We work out of the main floor of my home on Edward Street in Marketville. Number 300. It's a Victorian
detached on the corner of Edward and Water."

"The place that used to be a physiotherapist's office?"

"That's the one."

"I have another engagement tomorrow, but I can do
first thing Thursday morning, say around nine? Ask
Chantelle to come along."

"I'll do that. Do you prefer coffee or tea?"

"Coffee, black and strong," Lorna said. "I'm going to
need the caffeine. Something tells me I won't be sleeping much before then."

She hung up before I could comment.

I CALLED CHANTELLE and told her about the meeting
Thursday at nine, promising to update her on Eleanor
if she showed up early.

"How early?" Chantelle wasn't much of a morning
person, the reason she took so many late afternoon and
evening shifts at the gym.

"Seven thirty should do it. I'll have the coffee ready."

"What about your homemade carrot date muffins?"

"You're in luck. I have some in the freezer. I'll take a couple out to thaw."

"Heated with butter?"

"Yes to both."

"Okay, then. See you at seven thirty. And Callie?"

"Yes?"

"I would have settled for coffee and toast."

"I know. But you'd have been grumpy."

Chantelle laughed. "You're probably right." She was still laughing when we hung up.

I phoned Jeanine Westlake next. A recorded greeting told me that everyone at New Beginnings Center for Life was out at the moment, but to leave a name, number, and brief message. I did as instructed, curious about the company name, and wondered if it was a nod to Brandon's partially finished tattoo of The Fool.

A quick internet search revealed a simple website with a home page listing the Center's services: family or individual counseling, computer skills upgrading, and résumé preparation, along with the slogan, "Let us help you find your way." It wasn't exactly "Let us help you find yourself," but it was darned close.

On the bottom left-hand corner of the page there was a photograph of an attractive woman in her late twenties or early thirties, captioned Jeanine Westlake, MSW. Had she gotten her Masters of Social Work and started her practice with the hope of finding Brandon? Or was the objective to stop another family from going through the same pain the Westlakes had experienced? I suspected it was a bit of both, but Jeanine would be the one to fill in those blanks.

I searched my contacts for Gloria Grace Pietrangelo's telephone number next.

Gloria answered on the third ring, her voice breathless. A middle-aged woman of generous proportions, I could picture her in her usual attire: black turtleneck and olive green cargo pants with matching vest, the pockets filled with a jumble of photographic accessories.

"Callie, it's so great to hear from you. I've been meaning to call you forever but I've just been crazy busy. I started teaching photography part-time at Cedar County College, and that, along with running the studio…let's just say I never seem to have a spare minute. But enough about me. I read about Past & Present Investigations in the *Marketville Post*. Congratulations. That's so exciting."

"Thank you. In fact, Past & Present is the reason for my call. I'm hoping you can shed some light on an old case we've taken on. Or should I say cold case."

"I should have known," Gloria said with an exaggerated sigh. "And here I thought you were calling to come by for tea and blueberry scones."

"I'm always up for tea and scones."

"I'm teasing, you know that, though the offer of tea and scones is a standing offer. Now, in all seriousness, what's the case? I'm not promising I'll remember it, but I've kept all of my old interview notes, can't seem to bring myself to purge them. I'd be happy to share whatever I have with you if it will help."

"Thank you. The case involves a twenty-year-old boy who left home to find himself in March 2000— without a scrap of ID or a hint of a destination. No one has seen or heard from him since, although as you can imagine, his family wants closure."

"Closure is a television term that doesn't exist in real life. There are always loose ends and unanswered questions, and both come with heartache."

"The missing boy's name is, or was—"

"Brandon Colbeck," Gloria said. "I remember the case well. I've always believed that every single member of that family was holding something back, not that the police courted that view. If they had, the case may well have been solved by now."

"Are you saying that the family lied?"

"Lied? I'm not sure I'd go that far. Withholding an inconvenient truth that may have put them in a compromising situation? Almost certainly. Find out their secrets, Callie, and you just may discover the truth."

TEN

I ARRANGED TO meet Gloria Grace at her studio in Barrie at noon the following Monday. It was almost a week away, allowing me time to interview the family members first, something we both felt was advisable. Nonetheless, I was looking forward to seeing her again, and guardedly optimistic that she'd be able to add something to Brandon's story.

I'd just finished documenting what I'd discovered so far—a nod to the late Sue Grafton's detective, Kinsey Millhone, and her investigative methods, albeit without the index cards and the all-purpose black dress—when my phone played its familiar *By the Light of the Silvery Moon* ringtone. The call display read "New Beginnings" and I picked up before it went to voice mail.

"Past & Present, Callie speaking."

"Jeanine Westlake. Sorry I missed you earlier, I was in a session. I've been expecting your call."

"I appreciate you getting back to me so quickly. I was hoping we could meet to discuss your brother's case."

"My first session tomorrow starts at ten a.m. Does nine o'clock work for you? The Center is located at 15 Edward Street in Marketville, Unit B."

The time worked, though I couldn't pinpoint the location. "I'm at 300 Edward, and I shop and dine on Edward Street all the time. I don't recall seeing New Beginnings."

"We're on the second floor, above Spinners. There's a sign on the door leading to the upper level, but there's no reason to notice it unless you're specifically looking for us."

Spinners was an indoor cycling studio, a form of exercise that held little appeal to me, though a few people in my run club were enthusiasts. "I know the place."

"See you then," Jeanine said, and hung up before I could ask anything else. Like mother, like daughter. I wondered how closely their stories would match.

WITH MY PHONE calls out of the way and nothing scheduled until the next day, I was left with a couple of hours to kill before dinner. I decided to contact Lucy Daneluk, the administrator for the Ontario Registry of Missing and Unidentified Adults, and drafted up a quick email, rereading it twice before hitting SEND.

Dear Ms. Daneluk,
My name is Calamity Barnstable and I'm a partner with Past & Present Investigations. Your website was mentioned in an article in the Marketville Post in regards to a missing adult, Brandon Colbeck, your file number ONT-2000-03-09-1. Our firm has been commissioned to investigate Brandon's disappearance. While I realize you may have no additional information beyond what is listed on his profile page, I'm hopeful that you can find the time to meet and/or speak with me.
Sincerely,
Calamity Barnstable

It was a long shot, but I've learned that even the slimmest lead can yield something of importance. Which led me to my next mission, googling tattoo parlors in Marketville. There were three listed, all with multiple reviews and ratings averaging 4.0. Two were at the edge of town, the closest to me was Trust Few Tattoo, located on Poplar Street, which ran east-west off the upper north end, and less desirable section, of Edward. The proprietor was listed as Sam Sanchez, tattoo artist.

I slipped the photocopies of Brandon's pictures and the sketch of his partially finished tattoo into a manila folder, grabbed my purse and a light jacket, and headed out the door. It was time to pay a visit to Trust Few Tattoo.

POPLAR STREET WAS a mixed bag of retail, commercial, and questionable residential. Real estate ads liked to suggest that it was a neighborhood in transition, though which way it was transitioning was uncertain.

Trust Few Tattoo was sandwiched in with Triple P Pizza, Pasta & Panzerotti, and Totally Tempting Thai. The building itself was narrow, with a red brick façade and charcoal board and batten framing a gilt-lettered window and canary yellow door. Food smells from both restaurants wafted out to the street and I knew I'd be getting takeout for dinner.

I opened the door and was greeted with the droning sound of a tattoo machine. My senses were further assaulted with the sickly-sweet smell of industrial strength sanitizer and walls completely covered with framed pages of brightly colored tattoo designs.

The front desk attendant was leaning on a glass display case full of various jewelry items, half of which I wouldn't know where to put. She glanced up from her smartphone when I walked in. I wasn't sure if it was the head-to-toe look she gave me, or her heavily tattooed hands and fingers that made me feel slightly out of place. She stood up and favored me with a gap-toothed grin.

"Hey, welcome to Trust Few. I see you're checking out the flash. What can we do for you?"

The flash? The dazed expression on my face must have given me away, because the shop assistant's grin broadened.

"The generic drawings," she said, waving her intricately patterned hands. "They're called flash. Not as popular as they were once, if I'm being honest. Most of our clients are looking for custom work, unless, of course, they're underage or impaired. Sam won't work on either. But flash still makes nice wall art, don't you think?"

I nodded and then got straight to the point. "I have some questions about a tattoo." I felt a flush of embarrassment creep up my neck. Why else would I be here, if not about a tattoo? "I was hoping you could help me."

"Sure." She pulled a large day planner out from behind the jewelry-filled display case, and her arms opened to reveal a tattoo of a bear trap inside her left elbow. I winced, thinking of the pain.

The assistant caught my look and laughed. "Don't worry. We never do ditch tattoos on newbies."

Ditch tattoos? Once again I must have looked clueless, because she elaborated.

"Inside the crook of an elbow is called a ditch tattoo, and yes, it hurts like hell. Not as much as this one did, mind you." She raised her right arm to reveal a black rose covering her armpit. "Anyway, Sam's with a client right now, but I can probably slip you in for a consult in a few minutes. When and what were you thinking of getting tattooed?"

I shook my head. There was nothing in this world that I cared enough about to have it permanently inked on any part of my body. "The tattoo isn't for me." I reached into my bag for the photocopy I had brought of Brandon's tattoo. "I have some questions about someone else's tattoo, and I was wondering if you could help me?"

The shop assistant eyeballed me further, her former grin transformed into something resembling a scowl. "Like, what kind of questions? Is it infected or something? Because we usually recommend the person comes in so we can look at it..."

I placed the photocopy of the tattoo on the counter as the girl trailed off. As she spun the image around to face her, I was able to make out the tattoos on each of her digits—what initially had appeared to be random shapes and lines were actually symbols of the Major Arcana. Thank heavens for Pinterest.

"I like your finger tattoos," I said, quickly realizing how hokey the words sounded.

"Thanks." She extended both hands so I could take a closer look. "Sam is big on mystical things. She wanted to practice, so I said she could give me a few finger-bangers."

Flash. Ditch tattoos. Finger-bangers. I was getting a primer on tattoo talk. I wondered what kind of monopoly you placed on your own skin to let someone randomly practice tattoos on a place as visible as your hands. I also felt my pulse quicken as I realized that I'd made the right choice in selecting Trust Few, though I felt moderate surprise at the fact that Sam was a woman.

I'd expected Sam Sanchez to be a big, burly, intimidating biker-type. It served as a reminder to let go of any preconceived notions. That type of thinking could block an investigation. I pulled myself out of my thoughts when the shop assistant spoke.

"What do you want to know about this tat…oh, I'm sorry, I didn't get your name?"

"Callie," I said, extending a hand. The assistant shook it, and I was surprised at how soft her hands were, despite their harsh exterior.

"Tash," she said. "Nice to meet you."

"Likewise. As for the tattoo, I'm curious about the young man who got it. That is, if he got it here."

"It looks like it might be Sam's style, but she'd be the expert on that. C'mon around and we can ask. Like I said before, she's with a client, but they've been at it for quite a while. I'm sure they can both use a break." Tash waved me around the desk.

I picked up the photocopy and followed her down a narrow hall. More tattoo flash was on the walls, along with a neon Jägermeister sign and a framed poster of The Tragically Hip's *Man Machine Poem* final concert in Kingston on August 20, 2016. Three small offices opened into the hallway; the one at the end of the hall had its door slightly ajar and I could hear laughter mixed with rock music and the buzz of the tattoo machine. Tash rapped on the door three times and pushed it open.

"Hey, Sam, sorry to bug you, just wondering if you can help this lady out with a question about a tattoo?"

The buzzing stopped. "Sure."

Tash moved out of the way and I took it as my cue to step into the doorway. A thirty-something woman wearing combat boots, a sleeveless black Nine Inch

Nails T-shirt, and torn jeans with more rips and holes than denim looked up at me and nodded. A tattoo of a woman on a bucking brown horse took up most of her lower right arm. The words "Cowgirls don't cry" were written above it, with a green heart below circling "We can be heroes." The image reminded me of the 1950s Calamity Jane movie poster I'd discovered in the attic of Snapdragon Circle, and I wondered if there was an equally personal meaning behind her artwork. There were countless other tattoos on her legs, arms, chest, and I imagined, on body parts I couldn't see or begin to imagine, but I didn't want to stare.

"Hi," I said, holding out my hand.

"Ah, sorry. Sterile environment." Sam held up two latex-gloved hands. Her current client was lying face-down on a padded table, and turned her head away from the wall to face me. I tried to look at what was being tattooed on her lower back, but couldn't make it out. Sam put the tattoo machine down on a stainless-steel countertop, the surface covered in industrial grade paper towels, and gave me her full attention. Her cornflower blue eyes were in stark contrast to her long dark hair, which had been shaved on one side. Under the buzz cut I could see "Sanchez" and I found myself wondering how much getting your scalp tattooed would hurt. I figured a lot, maybe as much or more than a ditch tattoo, maybe even more than one under an armpit. I had no plans to get any of them.

"Tash says you have a question about a tattoo?" Sam smiled, showing off a row of perfect white teeth, made whiter by the deep plum lipstick she was wearing. I wondered what made her eyetooth gleam so brightly until I noticed the tiny diamond adhered to it.

I held up the photocopy of the partly finished tattoo. "Do you recognize this?"

Sam cocked her head and peeled off her gloves, throwing them into the trash. She took the photocopy from me, her expression serious as she studied it from every angle.

"This might help to jog your memory," I said, and offered the newspaper photograph of twenty-year-old Brandon Colbeck. "It was taken a few years back." I omitted the year. Sam either remembered Brandon and his tattoo, or she didn't. There was no point planting seeds that might otherwise not be there.

Sam looked up at me, then turned her attention back to the photocopies, her fingers tracing the outline of The Fool tattoo over and over.

"Yeah, I remember this tattoo," she said, finally. "I never got to finish it, though…"

ELEVEN

THE SOUND OF a throat clearing served as a gentle reminder that we weren't alone. Sam handed back the photocopies and smiled at the young woman lying on the table.

"Long enough break. Come back in an hour and we can talk more. We'll be done by then, she's my last client of the day."

I could grab a bite to eat and then stroll around the neighborhood to check out some of the other shops. "Sounds like a plan. What can you tell me about the food from the restaurants on either side?"

"Triple P has decent pizza if you like a thick bread-like crust—"

"I'm more of a thin crust kind of girl."

"In that case, I'd recommend the veggie panzerotti, which is stuffed to the brim with mozzarella, mushrooms, bell peppers, onions, and whatever else you want them to throw in there. The pasta's nothing special, with the exception of the chicken lasagna in a to-die-for béchamel sauce. It's decadent enough to be almost worth the calories."

"And the Thai place?"

Sam shook her head. "Not as totally tempting as the name might suggest."

I apologized to the client for interrupting her time, thanked Sam and Tash, and made my way to Triple P, where I waffled between ordering the veggie panzerotti or the chicken lasagna. In the end I selected the lasagna. What can I say? I'm a sucker for creamy sauces.

It was worth every single calorie.

THE STROLL ALONG Poplar Street revealed an eclectic mix of businesses. A secondhand store—perhaps more aptly described as third or fourth hand—took up the largest square footage, whereas a magic supply company was literally stuffed into a space not much larger than a storage locker. Rounding things out were a clothing consignment "boutique," unisex hair salon, the posters in the window faded with time, and a new and used bookstore, where I picked up a paperback copy of *A Hole in One*, a mystery set in nearby Lount's Landing, along with a non-fiction history of Marketville, both signed and in the "local authors" section. I'd never heard of either author, but the store's owner, a fresh-faced blonde who introduced herself as Francis, assured me both books were popular. I added a gently worn copy of John Sandford's latest Prey novel to my purchases and left with the promise to return.

There were three more restaurants, one Mexican, one featuring "authentic Indian cuisine," and a nondescript diner serving all-day breakfast and "the best burgers in Marketville." I grinned at the all-day description, given that the diner's hours were from seven a.m. to three p.m., but I made a mental note to come back and try it the next time I needed cheering up. There's nothing like reading a day-old newspaper while eating bacon, eggs, and home fries to set the world right again.

The sign on the door of Trust Few said Closed, but Sam was waiting for me when I returned. She'd changed from ripped jeans into a black denim mini and exchanged the Nine Inch Nails T-shirt for a flannel lumberjack-style shirt in black and red plaid, the sleeves rolled up, shirttails tied at the waist. The combat boots remained. There was no sign of Tash. Sam favored me with a narrow-eyed stare and I got the feeling something had changed in the hour since I'd left.

"Tash and my client said maybe I should be a little more cautious about how much I share. What's your interest in this case? It was a long time ago and you don't look like a cop."

"About nineteen years, to be exact, and you're right, I'm not a cop. I'm the co-owner of Past & Present Investigations on Edward Street. The young man in the photo, his name is, or was, Brandon Colbeck. He left home in March 2000. No one has seen or heard from him since. At least no one who has come forward. His family would like to know where he went, what happened to him, and whether he's dead or alive. I'm trying to get some answers."

Sam nodded. "I remember reading the story in the *Marketville Post* a couple of years back. A sad story, and if they'd mentioned a tattoo I might have put it together before now. I vaguely remember thinking, at the time, that the guy looked familiar, but he could have been someone I saw around town. It's not like the police came to see me."

"Sometimes details are purposely omitted so the police can weed out false leads and attention seekers. But it's possible that the reporter who wrote the story didn't know about it." I wondered when that detail had been added to the Registry and made a mental note to ask Lucy Daneluk if I had the opportunity. It also made me question why the police hadn't paid Sam a visit. I felt the first frisson of doubt. Was Sam simply looking for free publicity at the family's expense?

"I don't mean to go all *Hawaii 5-0* on you, especially since I'm the one who's come to you, but you make a good point about the police. Why wouldn't they have come to see you? Marketville doesn't have many tattoo parlors."

Sam shrugged as if the answer was obvious. "Probably because Trust Few didn't open until 2003."

Three years after Brandon left? "I don't understand. You said you remembered the tattoo and that you never had time to finish it. Are you saying that Brandon was here in 2003 or later?"

"No, it would have been in 2000, and I remember that one because it was my first tattoo. I was apprenticing at the time, worked at the back of Nature's Way."

Sam must have noticed my confusion because she clarified. "Now it's Sun, Moon & Stars, the place with the psychics, beads, and crystals. But back then it was Such & Such Tattoo." She barked a laugh at the expression on my face. "I know, terrible name, right? But Dave, that was the owner, he couldn't think of a name when he was setting up the shop, kept calling it Such & Such and I guess it stuck."

I hadn't seen Such & Such in my Google search. "Where did it move to?"

"Oh, it didn't. Dave was a great artist, but a terrible businessman. He closed the shop in August 2003. I could easily have found work somewhere else, but I took the plunge and bought this place. It used to be a hardware store, but the couple who ran it couldn't compete with the bigger chains moving into town, and the location wasn't exactly prime." Sam chuckled. "You think Poplar Street is in transition now, you should have seen it back then. Anyway, it's turned out to be a good investment, though the first two years were a struggle."

"I'm surprised the owner of Such & Such couldn't make a go of it, what with tattoos being so popular."

"Ah, but we're talking the late nineties to early two thousands," Sam said. "There was still social stigma attached to tattoos, especially in small towns. Cities were another story, especially where twenty-somethings were running dot-coms. That was mostly in the U.S., but it filtered into Vancouver and Toronto. I started seeing eighteen-year-old hotties in first year uni getting tramp stamps, though something like a butterfly on the ankle was more common. But Marketville? Tattoos were still associated with bikers, gang members, prisons, and sailors."

"When did it change?" I asked, thinking of Brandon.

"In 2005, a guy named Ami James linked up with network television to run *Miami Ink*, a reality TV show out of his South Beach parlor, 305 Ink, which he later renamed Love Hate Tattoo. The show made stars out of James and artists like Kat Von D, and before long singers and celebrities were lining up to get their own ink. Big stuff too—full sleeves and such. Tattoos went mainstream. Today, thirty-six percent of adults have at least one tattoo." Sam grinned. "Something tells me you're not going to be one of them. Needle phobia?"

"More like commitment phobia," I said, thinking about Royce and my reluctance to take our relationship to the next level. I envisioned "Royce" in fancy script on my bicep and winced. "I can't imagine getting a tattoo."

Sam laughed. "No biggie. Believe it or not, I spend

a fair amount of time convincing people not to get tats. I always advise against getting a tattoo of a partner's name. If the relationship fails, you're stuck with it somewhere on your body or trying to cover it up. Then there's superstition. Many people believe such a tattoo jinxes a couple. As for commitment phobia, you'd get over that soon enough, after your first tattoo. In my experience, most folks, once they get one, get another, and another. It can become as addictive as any drug." She grinned. "At least that's what I count on."

"You're probably right. Everyone I know with a tattoo has more than one. But back to Brandon. Tell me everything you remember. Even the smallest detail can make a big difference."

"Right, okay. Well, like I said, I was working at Such & Such as an apprentice, not that Dave needed one given how little business was coming through the door. But I showed him some of my sketches, mostly astrological and tarot stuff, and he said I had talent." Sam smiled at the memory. "'Raw undeveloped talent' is actually how he put it. For the first few weeks, I acted as a receptionist, janitor, bookkeeper, and observer, though Dave also had me frame some flash for the walls. It was the beginning of March when Brandon came in. There was an ice storm raging outside to remind everyone that winter wasn't over, no matter what the groundhog said. Dave muttered something along the lines of, 'What would prompt a kid—he might have said 'college kid,' to come for a tattoo on a hellish day like this?' Brandon came in with a book about tarot, the corners all dog-eared, and told us he wanted to get tattoos of all the Major Arcana. Dave laughed at that, asked him if he expected to get them all done in one day, and the kid…he said he was twenty but he looked younger than that…blushed and said something like, 'Of course not, I want to start with The Fool.' And I remember asking, 'Is that because it's the first card in the deck?' And Brandon shook his head and said, no, he was planning to go on a fool's journey."

I sat up straighter, thinking back to what Misty had told me earlier. "Were those his exact words? A fool's journey?"

Sam nodded. "I knew what he meant, because I'd studied tarot, but Dave didn't have a clue and he made a joke about it. Brandon got seriously pissed and I thought he was going to leave, but I explained to Dave that many believe the Major Arcana represents The Fool's Journey. After that, Brandon insisted that I be the one to tattoo him, and he asked me to pattern it after the Rider-Waite deck like the cards in his book. I didn't tell him it was my first tattoo, and since it was his first, he didn't know what to expect, or how long it would take. We had some flash for tarot, but he wanted an original. I took a few minutes to sketch it and get his okay. I free-styled The Fool's robe and the sun, added a few filigrees with a marker before getting started. The slight differences between the tattoo in your sketch and the Rider-Waite deck is another reason I recognized it as mine."

"How long did it take?"

"About three hours, much longer than it would take me today," Sam admitted. "Apprentices are notoriously slow, but the hourly rate is much lower, so it all works out, or at least that's the theory. Anyway, Brandon started getting antsy, and I remember being glad I hadn't gone into it beyond the sun and the top half of the robe, not to mention the filigrees. But I got where he was coming from. Three hours was a long time for him to sit still under the hot lights, and my shoulders were aching from being hunched over for so long. We made an appointment for the following week. He never showed."

"Did he call to cancel?"

"Nope. Not a word. I figured he thought I was too slow and was going to get someone else to finish it. Dave told me not to take it personally, but I did, you know? It shook my confidence for a while, but I got it back. I owe Dave for that, too. 'Never give anyone the satisfaction of thinking they broke you,' he'd say, whenever I got to feeling sorry for myself, didn't matter if it was a hard-to-please client, a cheating boyfriend, or the fact that the moon was full and I felt like howling at it."

I had to grin at the thought of Sam howling at the moon. I've felt like doing that myself, sometimes, not that I'd ever admit it to anyone. "Dave sounds like a standup guy. I'd like to talk to him."

Sam gave me a sad smile. "So would I. Unfortunately he went to that big tattoo parlor in the sky two months after the shop was shuttered. Pancreatic cancer. He never stood a chance." She pointed to the Cowgirls Don't Cry tattoo. "The first time I heard this Brooks & Dunn song, the one featuring Reba McEntire, I thought about Dave. That was fall 2008. I got the tattoo in his memory a few weeks later. I think he would have liked it."

"I think so, too," I said, not that I'd ever heard the song.

"Yeah, well… Reba's quoted as saying you need three things in life—a wishbone, a backbone, and a funny bone. I kind of think this tattoo has a bit of all of that in it. Of course, I didn't tattoo myself, but it's my original artwork."

I could see it: the sense of the hope for the future, the strong woman, the elements of whimsy. "I do believe you captured it perfectly."

"Yeah? Thanks. Anyway, I'm hoping to pay it forward, you know? That's what I want to do with Tash when she's ready. But enough about me, about Dave. Do you have any other questions about Brandon and his half-finished tattoo?"

"Just a couple. Today, would the tattoo look much the same? Or do they change with age? What if he'd had it colored in?"

"All tattoos blow out over time, the lines get thicker, blacks turn a bit gray, the shapes don't look as clean. If he'd gotten the entire tattoo done and colored in shortly thereafter, and never had any touch ups, it would definitely have faded. Vibrant colors like bubblegum pink, sunshine yellow, and bright green fade faster than darker colors like crimson reds. Watercolors tend to fade the fastest. But all colors fade."

"Which means, if someone got the tattoo as recently as a year or two ago, you could spot the difference."

"Almost certainly." Sam cocked her head, blue eyes curious. "Why? Do you think someone might be trying to impersonate Brandon?"

"Just covering all the bases," I said, unwilling to share news of the call to Eleanor. "I never know what's going to be important and as you can tell, my knowledge of tattoo art is sorely lacking."

Sam nodded, but I could tell she wasn't buying the explanation. I pulled out the age-progressed sketches of Brandon, hoping to smooth out the moment. "This is what the police artist thinks he might look like now."

Did I imagine a slight intake of breath? I watched in silence as she compared both sketches, placing them side-by-side, her fingers tracing every line as if she was memorizing them.

"He's a good-looking man," she said. "I wasn't expecting that. I guess in my mind he was still twenty. Crazy, eh?"

"It's natural to remember people as we saw them last, not as they might have aged."

"He had a nice smile, I do recall that. Good teeth. Of course, the police never sketch anyone smiling, always with the lips closed."

"I didn't know that," I said, wondering why Sam knew this odd bit of information.

"Oh yeah. A closed mouth expression doesn't change much over the years, whereas teeth do. They chip or yellow, people straighten them or lose them. It's one of the reasons you're not allowed to smile in a passport photo. When a mouth is open, it makes it difficult for facial recognition to work properly."

Sam tapped on the clean-cut version. "I can't imagine the young man who wanted to go on a fool's journey would grow up to look like a banker, though. If he's alive, my money's on the shaggy-haired, scruffy look. But who knows, right? Maybe he decided he wasn't cut out for a fool's journey after all."

"Do you recognize him?"

"If you're asking if these sketches remind me of the guy who walked in here on an icy March day looking for his first tattoo, no."

There was something evasive in the way she'd answered. I reworded the question. "What I meant is, have you seen him? The man in these sketches?"

"That would be another no."

I pushed back my disappointment, realizing it was irrational at best, and ridiculous at worst. What had I expected? "Did Brandon say anything about where the journey was going to take him?"

"He was planning to follow the path of the Major Arcana and get tattooed along the way. He didn't elaborate about the where or the when." She paused, her cornflower blue eyes appraising me. "Did you ever consider that Brandon Colbeck might not want to be found?"

Did Sam know more than she was saying? Was Trust Few more than the name of a tattoo parlor? Or had it simply been a rhetorical question?

"I have. But if he stays missing, his family will keep waiting, alternating between hope and hopelessness. I can't imagine living that way, can you?"

Sam shook her head. "No. No, I can't. Then again, some of the tattoos I've done, the stories behind them could break your heart. People tell tattoo artists things, like we're bartenders or something." She stood up, arching her back. "I'm sorry I couldn't be more help."

"There's nothing to apologize for. You were more than generous with your time, and I know more now than when I came." I pulled a business card from my purse and handed it to her. "Call me if you think of anything else."

"Sure." She walked me to the front door and opened it, a not-so-subtle hint that it was time for me to go.

"Can I ask you one more question?"

The narrow-eyed stare was back, but she gave a grudging nod.

"Why Trust Few?"

Sam smiled, the diamond chip in her front tooth glittering in the early evening light. "Love many, trust few, and always paddle your own canoe." She gave me a fist bump before turning back into the shop, her toned legs accentuated by tanned skin and body art. I squinted to make out the tattoo that covered most of her left shin and calf and finally nailed it: a pistol with four aces above it, the words, "Smith & Wesson Beats 4 Aces" circling the image.

Not a woman to be trifled with. I just wished I could shake the feeling that she was holding something back.

TWELVE

I ARRIVED HOME, placed my book purchases on the table, grabbed my notebook, and wrote down every detail of the meeting with Sam Sanchez. Royce didn't get it, but Chantelle understood. We were both journal book nerds, and I suspect my father's "A dull pencil is sharper than the sharpest mind" mantra had a lot to do with my habit. It was as if, having gotten everything down on paper, I was able to let my mind process what was important and what was periphery. In two or three days, I would transcribe everything into a Word document on my computer. By the time I recorded it as an official report, the words would be succinct and any conjecture clearly defined. Right now, it was all about not forgetting.

It took me two hours to recall and record everything, from my first impression of Sam, right down to her primer on *Miami Ink* and the way tattoos faded. Once done, I read it over, line by line, adding a word here and there, underlining some, adding comments in the margins, until I was satisfied that I hadn't forgotten anything. I flipped open my tablet and typed "Cowgirls Don't Cry Brooks & Dunn" into the search bar. A YouTube video popped onto the screen with more than twenty million views and over one hundred thousand Likes. I wasn't unfamiliar with country music—my father had been a big fan, and I listened to the local country station when I wasn't tuned into talk radio—but I'd never heard this song.

The video and lyrics told the story of a father who teaches his daughter that life isn't always easy, but that you have to ride it out. The daughter grows up to marry a cheating husband who comes home late every night, despite their own little girl, but remains stoic because, as the title goes, cowgirls don't cry. There's a tearjerker ending when her mama calls to tell her that her father is dying. I watched it a couple of dozen times, enjoying the voices of Brooks & Dunn blend with Reba McIntyre's distinctive Oklahoma twang, then read and reread the lyrics. Was Dave a mentor, as Sam had implied, or had they been father and daughter? Was that what she'd been keeping back? I went over my notes once again, looking for what I might have missed. Nothing stood out, but I'd let it percolate. If there was anything there, I would find it on transcription. In the meantime, it was time to check my email.

There was the usual influx of stuff: recipes from Kraft.com, posts from blogs I'd subscribed to, notifications from Amazon, Facebook, Twitter, and Pinterest. I skimmed through them all, zeroing in on a reply from Lucy Daneluk, the administrator for the Ontario Registry for Missing and Unidentified Adults.

Hello Callie,
Thanks for reaching out. I'd be more than happy to talk to you, though I'm not sure how much help I can be. I'm in the Ottawa area, but as luck would have it, I'll be in Toronto for a conference this coming weekend. The drive to Marketville from Ottawa takes about five hours with a couple of pit stops, the same length of

time it takes to drive to Toronto, and I'm always up for a road trip. If I leave at nine a.m. Friday, I should be there by two o'clock. I know it's short notice, but are you available? I can drive to Toronto from your place after the rush hour craziness subsides on the 404-Don Valley Parkway.
Over to you,
Lucy

It was a stroke of luck I hadn't expected. True, Daneluk may not have any additional information, but her willingness to meet was encouraging. I drafted up another email before she had time to change her mind.

Hello Lucy,
Thanks for your prompt response. I'm most definitely available to meet with you this Friday afternoon. My address is 300 Edward Street, Marketville. Please plan to stay for dinner, if you can, and let me know if you have any dietary concerns so I can accommodate them.
Looking forward to it,
Callie
PS: Do you mind if my business partner, Chantelle Marchand, joins us?

I'd no sooner hit the Send button when the reply came in.

Hi Callie,
Dinner sounds wonderful. I literally eat anything and everything so whatever you want to serve works for me, especially as I look toward two days of hotel and restaurant food. Thank you for offering.

See you Friday approx. two p.m. Would love to meet your business partner, too.
Cheers,
Lucy

I forwarded the email string to Chantelle, hoping it wouldn't conflict with her schedule at the gym. Then I started planning Friday's menu: Brie and asparagus quiche, mixed greens with balsamic dressing, angel food cake with fresh strawberries and a dollop of strawberry whipped cream for dessert. That done, I got ready for an early night. Tomorrow was going to be a big day, and I needed to be refreshed and ready.

THIRTEEN

I MADE MY way down Edward Street to the office of New Beginnings Center for Life, looking for my landmark, the Spinners cycling studio. Today there were a dozen hardcore cyclists going through their workout, led by a finely muscled, gray-haired woman who appeared to be in her late fifties. Unlike the rest of her sweat-drenched group, she barely had a glint of perspiration on her six-pack abs and ropey thighs, even when she stood upright to pedal. A tattoo on her upper right arm featured a large red dot over a capital M. I recognized it from my days with the two-timing triathlete as an Ironman tattoo, and knew you only got the tat if you'd actually managed to complete the 2.4-mile swim, 112-mile bike, and 26.2-mile run within the seventeen-hour time cutoff.

The woman saw me looking and waved, a kickass grin on her weatherworn face. I waved back, embarrassed to be caught in the act of voyeur, and slunk away to the adjacent door stenciled with small black letters: New Beginnings Center for Life. Jeanine Westlake, MSW, Upper floor. Pull to enter. Ring bell twice.

I did as instructed and wound my way up a narrow staircase with a few rickety steps. The entrance to New Beginnings Center for Life opened to a waiting room that could have been any medical walk-in clinic in the county: a water cooler with tiny, triangular paper cups attached to a side holder, a dozen straight-backed chairs, seats and backs upholstered in gunmetal gray tweed, a couple of glass-topped end tables tucked into the corners, an oversized wicker basket filled to over-flowing with back issues of *Social Work Today*, *Healthy Living*, and that quintessential Canadian staple, *Chatelaine*. A reception desk was positioned next to a long hall, which I assumed led to the office of Jeanine West-lake. In short, everything you'd expect to see with the exception of dozens of brightly colored origami birds, in varying shades of pink, aqua, purple, and teal, some perfectly folded, some less so. Suspended from the ceiling tiles, the paper shimmering under the fluorescent lights, they lent a sense of whimsy and hope to an otherwise sterile room.

A pointy-nosed receptionist greeted me with a caustic glance and I was momentarily reminded of the Wicked Witch of the West in the *Wizard of Oz*. I half expected her to call me "My Pretty," and was almost disappointed when she didn't. There was an oversized daily planner on her desk, each column and time slot filled with a scribble presumably only she could decipher. Job security at its finest. "Name?" she asked, her voice as strident as her appearance.

I gave her my most ingratiating smile, hoping it would thaw her out some. "Callie Barnstable. I have a nine o'clock appointment with Jeanine Westlake."

Pointy-nose sniffed, took a yellow marker from a stoneware mug filled with various writing implements, and highlighted my name next to 9 a.m., the first appointment of the day. "You're early. It's only 8:54." The frost in her tone implied that I was hours early versus mere minutes. I'd done something to seriously set this woman off, though I had no idea what it could be.

"I like to be punctual. I view it as a sign of respect."

That seemed to mollify her because she attempted a smile. "Have a seat. Ms. Westlake will be with you in four minutes."

Exactly four minutes later, a young woman wearing black slacks and a white silk blouse strolled into the room. "Jeanine Westlake. You must be Callie. Welcome."

She looked younger than thirty-one and I was reminded of Sam saying much the same about Brandon at age twenty. "Thanks for seeing me on such short notice." I pointed to the ceiling. "I'm fascinated by your origami birds. It must have taken days to make so many."

Jeanine laughed, a soft, tinkling bell-like sound. "Oh, they're not all mine. Studies have shown the art of folding paper to be therapeutic. Each bird is made from a single sheet of paper, without any cutting or glue. In teaching my clients the technique, they build attention and focus, frustration intolerance, and self-esteem. Simply put, my clients can replace 'I can't' with 'I can.' But you didn't come here to discuss origami. Follow me to my office where we can talk."

I followed, dropping my voice to a whisper. "I don't think your receptionist approves of me."

"It's not you she disapproves of, it's the rehashing of Brandon. She thinks it's time to let him go. She's probably right."

"I'm only trying to help."

"Are you? Well, I suppose we'll see how things turn out this time. My office is the third one on the left."

She chuckled. "The corner office, with a five-star view of the back alley. Some interesting sights back there after sundown, not that I make it a habit of staying past five. There are two other offices. The largest one has a window overlooking Edward Street. We use it for training, anything from interview preparation to updating computer skills. I have an assistant, a retired high school teacher, who takes care of that side of things. The smallest is not much bigger than a broom closet. It has basic office supplies, and a four-in-one printer that scans, copies and faxes—not that many folks fax anymore. Mostly, our clients use the space to print or send out résumés."

Jeanine reminded me of her delicate origami birds: petite, with translucent skin, a heart-shaped face with a tiny triangle of a nose, pale blue eyes, a petite frame, streaked blonde hair cut short, and a chirpy, sing-songy voice. Even her choice of jewelry was delicate: amethyst stud earrings, a simple silver necklace with an amethyst pendant that reminded me of the Inuit inuksuk, and a single ring on the fourth finger of her right hand, a silver filigree band with an amethyst inset in the center. And yet I knew, given the work she was trying to accomplish and her past history, that beneath the seemingly fragile exterior would lie a far tougher interior. Not jaded, not yet, but I expected the day would come. The thought saddened me. I searched unsuccessfully for any resemblance to her half brother, either in his twenty-year-old self or the age-progressed sketches.

"I take after my mom's side of the family," Jeanine said, as if reading my mind. "I figure Brandon took after his biological father, not that he or I ever knew who that was. It was one of the things that haunted him, the not knowing." She pushed open the office door. "Come in and have a seat."

Unlike the reception room, there were no origami birds hanging from the ceiling. There was also no desk. Instead there was a round glass-topped dining table with brushed stainless steel legs, surrounded by four black leather kitchen chairs, two more stacked in the corner. The walls, painted stark white, were without ornamentation, the sole exception a framed university diploma by the door from Dalhousie University for Jeanine Rebecca Westlake. It was the only personal touch.

Jeanine smiled. "Not what you were expecting?"

I admitted it wasn't.

"I find the round table approach far more conducive to sharing than me sitting behind a desk trying to look all scholarly. I'm too short to carry off the authority figure act with any credibility and I'm not an authoritarian. I'm here to listen, and hopefully provide guidance. Admittedly the space is a bit barren, but I assure you there's nothing Freudian about it. I'm looking for the right artwork, just haven't found it yet. When I do…" Her voice trailed off. "But enough banalities. You're here about Brandon. I'll tell you what I remember. I warn you, it's not much. I was only twelve when he left, and my parents and the police have been down the 'Find Brandon' road many times over the years. If he's alive, he doesn't want to be found."

Sam Sanchez had said much the same thing. And yet, my job was to do my best to find him, or at least what became of him. "Is that your belief? That your brother is alive and doesn't want to be found?"

Jeanine managed a tight-lipped smile. "If you're asking if I think the call to Nana Ellie was legit, the answer is no. Do I believe Brandon is alive and hiding out somewhere? I'd say the odds are remote, but I suppose anything is possible."

"Can we go back then, to the time just before he left home? The newspaper article quoted you as saying there had been tension in the house."

"I wasn't about to drag our dirty laundry in front of the world, but tension was an understatement. Even as a little girl, I could sense things were always strained between Dad and Brandon, like a blister waiting to burst, and they got worse with every passing year. Maybe things would have been different if Dad had adopted Brandon, but he didn't. You'd have to ask him why. I was never given a reason, and to the best of my knowledge, neither was Brandon."

"In the newspaper article, your mother is quoted as saying that he treated Brandon like his own son."

"Don't believe everything you read. My mother has a tendency to whitewash the facts. Most of the time, I don't think she's even aware of it. Denial can be a wonderful respite from reality. But my father would have taken a very dim view of her saying anything else. A very dim view."

"What about you? Were things strained between you and your father as well?"

"Far from it. My childhood experience was quite different from Brandon's."

"Yet you were raised in the same house."

"Yes, though with completely different styles of parenting. Not as unusual as you might think, and in many households one parent will favor one style, while the other parent may favor another."

"Good cop, bad cop," I said.

"Something like that. Shall I go into detail? Or do you know all of this already? I don't want to bore you."

I shook my head. "Trust me, I won't be bored, and my knowledge of raising children is zero. I don't have kids, and as odd as it may sound, none of my close friends do either."

"Also not entirely unusual. We often hang out with people in the same social circles. Young moms tend to gravitate to other young moms, career women to other career women. There are exceptions, of course. Childhood friends, for example. One friend may have children, the other may not, but the bonds of youthful secrets serve to keep them connected. Even so, those friendships often drift apart until the children are much older and involved with their own circle of friends." Jeanine leaned back, her eyes locked into mine. "What were your parents like?"

"My father raised me on his own from the time I was six."

"And your mother?"

"Not in the picture." I wasn't here for a consult, and hoped that the clipped tone of my voice made it clear.

A pink tint flushed Jeanine's pale skin. "Sorry, occupational hazard, being inquisitive. I wasn't meaning to pry."

Now it was my turn to blush. "An overreaction on my part, it's a sensitive subject. You were going to tell me about parenting styles."

"There are three different styles of parenting," Jeanine said, slipping into counseling mode. "Four styles if you consider uninvolved or neglectful a style. Some do, some don't. I fall into the latter category. At any rate, in the 1960s, Dr. Diana Baumrind, a psychologist, conducted a study, from which she developed her Pillar Theory. That theory draws relationships between basic parenting styles and children's behavior as a result. The styles are defined as authoritarian or disciplinarian, permissive or indulgent, and authoritative. Are you with me so far?"

I nodded.

"Let's start with authoritarian. Abusive parents usually fall into this category, but that doesn't mean that all authoritarian parents are abusive. They do, however, expect their children to obey every instruction without question. Punishment tends to be harsh and swift when rules are broken. There's seldom room for negotiation, little or no patience for disobedience, and there's a tendency to be unresponsive to a child's emotional needs. Another trait of this type of parent is that they will withhold love and affection if the child misbehaves, or shame them, something along the lines of, 'Why can't you ever do anything right?' or 'How can you be so stupid?' This is considered psychological or emotional manipulation. It's all about maintaining the upper hand. This type of behavior can also be found in other relationships, and it's never healthy."

"You said each style had a behavioral consequence."

"There are always exceptions, but in general children of authoritarian parents have lower self-esteem. They grow up to associate obedience and success with love, and they are very good at following rules. However, because they have rarely been given options, instead being told exactly what to do and when to do it, they may lack self-discipline, which can lead to problems when the parent is not around to supervise their behavior. There's also an increased risk of anxiety or depression."

I thought back to my own childhood. My father had never been abusive, but there had definitely been house rules that I'd been expected to follow. "I don't agree with psychological battering, but isn't it important for children to have established boundaries?"

"Absolutely," Jeanine said, "but most developmental experts agree that authoritarian parenting is too punitive and lacks the warmth, unconditional love, and nurturing that children need."

"I take it the permissive parent is the polar opposite of the authoritative parent."

"Exactly. In this parent-child relationship there are few boundaries. The emphasis is on freedom versus regulation, friendship versus parenting. The parent rarely enforces any sort of punishment as a consequence of poor behavior. In fact, the parent will sometimes resort to bribing their kids with toys, candy, or another reward to get them to behave, i.e. 'if you stop stomping your feet, I'll buy you an ice cream cone." It sounds idyllic for the child, and in truth, these types of parents are very nurturing, but the outcomes have proven to be poor. Without rules and guidelines, these children never learn limits, and studies have also linked permissive parenting to low achievement. If there are no expectations to meet, there's nothing to strive for. As a result, they can be ill-prepared for the real world, where there is an expectation of taking charge and accepting responsibility for actions or inactions."

Neither style sounded like my father. I found myself intrigued on a personal level. "What about the authoritative style?"

"This is the one recommended by parenting experts. Here, the parents have high expectations, but they also provide the necessary resources, tools, and emotional support to ensure the child's success. They encourage independence and ask for the child's opinion, but unlike the permissive parent, they don't rely on it as a means of making a decision, and unlike the authoritarian, they are open to discussing options. There are limits, expectations, and consequences. When necessary, discipline is fair, consistent, and measured. These children are self-confident in their ability to learn new skills and have good emotional and social interactions with others." Jeanine smiled. "Something tells me your father was an authoritative figure. Not that I'm trying to pry."

I smiled back. "I take it as a compliment. And yes, he did try to raise me that way. Certainly no amount of foot stomping or holding my breath would have resulted in getting a reward, and while he was strict, he was always fair, and never abusive, emotionally or otherwise. But let's get back to your household and your parents. Which style did they favor?"

"A fair question, and a good one. In a lot of ways, it was like Brandon and I were raised in two different households. Then again, we were very different kids. If my parents asked me to do something, I did it without question."

"I gather that wasn't the case with Brandon."

"I was eight years younger, so a lot of stuff went over my head, but I saw early on that defiance never led to a good outcome. As a result, Brandon was always being compared to me. 'Why can't you be more like your sister?' That sort of thing."

"He must have resented you."

"You would think so, but no, he didn't. If anything, he tried to protect me. There were lots of examples, but the one that stands out would have happened when I was about eight. I dragged a kitchen chair over to the countertop and climbed up on it. My objective was to get my mom's blue-and-white teapot to take to my teddy bear tea party, but I slipped and the teapot crashed to the floor, breaking into a thousand pieces. Brandon heard it and came flying in, a look of terror on his face. He told me to run to my room and keep my mouth shut."

"Let me guess, he cleaned everything up and took the blame for the teapot."

Jeanine nodded, her expression grave. "My father gave him the belt that day while I watched and listened to every flick as the leather hit his back, but Brandon never cried. My guess is he never even flinched, which, of course, enraged my father all the more. Later on, it occurred to me that my father knew it was my fault. Why would a sixteen-year-old boy want a teapot? So watching Brandon get the strap for my misdeed was my punishment, too. That's the day the dynamics started to change."

"In what way?"

"Until that day, Brandon had always made an effort to follow the rules. Though he defied Dad, he was otherwise quiet, studious, and tidy. He was also a bit of a dreamer, another thing that drove my father nuts. But after that day, Brandon pulled the 'you're not my father card.' Whatever Dad asked Brandon to do, from pass the salt to shovel the driveway, that became his stock reply." Jeanine gave a dry laugh. "You can imagine how that played out. My father couldn't argue the fact. It was true. And Brandon had already demonstrated that no amount of physical punishment was going to make him give in."

"Where was your mother in all this?"

"She'd try to make up for it by being too permissive when Dad wasn't around, which only served to confuse him. But she fell in line when Dad was around."

"The newspaper article also said Brandon had been a straight-A student, at least until his second year of college. That must have pleased your folks, if nothing else."

"Yes and no. Certainly they never had to worry about Brandon's marks. That boy was brilliant. I had to study night and day to make the honor roll, and even then I didn't always succeed. Half the time, Brandon didn't even bring his books home, and when he did, he'd just leave them in his backpack by the front door. It was one more thing to get under my father's skin, especially since he couldn't say much about it. Brandon was consistently in the top quarter of his class, often the top of it. He could have had his pick of any college or university, but Dad insisted on Cedar County College in Lakeside, and no residency for him either. Brandon was forced to commute back and forth on the GO."

Taking the GO train to Toronto was one thing. The GO bus to Lakeside would involve multiple stops and a very slow ride both ways. I could imagine a young Brandon making the daily journey and resenting every minute of it, the resentment for his stepfather intensifying with every trip. "Was money an object?"

"Dad claimed it was a financial decision, but I know it was just his way of being in control." She shook her head. "Maybe if he'd given Brandon a little more freedom, allowed him to go somewhere out of province, or at least out of the county, he wouldn't have felt the need to run away to find himself."

"Brandon's marks slipped to the point of flunking out in his second year and he dropped out. Why do you think that was?"

"I wish I knew. He just kept withdrawing deeper into himself. By the time he left, his closest friends hadn't talked to him since before Christmas."

"Drugs?"

"It fits in theory, but I don't think so, at least not beyond the experimentation stage. I certainly never saw any evidence of it and if he had a problem, my father would have been the first one to deal with it—and not in a constructive manner."

"Something changed him enough to start flunking out."

"I know that he became increasingly obsessed with finding his biological father. It was the source of many arguments between him and our mother, but she refused to tell him who the guy was, or why it was such a big secret. Sometimes I think if she'd told him, Brandon wouldn't have left home. But then I think, what good comes out of laying blame? It's not going to change the outcome, is it?"

The bitterness in Jeanine's voice surprised me. It was time to hit her with the question I'd been saving for just such a moment.

"Did Brandon ever talk about going on a fool's journey?"

"A fool's journey?" Jeanine's brow wrinkled in concentration. "No, although…"

"Although?"

"My father. As far back as I remember, he would

taunt Brandon by calling him a fool. 'Don't be such a fool.' 'Only a fool would do something like that.' Sometimes Brandon would bait him, say stuff like, 'look what the fool did, got himself an A-plus in Calculus.' But mostly he'd just slink into his room and slam the door, trying to shut it all out."

Her answer came a little too fast, and the skeptical side of me remained unconvinced. "The tattoo your brother got, it's the top half of The Fool, the first card in the tarot deck. Some people claim the tarot is The Fool's Journey."

"I don't know anything about tarot," Jeanine said, defensive, her face flushed.

"But you knew something." Relentless, picking at the scab and not entirely proud of it.

A big sigh and then, "Yes, I knew what the tattoo was, or at least, what it was going to be. Brandon talked to me about it for weeks before actually going under the needle. For all his bravado, I think he was worried about Dad's reaction. My father doesn't have much use for tattoos, calls them trailer trash art." Jeanine grimaced. "He can be a bit of a bigot, as you'll find out for yourself when you interview him." A pained look flicked across her face and I wondered how much she and her mother had endured over the years, or if all the vitriol had been targeted at his stepson.

"Did your father find out about the tattoo?"

"Not at the time. Brandon kept his arms covered. But he showed me. He was so proud of it, said he was going back the following week to get the outline finished. He kept going on about the tattoo artist, some guy named Sam who was totally into tarot, too."

"A guy named Sam?" I asked the next question, already knowing the answer. "Did the police ever find him?"

Jeanine bit her lip. "I didn't tell the police or my parents about that tattoo for two years. It's my one regret, and it's a big one. I wanted to keep Brandon's secret. I never thought he'd stay away forever. I assumed that he'd come home stronger than when he left, that he really would find himself a new beginning. When he didn't call or write…when the police said there were no other leads to follow up…that's when I told them, that's when they had me describe it for the police sketch artist. Not that it did any good. By the time they linked it to Such & Such Tattoo, the business had gone under and Dave Samuels had died."

"Dave Samuels?"

"The tattoo artist and the owner of Such & Such. His name was Dave Samuels, Sam for short, I guess. Sorry, I'm usually more articulate."

Dave Samuels. Sam Sanchez. A whole lot of Sams going on. I wondered what it meant, or if it meant anything. I pushed the thought aside for the moment. The delay in telling the police about the tattoo at least explained why Sam Sanchez had never been interviewed.

"You just said blaming your mother wouldn't change the outcome. And yet you blame yourself. Why? You were just a kid at the time, doing what you thought was right to protect your brother. You're an innocent bystander."

"I stopped being innocent the day Brandon got the belt on my behalf. Any hope for staying a kid died when Brandon left home. You grow up in a hurry when your parents are at each other's throats blaming one another twenty-four seven, or when they stop talking and the silence becomes deafening. I never thought of Brandon as a half brother, and for all his 'you're not my father' talk to my dad and the fact he wasn't adopted, I know he never thought of me as anything else but his little sister. We loved each other. We had each other's backs."

"You still miss him." A statement, not a question.

"Every day of my life. It's why I started the Facebook page, not that it ever resulted in anything. It's also the reason I went into social work, to help other families that are going through what my family did. But you have to want help, to accept that you don't have all the answers. My mother just closed off from the world. My father went on with his life as though nothing had changed. Sometimes I question if they really want to find Brandon."

An odd thing to say. "Why do you think that?"

"I don't know. They didn't file a missing person report until early August, four months after he left home. And when Nana Ellie got the call from the man claiming to be Brandon, I had the very distinct impression my father was more upset with the possibility of him turning up than it being a scam." Jeanine's hand flicked an imaginary strand of hair from her face and I noticed a small tattoo on the inside of her wrist for the first time. I couldn't be sure, but it looked like one of her origami birds. I wondered when—and where—she'd gotten it.

"What about your mother? What was her reaction to the call?"

"You'll have to ask her. We stopped communicating years ago. Now if you'll excuse me, my ten o'clock should be here in six minutes." Jeanine got up and opened the door. I walked out under the canopy of origami birds and heard the pointy-nosed receptionist sniff loudly as I made my way out of the windowless waiting room, down the stairs, and onto Edward Street. Inside Spinners, the cyclists were doing calf and quad stretches next to their bikes, fluffy white towels draped around their necks, smiles plastered on their sweat-drenched faces. I envied their feeling of accomplishment, their work done, mine just beginning. A thought struck me and I grinned at the irony of it. Maybe I was the one on a fool's journey.

FOURTEEN

BACK HOME, I went through the ritual of writing everything down in my journal, closing my eyes every now and again as I tried to recall an exact quote or an expression on Jeanine's face during the interview. She'd been more open with me than I'd expected, and yet, as had been the case with Sam Sanchez, I was left with the distinct feeling she was holding something back.

But what? I believed her when she said she didn't know anything about tarot and The Fool's Journey. I tapped my pen against the table. Could it relate to her mother? Perhaps the reason they stopped communicating? It would be something else to ask Lorna. I just hoped she was prepared to answer.

CHANTELLE MIGHT NOT be a morning person, but she's punctual. I like that in a person. I gave her my journal to look over while I got the coffee and muffins ready.

"Good notes," Chantelle said, when she finished. "Comprehensive. Your recall never fails to amaze me, but wouldn't it be easier to tape the conversations?"

"Definitely, but someone like Sam Sanchez would have clammed up if I'd suggested it. Jeanine, too, I suspect. And it wouldn't be ethical to record them without their knowledge. Anyway, writing it down like this helps me to crystallize my thoughts. Now that you've read the notes, what's your first impression?"

"Sam Sanchez is an interesting character. You wrote that you thought she was holding something back. Any idea what it might be, now that you've had a day to think it over?"

"It has to be Dave Samuels. She spoke of him as if her were a mentor, but I think he was more of a father figure."

"That could explain the Cowgirls Don't Cry tattoo. Have you seen the video? Really good."

"I have, and I had no idea you liked country music. How did I not know that?"

"To be honest, country is more Lance the Loser's thing, but I'm a big Reba fan. Did you ever watch her TV show where she plays a divorced mom with three kids?"

I shook my head.

"Her teenage daughter gets pregnant, marries the teenaged boyfriend, and the two of them move into Reba's house while they finish high school. Reba's ex-husband is a dentist and his new wife thinks she's Reba's best friend." Chantelle blushed. "I loved that show. I actually own all six seasons on DVD."

"Good to know," I said, without any intention of borrowing it. Chantelle caught my sarcasm.

"Apparently not. So—what did Misty say?"

Sometimes Chantelle changes directions fast enough to give me whiplash. "What did she say about what?"

"About Brandon going on a fool's journey."

"I, uh, I haven't told her yet." I felt like an idiot. It was such an obvious thing to do.

"Have you looked at the website? She did a great job of setting up the 'Find Brandon' page."

I shook my head.

"There's no time like the present," Chantelle said, pushing my tablet towards me.

I opened the browser to our home page. Two clicks took me to the headline: Help Us Find Brandon Colbeck, along with a brief summary. She'd also included his photograph and the age-progressed sketches, all three clearly labeled, as well as the sketch of the half-finished tattoo with a caption indicating it was The Fool, and a link to the article in the *Marketville Post*. No comments or shares yet, but it had only been posted for a few hours. At the bottom of the page there was a link to Misty's Message page, with "*To Read More About The Fool in Tarot, click here*" in bold italicized text. I clicked.

The post included a large image of the Rider-Waite card in the upper left corner.

The Fool (0)

The first card in the Major Arcana, The Fool depicts a young man dancing on the edge of a mountain cliff, his face tilted with reverence toward the sun. Notice the attention to detail: the small white dog leaping with abandon by his right foot, the boy's wavy golden hair topped with a small cap sporting a flowing purple feather—we will see the same feather on the child in the nineteenth card, The Sun—the jewel-toned flowered tunic over a white long-sleeved shirt, the bright yellow calf-length boots, the single white rose in one hand, the long stick slung over his shoulder, a small brown bag tied to the end of it. Some believe the bag contains his life experiences, others his memories of past lives; whatever the case, he carries it lightly, without any sense of burden.

The imagery evokes a sense of freedom, of a journey ready to begin. Even the card's number is meaningful: an egg-shaped zero, from which new life will begin. Only one other card in tarot features someone dancing—number 21, The World, the final card in the Major Arcana. Signifying the end, it features a woman centered inside an egg-shaped wreath, the journey coming full circle.

I flipped the tablet closed. "She did a nice job."

Chantelle nodded. "Do you think we should let her know we appreciate what she's done here, maybe send her an email?"

I picked up the phone. "I do, and it will be even more meaningful if we call her."

"Uh, Callie, I appreciate the sentiment, but it's not even 8:30. Not everyone is up at the crack of dawn."

"For your information, dawn cracked at 5:35, but I take your point. I'll text her to call me when she's up." I sent the text, smiling as I wrote it. Chantelle liked to tease me about my perfectly worded and spelled texts, but I just couldn't bring myself to abbreviate you're to *yur* or worse, *yer*, and seriously, how difficult was it to add an apostrophe? "Call me if you're up."

Misty rang me within a minute, her voice breathless. "Did you see the page? Is it okay? I shared it on all the usual social media platforms."

"You've outdone yourself, but the journey is just beginning, pun fully intended. Are you up for more work?"

"I thought you'd never ask."

I updated Misty briefly on my visits with Sam Sanchez and Jeanine Westlake. "According to Sam, Brandon was planning to go on a fool's journey. Jeanine claims to be unaware, though she admitted he'd gotten heavily interested in tarot. I'm inclined to believe her about not knowing about The Fool's Journey, but I get the impression she knows more than she's saying. So is Sam, or at least that's my gut feeling. Do you think you could create a post about The Fool's Journey? The history behind it?"

"I could definitely do that," Misty said, a lilt in her voice. "What if…what if I followed it up every few days with the next card in the Major Arcana to create a better understanding of the cards?"

"Hmmm… I'm not sure how you'll be able to tie it into Brandon, given we don't know where he is or if he's even alive."

Misty's silence spoke volumes. She'd come up with a concept and all I had done was naysay it. "I'll tell you what. I'll enter my interview notes from Sam and Jeanine in Word and send them to you in the next couple of days. It's a long shot, but you may be able to find a nugget of something that will tie in with the cards. If so, I don't see the harm in trying it. But let's start with The Fool's Journey, okay? I think it's the key to this case, and I don't want to dilute the importance of that with a bunch of posts, even if they are interconnected. Besides, we may find, in time, that one card is more important to the investigation than another."

"I totally understand," Misty said, and I could hear the enthusiasm creep back into her voice.

"Okay, good. Chantelle and I are meeting with Lorna Colbeck-Westlake in about thirty minutes, so there'll be that one coming as well. I don't have an appointment yet with Michael Westlake—Lorna has promised to set that up for me—and at this stage we still don't know the name of Brandon's biological father. I'll update you whenever I have that information."

"I'll get working on The Fool's Journey post as soon as we hang up." Misty paused. "And Callie? Thank you for including me. It means a lot that you trust me with this."

"Thank *you*, Misty."

I disconnected and smiled at Chantelle. "She's on it."

The phone rang. I glanced at the call display expecting to see Misty calling back. Instead it was Shirley Harrington. "Hey Shirley, what's up?"

"Sorry to call you so early, but I figured you'd be up and I want to head down to the Cedar County Reference Library when it opens. I've been going through the archives of the *Marketville Post*, but so far all I've found are a few articles on Eleanor Colbeck's philanthropic initiatives. I can't imagine they'll be helpful, but I've printed them nonetheless. There's been nothing else so far, but it's early days. Everything earlier than 2009 is on microfiche."

I knew how tedious that could be and sent her a silent hug for tackling it. "I appreciate the update, though there's no need to call unless you've got anything riveting. In the meantime, keep digging."

"I plan to. At least the *Toronto Star* will be easier since the Toronto Public Library has everything but the past three years digitalized."

A thought crossed my mind. "Actually, it's probably good that you called because I have four more names for you to check out."

"I've got a pen and paper handy."

"Samantha, a.k.a. Sam, Sanchez. She's the owner of Trust Few Tattoo on Poplar Street, established sometime in 2003. The other name is Dave Samuels. He owned a tattoo parlor called Such & Such. It was in the Nature's Way store, at the back, where Sun, Moon & Stars is now. I'm not sure when it opened but my guess is the late nineties. He closed the shop in August 2003, died shortly thereafter."

"Samantha Sam Sanchez. Trust Few Tattoo. Dave Samuels. Such & Such Tattoo. Got it. What are you expecting me to find?"

"The *Marketville Post* may have something about Such & Such Tattoo closing. The *Post* or *Star* may have an obituary for Dave Samuels, which could prove enlightening."

"Nothing like reading a good obituary," Shirley said, a chuckle in her voice. "I'll be in touch."

Shirley might chuckle, but I knew only too well the truth of that statement. Obituaries could be more than a record of when someone was born and when they died. A statement like, "Donations to Cancer Society or Heart & Stroke" and you could pretty much guarantee the person died of cancer or something cardiac related. "Died suddenly" often meant by suicide, especially when combined with a call for donations to a mental health organization. But it was more than that. The best obits listed family members: parents, children, brothers, sisters, aunts, uncles, cousins, nieces, nephews—that's where the magic lay.

I turned to Chantelle. "You know, we have a great team." We were clinking our coffee cups together when the doorbell rang.

FIFTEEN

LORNA COLBECK-WESTLAKE wore a beaded, off-white macramé vest over a rainbow-hued, long sleeved, tie-dyed T-shirt, a woven brown leather bracelet with fringes, and faded acid wash jeans. I found myself checking to see if the hems were bellbottomed and frayed, circa 1978. A vague memory surfaced: sitting at the kitchen table with my mother, a gridded board, twine, and colored beads in front of me as she attempted to teach me a few simple knots. The memory surprised me, but that was what remembering her was like, random thoughts drifting in when I least expected them. I shook the thought aside and focused on Lorna.

Jeanine definitely took after her, at least physically. Like her daughter, Lorna was petite, with delicate facial features and pale blue eyes, but where Jeanine's highlighted blonde hair had been cut short, Lorna's gray-streaked curls had been twisted haphazardly into a messy bun, strands spilling out at odd angles. Lorna looked to be in her late fifties, too old to carry off the look, but somehow she succeeded. I wondered how this free spirit had managed to marry, and stay married to, an authoritarian like the Michael Westlake their daughter had described. I'd expected someone bottled up, tight and prudish.

"Welcome to Past & Present," I said, realizing that I'd let her stand in the hall longer than could be considered polite. "I'm Callie, and this is my business partner, Chantelle. Have a seat at the table and I'll bring you a coffee. Mug or cup?"

"Mug. The bigger the better. Black, no milk, no sugar."

I bustled into the kitchen, eager to get started. Chantelle was already chatting with Lorna when I came back.

"Lorna was just telling me that she filed for divorce yesterday," Chantelle said. "Irreconcilable differences."

Her other appointment, the reason she couldn't see us yesterday. I wondered what would be considered an appropriate response and settled for, "I'm sorry."

"There's no need to be sorry. Our marriage was on a slow path to destruction from the day Brandon left home. Michael and I both blamed each other, though no one could have blamed me any more than I blamed myself. Michael said I was too soft. I said he was too hard. Both statements are equally true." Lorna gave a resigned shrug. "My daughter has labels for such things, as you no doubt learned when you met with her yesterday."

"I was under the impression you no longer communicated."

Lorna barked out a bitter laugh. "Is that what she told you? You mustn't take Jeanine so literally. We talk, most days, in fact. We just don't talk about anything of substance. The weather, how the Raptors are doing, how much the house down the street sold for. I started losing Jeanine somewhere in her teens, my fault, not hers. I was too consumed with guilt and grief to be a proper parent. Every day, every week, every year that ticked by without word of Brandon closed me further off from the world. Michael, on the other hand, handled things with more resilience. Once Brandon was gone, whatever little affection Michael felt for him was quickly and efficiently transferred to Jeanine. He's like that. Efficient with his emotions."

Efficient with his emotions. Interesting. "Jeanine implied that Michael was tough on Brandon."

"Tough? That's a nice way to put it. He bullied Brandon and bubble-wrapped Jeanine. It's probably the reason she went into social work. If so, at least Michael and I did something right as parents. She's done well for herself in trying to help others. Unfortunately, one of those others isn't my son." Lorna looked down at her clothes as if noticing them for the first time, then ran a bird-like hand through her hair. I noticed she was still wearing her wedding rings.

"I don't think she'd approve of my new look, though admittedly I'm not usually quite so bohemian. Found these at the back of my closet, couldn't believe I'd kept them, or that they still fit. The one positive of being a frayed sack of nerves for the better part of two decades. I can't keep weight on, even when I binge, which truthfully isn't often, and I'm a manic exerciser. I tried drinking to excess for a while but it didn't help. I usually favor well-cut slacks and silk blouses, and my hair is usually wrestled into a French braid or something equally reserved. I'll probably go back to that look in a day or two. Right now, I'm enjoying this retro phase." She laughed again, embarrassment replacing the bitterness. "Listen to me blathering on about my wardrobe choices. You wanted to talk about Brandon. Let's talk. Though I can't imagine I'll have much to add beyond what you've already been told or read."

"Jeanine also told us that Brandon had become increasingly interested in learning about his biological father." I didn't add that she'd told us about Brandon's "you're not my father," rants, though by the tight expression on Lorna's face, she knew that we knew. I continued on. "Chantelle is an expert in genealogy. We thought if she prepared a family tree for Brandon, it might provide a direction to take."

"What you're actually asking is for the name of Brandon's biological father. The rest is window dressing."

Chantelle blushed. "We're not trying to be invasive, but it's important to explore all avenues. The more information we have, the better chance of success at finding a connection."

"I don't think you're trying to be invasive, but the police have already asked these questions."

"Then let's start with what you told them," I said, and Chantelle nodded her agreement.

Lorna assessed us both. "Okay, sure. What harm can it do after all these years? Brandon's father was a guy I met in a bar one night. He was maybe early thirties, though he could have been younger or older. I was underage, over-served, and feeling amorous. He was handsome and charming and laughed at all of my jokes. When he offered to drive me home, I agreed, though we both knew it would be more than that. We drove into the Cedar Park Soccer Field and made love under the moon and stars. He even had a blanket. At the time it seemed romantic, and neither one of us thought about using protection. I found out I was pregnant six weeks later. I went back to the bar, looking for the guy. Never saw him again. No one had. My guess is he was just driving through."

"What was his name?" I asked.

Lorna blushed. "He said his name was Alexander, but it could have been anything. We didn't get to last names. I remember he had a tattoo of an eagle across the top of his back, went from shoulder to shoulder. I'd never known anyone with a tattoo."

"What did he look like?"

"Like the age-progressed sketch of Brandon. The one with the beard. When the police first showed me that sketch, I couldn't believe it. I mean, I knew Brandon took after the man who knocked me up, but to see him as an adult…" Lorna bit her lip. "You'd think something like that would bring me comfort, but instead, it broke my heart."

I sat there, not sure of what to say. Chantelle came to the rescue.

"Do you remember the name of the bar? Where it was?"

"Sure. It was on the corner of Lancaster and Water, long gone and replaced by a strip mall. It was called the Running Jump, though locals called it the Running Dump, a reputation well deserved, I assure you. Not a place for nice girls. Then again, I wasn't a nice girl, or at least I didn't want to be, gave my parents plenty of room for concern during my teen years. That changed after I found out I was expecting. I never once thought of having an abortion or giving my baby up for adoption. I wanted to be a good mother. I think I was, for a while. We'd go to my parents' cabin in the summer and swim and fish and hike. Then I met Michael at work. I thought he'd be good for us. A boy needs a father, you know, and Brandon was seven. So we got married, and I got pregnant pretty much right away, and any talk of adopting Brandon went by the wayside."

"Jeanine said that you never told Brandon about his biological father."

"That's where she'd be wrong, not that I've ever told her differently. I did tell him. I told him a couple of weeks before he left to find himself. That's why it haunts me. Day and night, the thing that makes me believe my son left with the intention of never returning home."

I felt clueless. "What is it that haunts you, Lorna?"

"He took his laptop, clothes, even his toiletries. But he left his ID behind, the one thing that identified him as Brandon Colbeck. Without that, he could be anyone." Lorna looked at us, her cheeks stained by tears. "He could be anyone, couldn't he?"

I didn't have an answer for that. Neither did Chantelle.

SIXTEEN

Lorna had no sooner left when my phone rang. I checked the call display. Royce. I'd had a handful of voice mail messages and texts from him asking me to call him. I showed the phone to Chantelle who made an "answer it" gesture.

"Hi, Royce, I got your messages, but I've been busy with this new case. In fact, Chantelle's here now."

"I'd like to come by when you're free. Later on today, after she leaves."

No preamble, just, "I'd like to come by when you're free." It might have been nothing more than annoyance at my not calling him back, but I sensed something more in his terse tone. "Do you want me to make dinner?"

"No, that's okay. Just text me when Chantelle leaves and I'll swing by. There's something I need to talk to you about, and I'd rather do it in person."

"Will do," I said, and hung up, a disconcerted feeling seeping into my bones.

"Royce coming over for dinner later?" Chantelle asked.

"He says he doesn't want any dinner. He does, however, have something he needs to tell me."

A raised eyebrow. "Hmmm. How's it going with him, anyway?"

"If you'd asked me an hour ago, I would have said we were figuring out our relationship."

"And now?"

"I'm pretty sure he's coming over to break up with me. Royce would be chivalrous like that. He wouldn't do it over the phone."

"Are you misreading the situation?"

"Maybe, but I don't think so." I caught Chantelle's sympathetic glance and felt my defense mechanisms kick into overdrive. I didn't want or need her pity, especially over some guy where my feelings were as yet undefined. "Seriously, it's fine. I like him as a friend, and I'll admit to being physically attracted to him, but you know as well as I do that it's never going to feel right between me and his family, and family's important."

"You don't have to extol the virtues of family on me," Chantelle said, "but I think if you gave it some time, things would sort themselves out. If you like Royce, he's worth fighting for."

"The thing is, I've been in love twice before, and it felt different than this. More heat in the passion. More daydreaming about what our future together would look like, right down to the house we'd buy and the kids we'd raise. This feels more like… I don't know…best friends with benefits?" I thought back to the guy who dumped me on Valentine's Day when I was expecting an engagement ring. Then came the two-timing triathlete. Talk about clueless. At least this time, I'd be semi-prepared.

"There's nothing wrong with being friends with benefits if that's all you want," Chantelle said.

"Why am I sensing a but?"

"Because I think it's more a case of you've been in love twice before and been hurt twice before, and you don't want to be hurt again. God knows, I can relate.

Anyway, I should go, let him come over, get whatever it is he needs to say, said."

"Don't you think we should review what Lorna told us?"

"I think we should both write up our version of the meeting and compare notes on the weekend. Speaking of which, I can't make it when Lucy Daneluk comes over tomorrow. I have a…thing."

"A thing?"

Chantelle blushed. "If you must know, I've agreed to help Lance work on his family tree."

Lance. Not Lance the Loser. Was there a reconciliation going on that I didn't know about?

"I know what you're thinking, and no, it's not like that. As far as I know, he's still with Cleopatra."

Cleopatra was the name Chantelle had given to Lance's adolescent girlfriend, she of the porcelain skin, waist-length black hair, jade green eyes, and legs that went up to her ears. "If you say so."

"I do. Say so. Lance just received the results of his DNA test from Ancestry.ca, and there are a bunch of matches we want to drill down on to see if we can find out any more. He was adopted, you know."

"I didn't know."

"Oh yeah. I often think the main attraction to marrying me was becoming part of a big family. He and my brother, Bill, are still best buds."

Spoken without a trace of bitterness. Something was definitely brewing between Chantelle and her ex. She'd fill me in when she was ready and not a moment before. "I've been thinking of doing a DNA test," I said, "but part of me is worried that I'll dredge up more skeletons."

Chantelle laughed. "Your imagination runneth over,

Callie. Anyway, I'm off. Call me later if you need a shoulder to cry on."

I should have texted Royce as soon as she walked out the door. Instead, I took ninety minutes to write up my notes about our meeting with Lorna Colbeck-Westlake, and another thirty to reread them and satisfy myself I'd captured everything. Only then did I send a two-word text to Royce.

"I'm free," wondering if the words held a double meaning.

My phone pinged. "Be there in 60."

An hour. That gave me time to scoot out to the convenience store on Trillium Way and pick up a bottle of chocolate syrup and a pint of French vanilla ice cream. What can I say? I've had experience getting dumped.

ROYCE ARRIVED WITHIN the hour, and he looked good, his sandy brown hair slightly tousled. Then again, he always looked good. There was nothing wrong with the physical attraction side of things, at least from my standpoint. He gave me a quick peck on the forehead, like something you'd do to your favorite niece, and I was filled with a sense of déjà vu. The forehead peck is never a good sign, and I was reminded of the Justin Moore song, "You Look Like I Need A Drink."

"Can I get you something? Beer? Glass of wine? Soft drink?"

"A beer would be nice."

I went into the kitchen, grabbed a beer and a bottle of Chardonnay from the refrigerator, and took a mug and a wineglass out of the cupboard. I poured the beer slowly, not just to get the foam right, but because my hands had a slight tremble. I followed with the white wine, returned the bottle to the fridge, and took our drinks to the main room. Royce was sitting in one of the Arts & Crafts Mission oak chairs. He stood up, took the beer and clinked my wineglass. "Cheers."

"Cheers." I sat down. May as well cut to the chase. "What is it you needed to tell me?"

Royce took a sip of his beer, then came out with it. "I, uh, I've met someone."

Met someone? I'd been expecting a breakup but not because he'd met someone. "Oh."

"I met her at Porsche's play. When Porsche was Eliza Doolittle in *Pygmalion*. In Muskoka. There was a party afterwards. At night."

I nodded. I was supposed to go with him, but the reading of Olivia's will had put an end to that. I remember feeling slightly relieved at the time, knowing his mother, father, and aunt would also be in attendance. I nodded again, not quite ready to trust my voice. You'd think it would get easier, me being an old hand at this getting dumped business. It doesn't.

"Her name's Mercy," Royce said.

Mercy.

"She's an actress."

An actress. It just keeps getting better. I took a swig of my wine.

"Mercy Dellacorte," Royce continued. "She was Porsche's understudy. Also played the role of Clara Eynsford-Hill. Does commercials, too. You might recognize her from the one for that new Icelandic yogurt."

I shook my head, wondering what a Mercy Dellacorte would look like. I envisioned someone young, fresh-faced, movie-star-slender, with shoulder-length blonde hair, wispy bangs, and long, black eyelashes framing smoldering cobalt-blue eyes.

"I gather you were taken with her performance." I heard the snooty tone in my voice and cursed myself. I was trying to be an adult about this, and failing miserably.

"I'm sorry, Callie," Royce said, and he really did look sorry. "I thought you and I may have had something, but... I don't know. I just had the impression that you weren't committed to committing. I'm forty-one. More than ready to settle down and start a family before it's too late."

Too late? Men could have kids when they were positively geriatric. Just ask Mick Jagger or Richard Gere. "There's no need to apologize. You're right. I wasn't ready. I'm not sure why." I thought about adding, "It's not you, it's me," but figured that would be overkill. "I hope we can remain friends."

"I'd like that," he said, and I knew from the way he said it that it would never happen. Damn. Good renovators were hard to find. What was I thinking? Good guys like Royce Ashford were even harder to find.

He drained his beer and got up to leave. "I'll let myself out."

"Sure you can't stay for another? I can still make dinner."

Royce shook his head. "Mercy is waiting for me back at the house."

That explained the slightly tousled hair. "Ah. Well, then." I stood up, resisting the urge to trace my fingertip lightly along his jaw. "You take care of yourself."

"You too, Callie."

He left without pecking me on the forehead.

I CALLED CHANTELLE after inhaling the entire pint of ice cream, drenched in chocolate syrup.

"Hey," she said, picking up on the first ring.

"Mercy."

"Mercy?"

"That's her name. Mercy Dellacorte. She's an actress."

"Ah, geez. I'll be right over."

"No, seriously, stay put. I don't feel much like company right now. Actually, I feel kind of sick to my stomach."

"How much wine did you drink?"

"Just one small glass when Royce was here. It's the ice cream. A whole pint, with chocolate syrup."

"Taking ice cream therapy to a new level, are you?"

"Next time I'll skip the syrup."

"Next time?" Chantelle laughed. "You're the only person I know who prepares to get dumped before they even have a new man in their life."

"Just thinking ahead," I said, but she had me laughing with her. I hung up and made myself a cup of peppermint tea to settle my stomach.

Mercy Dellacorte. Her real name was probably something like Mary Dell or something equally benign. I smiled, comforted by the thought, and sipped my tea, letting my mind drift to wherever it needed to go. Mercy Dellacorte. Mary Dell.

Brandon Colbeck.

I took out my journal book and underlined Lorna's last few words: "Why didn't he take his ID?"

"Where are you, Brandon Colbeck?" I asked the darkening room. "And who did you become?"

SEVENTEEN

I WOKE UP early Friday morning with time to kill before Lucy Daneluk arrived at two p.m. I made tea, two slices of rye toast with peanut butter, and turned on my tablet to see if Misty had added the entry for The Fool's Journey to the Past and Present website. Instead I found myself googling Mercy Dellacorte.

As websites went, hers was pretty basic. The Home page included a brief bio, along with a photograph of Mercy sitting on a large boulder beside a lake. Mercy didn't look at all like I'd envisioned her. She was about my age, height, and weight, in other words late thirties, five-foot-six, and neither slender nor plump, with straight, dark brown hair cut in an unadventurous chin-length bob parted to one side. Everything about Mercy seemed ordinary—provided you were able to ignore the enigmatic half-smile and the come-hither sparkle in her black-brown eyes. Apparently Royce couldn't.

I studied her choice of clothes: black open-toed, wedge-heeled sandals, black tights, and what appeared to be a black camisole, covered by a flowing black and turquoise top in an abstract circular pattern, with patches of black crocheted bits along the sleeves and neckline. If I had to label the style of the top, it'd be a flouncy thing.

The bio was short and simple:

Born and raised in Toronto, Ontario, Mercy Dellacorte is a Canadian actress best known for her regional stage work. She is currently in *Pygmalion* as Clara Eynsford-Hill and recently played Gwendolen Fairfax in *The Importance of Being Earnest*. She was also a runner-up on season two of *Canada Bakes*.

I recognized the baking show and was forced to admit I'd caught it once or twice, although clearly I'd missed season two. I also knew that Royce had a sweet tooth, another plus for Mercy Dellacorte. I clicked on the link that took me to her Credentials page, which was more of the same, along with mention of the Icelandic yogurt commercial.

The Photos page included a collage of Mercy, Mercy, and more Mercy. My breath caught in my throat at a shot of her, champagne flute in hand, laughing backstage with Porsche and Royce.

I clicked off, annoyed with myself for the investment of time and the hollow ache in my stomach, and went to the Past & Present website, pleased to find The Fool's Journey entered. At the top of the page, Misty had included a fanlike spread of all twenty-two cards in the Major Arcana, placed in order from 0 to 21.

The Fool's Journey: A Brief History
This post will serve as a brief introduction to a new series tracing The Fool's Journey in tarot. Each of these posts will review the subsequent cards in the Major Arcana in order. (To read about the first card, number 0, The Fool, click here.) It is our hope that beyond serving as entertainment,

that one or more of these posts will resonate with readers, and help Past & Present find Brandon Colbeck. Comments are open below, or you may contact us using our secure form. We appreciate all shares on social media.

I stopped reading to test all three links: The Fool, Brandon Colbeck, and Contact Us. Each one opened to a separate page, leaving The Fool's Journey post open. Perfect. I went back to reading.

Many believe the Major Arcana is The Fool's Journey as he travels through life, making discoveries and learning along the way, until his journey is complete. Some believe the concept was first embraced by Eden Gray in her 1969 book, *The Tarot Revealed*, which delved into the meaning of tarot cards as they relate to fortunetelling, and played an integral part in the creation of the contemporary interest in tarot in general, and her interpretation of The Fool's Journey in particular. However, A.E. Waite, the designer of the card, wrote, some eighty years earlier, "he is a prince of the other world in his travels through this one."

Misty's Message: Be careful what you wish for: only those truly alone in this world have no one to miss them, and those left behind remain on an endless journey for the truth.

It was a powerful message. Time would tell whether it reached anyone who could help us. I logged off and turned on the TV, clicking On Demand to find back episodes of *Canada Bakes*, season two.

I'll admit to feeling somewhat smug when Mercy was cut after the pound cake in her Baked Alaska was too dry. I mean, seriously, how difficult is it to bake a moist pound cake?

EIGHTEEN

LUCY DANELUK ARRIVED bang on two p.m. Friday. I invited her in, explaining, without elaboration, that Chantelle wouldn't be able to make it.

Daneluk was an attractive woman in her late forties, with feathered bangs and shoulder-length hair highlighted with shades of copper and gold, lightly bronzed skin, and dark eyebrows over intelligent brown eyes. She sized me up briefly and nodded once, as if satisfied with what she saw. I motioned her to sit in one of the mission oak recliners under the kitchen pass-through, offering her a beverage of her choice. She opted for soda water with a slice of lemon if I had it. I did, and decided on the same for myself.

"You're younger that I thought you'd be," she said, settling in after I brought her the water.

"Thirty-nine. The big four-oh looms on the horizon."

"Growing old is a privilege denied to too many. Not that forty is old. Tell me how someone so young gets into the business of digging up the past?"

"It's a long story."

"I have time."

The way she said it made me realize it was her way of vetting me. If I wanted any information, I'd have no option but to tell her.

"My father died in an occupational accident two years ago." I've learned to refrain from prefacing it with "unfortunate," the term used on the day I was no-tified. "He left me a house in Marketville on the condi-tion I look into my mother's disappearance thirty years earlier."

Lucy glanced around the room. "This house?"

"No, it was on Snapdragon Circle in the Trillium Way subdivision, the house we lived in when my mom left. I sold it a few months ago, after…after closing the file on my mother." *Closing the file on my mother.* Well, that was one way to put it. I took a deep breath and sol-diered on. "I didn't want to stay there, and I didn't want to go back to working at a bank call center."

"I can imagine neither option appealed."

I glanced at Lucy, checking her face for a hint of sar-casm, and found none. "I purchased this property and started Past & Present with Chantelle. It's working out."

"Tell me a bit more about Past & Present. I gather you're the leader?"

"I guess so, yeah, because Chantelle also works as a personal trainer and fitness instructor at the gym, so she's less available than I am, and I have more invested financially. But we don't do everything ourselves. We have a team. Chantelle's specialty is genealogy and on-line research. Arabella Carpenter owns the Glass Dol-phin antiques shop in Lount's Landing. She actually referred us to our first case, a woman who came to her looking for ocean liner memorabilia that might lead to information about her grandmother. Shirley Harrington is a retired reference librarian. She has a passion for perusing old newspapers and records, which, trust me, is every bit as tedious as it sounds. And Misty Rivers is…" How did I explain Misty without coming across like a crazy person or losing Lucy as a source?

"I've been reading Misty's Messages on the Past & Present website," Lucy said, sparing the need for an explanation. "Very informative and professionally represented. I think her expertise in that area will come in handy as you search for Brandon Colbeck."

I breathed an inward sigh of relief. "It already has. She recognized the partially finished tattoo as the top half of The Fool, the first card in tarot. The drawing is representative of the Rider-Waite deck."

"I knew that, as did the police, not that the lead went anywhere. Fresh eyes might help."

"We'll be following that up," I said, unwilling to talk about Sam Sanchez or discuss my conversation with Jeanine Westlake. This meeting was about me gathering information, not giving it. I also didn't want to push Lucy into any one particular direction.

"I assumed you would. Am I right in ascertaining that this is only your second investigation under the Past & Present umbrella?"

"Yes, but rest assured, while we may not have experience on our side, we will do everything in our power to find him. Or at least find out what happened to him."

"Why?"

"Because that is what we were hired to do. Because I already feel invested in it. Because the family deserves answers."

"I'm glad you didn't say you were hoping to provide them with closure."

I sent a silent thank you to Gloria Grace. "My experience is there's never closure, no matter the outcome."

"You impress me, Callie," Lucy said, "and I don't impress easily. However, I'm not sure what you can do that the police haven't already done."

I felt my back stiffen. All this true confession stuff to get to that? "So I've been told, and yet, here we are." I tried to keep the edge out of my voice and knew I'd failed. It must have been the right response, because Lucy smiled, revealing a row of straight, white teeth.

"We are indeed. I like someone who doesn't give up. Ask your questions, and I'll do my best to answer them."

I should have gone straight to Brandon Colbeck's file and yet… "You didn't ask about the outcome of my mother's case. Why not?"

The smile broadened. "Perhaps I already knew the answer."

I felt a flash of anger and tried not to give into it. "You asked me how I got into digging into the past. Now you know." *Okay, so maybe not entirely successful with the anger quashing.* I took a deep breath and summoned up a smile. "Your turn on the hot seat. When did you start the Ontario Registry of Missing and Unidentified Adults, and what made you do it?"

"It wasn't a planned thing. I expect these labors of love never are, they just find us somehow. At any rate, it was the summer of 2003, and I'd been reading about the Doe Network—"

"The Doe Network?"

"It's a non-profit organization of volunteers who work with law enforcement to connect missing persons cases with John and Jane Doe cases. I was shocked at the number of people featured on the website. I volunteered because I wanted to work towards returning a missing loved one to her or his family. A few months later, I was asked to assume the position of Area Directorship for Ontario. My focus reverted to researching the cases we had on file via newspapers, and verifying the information with police. It seemed that with every new piece of information, I learned of yet another missing or unidentified person case."

Lucy took a deep breath, her warm brown eyes glistening with tears. "As I became more familiar with the cases, I thought about the parents who live without knowing what happened to their adult son or daughter. I thought about missing adults whose young children are left waiting for their return, and the parents who step in to raise their grandchildren while dealing with the pain of a missing adult child."

"I read on the Royal Canadian Mounted Police website that over 78,000 persons were reported to police as missing. I was shocked at the number."

"The numbers fluctuate every year, but it's always in the multiple thousands. Thankfully, in the vast majority of cases, the missing persons are located within days. Sometimes it's miscommunication. For example, the person is expected to arrive at a certain place at a certain time, but the time and meeting place are misunderstood, or the person gets lost and arrives late. These types of disappearances fall into the 'unintentional' category." Lucy put air quotes around the word unintentional, then continued. "There are also cases of dementia, Alzheimer's, bipolar disorder, psychosis, or schizophrenia, sometimes undiagnosed. Addiction can be a contributing factor. Then there are those who disappear while engaging in sports—boating, hiking, diving, backcountry skiing…"

"What about foul play?"

"Some cases are a result of human trafficking, homicide, or kidnapping, but these are in the minority, as are cases of those who disappear with the intention of committing suicide."

"And the rest?"

"Fall under 'deliberate disappearances.' The decision to disappear might be a way to escape a difficult situation like a bad marriage, a family breakdown, or financial difficulties. Some choose to leave family and friends behind to start a new life elsewhere. Some become drifters leading a transient lifestyle." Lucy shook her head. "Dealing with missing adults is a difficult issue, as you know all too well from personal experience. There is no law that prevents an adult from voluntarily picking up and starting a new life somewhere else. The situation is further complicated in cases where there is no clear indication of foul play. It's a delicate balance between respecting the adult's privacy, while trying to determine exactly what has happened to them. At the same time, family and friends of the missing person are left to grapple with feelings and situations for which there is no guidebook. I created the Ontario Registry of Missing and Unidentified Adults as a first step in helping those families."

"How do you upload a missing person case to the Registry?"

"I have four basic ground rules," Lucy said. "One: the individual disappeared from or in Ontario. Two: they were eighteen years or older at the time of the disappearance. Three: they've been out of contact for three months or longer. And four: a report has been filed with law enforcement. I also insist on the case number and the police agency handling the case."

"What about gathering the information? Is there a form to fill out?"

"There is, but before that happens I call the family member reporting the missing adult to flesh out as many details as possible."

"Do you remember every phone call, every case?"

"I do, though some haunt me more than others. I still remember the day I spoke to Jeanine Westlake. She wasn't like so many others I speak to. She was... the best way to describe it was hopeful."

"Jeanine? Not Lorna or Michael? I spoke to her yesterday. She didn't mention that."

"It was definitely Jeanine, and it was three years ago. She told me she'd learned about the Registry through a client at New Beginnings." Lucy shrugged. "I don't advertise. Most police agencies will tell families about the service, but some don't. The Registry wasn't open when Brandon Colbeck disappeared. It's understandable the family was unaware of our existence."

"You say she sounded hopeful. Why do you think that was?"

"She'd convinced a reporter from the *Marketville Post* to re-interview the family and run a story about Brandon. She was sure it would bring new leads, especially with the age-progressed photos and the sketch of the partially finished tattoo on the Registry. Unfortunately, it didn't. Unless you consider the scam call from a few months ago."

"You knew about that?"

"Yes, Jeanine called to tell me. Unconscionable."

"You don't think it was Brandon?"

"The police didn't seem to think so, nor the family. Are you less certain?"

"I haven't ruled it out or in. I'm hoping he'll reach out to me, whoever he is, though I'm still trying to figure out a way to get his attention. Eleanor Colbeck told me a few facts that weren't in the newspaper article. If he does contact me, I can vet him through that."

"You may just have come up with the solution," Lucy said. "The newspaper. If you could get the *Post* to run another article, that might get his attention. Or possibly a larger paper, like the *Toronto Sun* or *Star*."

"I'm meeting with Gloria Grace Pietrangelo, her by-line is G.G. Pietrangelo. She was the original photojournalist on the case in 2000 and a huge help when I was searching for my mother. I'm sure she still has connections, and she's offered to share her notes with me."

"Well, then, that's your angle. I hope it works."

"Now, enough shop talk. I promised you dinner. You must be famished."

Lucy laughed. "I could eat the arm off a bear."

I laughed with her. "My father used that expression. I've never heard anyone else say it, until now."

"Then that's another thing we have in common, beyond digging into the past."

"Well, I can't promise you any bear arms, but I did make an asparagus and Brie quiche and a radicchio salad. All I have to do is pop the quiche in the oven for thirty minutes. There's angel food cake with strawberries and whipped cream for dessert. In the meantime, can I offer you a glass of wine?"

"Do you have red?"

"Merlot, Cabernet Sauvignon, and Shiraz."

"Cabernet."

"Coming right up."

Lucy brought the conversation back around to Brandon after dinner. "I've been debating this all evening, whether or not to tell you. However, your investigation does have the full approval of the family, and I believe you should know." She shifted in her seat. "It's something Jeanine mentioned to me when we had our telephone interview. It's not on the Registry website because she left it out of her submission."

Curious. "What is it?"

"One of the things Brandon took with him, a folder with some sketches. It was missing when he left."

I wondered why Jeanine had neglected to mention that to me. Find out their secrets, Gloria Grace had said, and you just may learn the truth. This was the thing Jeanine had been holding back from me. I could feel it, taste it. "What sort of sketches?"

"*That* would be breaking a confidence. I'm afraid you'll have to ask her."

I planned to do exactly that.

NINETEEN

LUCY DANELUK LEFT early Saturday morning, refusing my offer of breakfast. "You've been far too hospitable already, and besides, there will be a buffet breakfast at the hotel. With the amount I'm paying for the conference, I want to be sure I capitalize on every freebie." She gave me a quick hug. "It was great to get to know you a bit better, and I hope what I've shared with you will help to bring news of Brandon."

"I hope so, too. At the very least, I have an understanding of the process, and new information to follow up with Jeanine Westlake. And I loved having you. If you're ever back this way, be sure to let me know. We'll do it again." I smiled, thinking about the enjoyable evening we'd had. It turned out that we had more in common than digging into the past. Both runners, we compared race events past and upcoming, and it turned out we were both registered for 30K Around the Bay in Hamilton come March.

"The same holds true if you're ever in Ottawa," she said. "And of course, we have to get together in Hamilton for a post-race celebration."

"You're on. I'll be in touch before that, regardless, to keep you posted on our progress."

Lucy nodded, her expression suddenly serious. "Be careful, okay?"

I was surprised at the warning. "Is there something you haven't told me?"

"Nothing I can substantiate and I have no use for gossip. But not everyone welcomes having the past dredged up. You find out things, about people, family members left behind, things they may not want you to know. Things that may break your heart."

Past experience had taught me that lesson all too well, especially the heartbreak part. I wanted to ask her more, to try to pry out the smallest hint of a detail, but she was in her car and halfway down Edward Street before I could formulate a question. It occurred to me maybe Lucy Daneluk had a secret or two she wasn't ready to reveal.

I WROTE UP my notes from my meeting with Lucy Daneluk while everything was fresh in my mind, careful to write legibly. Tomorrow I would transcribe all my handwritten notes into a Word document, and from that I'd start my own version of a family tree, with Brandon's name at the top, and everyone else's branching off with a key point or highlight. I hadn't tried to do that before, but it had been one of Daneluk's suggestions, and I liked it.

The meeting duly recorded, I heated up some leftover quiche for lunch, and pondered how best to approach Jeanine Westlake on the sketches. Coming up with nothing clever or particularly inventive, I opted to come straight out and ask her. I called, expecting to get voice mail, given it was a Saturday, and was surprised when Jeanine answered.

"Callie. I understand you met with my mother. I apologize if I gave you the wrong impression. We talk. We just don't *talk*."

"No harm done. Actually, I'm calling for another reason."

"Oh, what is it?"

"I met with Lucy Daneluk yesterday." I paused to let the name sink in.

"The woman from the Missing Adults Registry? You really are thorough, aren't you?"

"I *try* to be." I placed an emphasis on try. "I was hoping to ask you a couple more questions."

"Do you have time to pop down now? The office is closed, but I'm here doing some much-needed paperwork. Not my strong suit, I'm afraid. I'll do just about anything to avoid it."

It was a backhanded invitation, but I seized it. It would be better to see Jeanine's reaction than to try to gauge it over the phone. "I'll be there within the half hour."

"See you then."

I hung up, grabbed a jacket, and was out the door in minutes, the brisk walk down Edward Street serving to calm my nerves. Because despite my earlier resolve, I was nervous about questioning Jeanine about the sketches. She must have had a good reason to withhold the information from the online Registry, and for not telling me about them yesterday. What made me think that she would suddenly reveal all?

I made it to New Beginnings in record time and stopped long enough to watch the latest group of cyclists going through their paces. The same instructor was leading the way and she caught my eye and winked, motioning for me to come in and give it a try, her hands making a spinning motion. I grinned, mouthed "maybe next time"—as if—opened the door to New Beginnings and trundled up the stairs.

Jeanine was in the reception area, waiting for me, and, true to her word, searching through some files. "Callie, have a seat. My office table is cluttered with paperwork and folders. We'll be more comfortable here. Can I get you anything? We have one of those coffee pod machines in the kitchen."

"No, I'm good, thanks. It looks as if you're busy, so if you don't mind, I'd prefer to get straight to the point."

"That works for me. You mentioned that you'd seen Lucy Daneluk. A lovely woman and so passionate about what she does. I get the same impression about you."

"Thank you for the comparison. I am passionate about finding out the truth and as I said on the phone earlier, I try to be thorough. The thing is, I can only be as thorough as the information given to me."

Jeanine's face flushed with embarrassment. "I gather Lucy mentioned the sketches."

"She did, although she was reluctant to do so and provided no details, outside of the fact that there were sketches and that you excluded them from the Registry report as something Brandon would have taken with him. Was there any mention in the police report?"

"No. I know you're thinking that I should have told the authorities but I didn't want Brandon's reputation tarnished any more than it already was. The police were already looking into things like online gambling or drug abuse. I didn't need them to think he was into pornography, and I didn't want my mother to feel any worse than she already did. My father, his reaction... I don't even want to think what his reaction would have been."

"Back it up a bit. Are you saying the sketches were some sort of pornography? Do you think that was the reason Brandon had withdrawn?"

"I don't know, because I never actually saw the sketches. All I know is that a couple of days before he left home, I knocked on his bedroom door and went straight in. I did that all the time, you know? Anyway, he had this thin green binder, and there were plastic sleeves inside—you know the ones that you use for archiving paper?"

Thanks to my last case and an interview with an expert on ephemera, I knew more about archival sleeves than was necessary. "I do."

"Okay, so Brandon slammed the binder shut as soon as I walked in, and all I had was an impression of color, and I can't even tell you how many there were, maybe half a dozen, could have been more, could have been less. I asked him what they were and he said they were flesh art."

"Flesh art?"

Jeanine nodded. "Flesh art. I've never heard pornography called that before or since, but I was twelve and he may have been trying to protect me. I imagined sketches of naked women. After he left, I looked under his mattress and found some back issues of *Playboy* and *Penthouse*, but no binder, and no sketches. I took the magazines into my room and hid them under my mattress. I knew I had to dispose of them, and thought about putting them in the trash, but what if my parents searched the trash? That made me think the sketches might be in the trash. I checked, smelly and disgusting as it was, but there were no sketches and no binder. A couple of days later, I put the magazines in a plastic grocery bag, stuffed them into my backpack, and tossed them into a green garbage bin behind the plaza by my school."

I imagined a young Jeanine, frantically trying to help her brother, so sure he'd come home, so worried about what her parents would think. "And the sketches?"

"Don't you see? He must have taken them with him. In hindsight, maybe I should have told my mother, or the police, but I was so embarrassed for him…" Her voice trailed off. "I confided in Lucy Daneluk when we added Brandon's story to the Registry. She suggested that I put it in the report, but how could I? What would I tell my parents after all these years? Not to mention that I'd withheld information from the police."

I could understand her position except… "Are you positive he said flesh art?

Jeanine's brow wrinkled. "Why? What are you thinking?"

"I'm thinking he probably said flash art."

"Flash art?"

"As in tattoo flash. He'd just gotten a tattoo. Maybe he bought some flash art at the same time."

"Tattoo flash," Jeanine said, her voice soft. "All these years, no matter what I told anyone about my respect for Brandon, the police or my parents, his friends or reporters, inside me, I've thought the worst of my brother. Loved him and loathed him in equal measure."

"You were just a girl, it's understandable that you heard flesh versus flash. He slammed the binder shut, like it was something secret. Your actions, reactions, all perfectly understandable."

"Thanks for trying to make me feel better." Jeanine shot me a rueful smile. "Regardless, flesh art or flash art, I don't see how it's going to help find Brandon now. I can't even describe the sketches."

"Let me worry about the how, okay?"

"Okay. And Callie?"

"Yes?"

"Thank you."

"You can thank me by asking your father to call me. Your mother was going to do that, but now that they've filed for divorce—"

"She filed for divorce? When was she going to spring that one on me?" Jeanine shook her head. "What did I tell you? We talk, we just don't communicate."

"I'll let you get back to your paperwork," I said, mainly because I didn't know what else to say. I wondered if the family was this dysfunctional before Brandon left, if his leaving had caused the chasm or widened it.

TWENTY

I DECIDED TO pay a visit to Sam Sanchez, and wound my way along the side roads off Edward, eventually looping onto Poplar. Tash looked up when I walked into Trust Few. Once again I was greeted with the droning sound of a tattoo machine, the air redolent with the sickly-sweet smell of industrial strength sanitizer.

"Hey, welcome back," Tash said. "Callie, isn't it?"

"Good memory."

"Part of the job is to remember client names." She grinned. "Are you back to book a tattoo consult?"

"I was hoping that Sam might have a few minutes to talk to me. I was in the area." Not entirely true, but not exactly a lie.

"You're in luck. She's just finishing up with a client. Should be done in fifteen, and nothing else is booked for a couple of hours. It's been slow, especially for a Saturday. Grab a chair. Can I get you anything? Herbal tea? Coffee? Water?"

"No, I'm good. If you don't mind, I'm going to check out the flash art on the walls."

"Sure, we have binders, too, if you want to look at those."

"Binders?"

"Yeah." Tash pulled out a two-inch binder, longer than the traditional binder I'd envisioned, though about the same width.

"I'd like to see one of those. Do you have anything with vintage flash?"

"Vintage? How vintage? We have a few pages from the 1950s through to the '80s. Nothing older than that."

Given that I was born in 1980, I didn't like to think of the 1980s as vintage. "I'd say from the 1950s or '60s."

Tash located a couple of binders and brought them over to me. "Have at it."

I started with a binder labeled "1950s." There were pages of horseshoes, anchors, roses, mermaids, and apple-cheeked cherubic women. What struck me most was the innocence of the art; even the snakes and dragons were reminiscent of classic cartoons. I was still flipping through the pages when Sam slipped into the reception area. I took in the black leotards, denim skirt, combat boots, and Metallica T-shirt and felt an irrational flush of envy, knowing I could never carry off that look, even if I'd wanted to. Which, I reminded myself, I didn't.

Sam thanked her client, letting Tash take care of the payment, and motioned for me to go back to her work area.

"I didn't expect to see you again," she said. "Certainly not quite this soon. I take it from your sudden interest in vintage flash that you learned about the ones Brandon purchased from Dave. I wondered if you'd find out about that."

"Why didn't you tell me?"

Sam shrugged. "I figured if you were a decent investigator, you'd find out. If you weren't a decent investigator, you didn't deserve to know."

"And just how did you think I'd find out? Through a tarot reading?" I wanted to bite the words back as soon as I said them, but it was too late.

"No need to get snippy," Sam said, though she seemed unperturbed. "The newspaper article said he took his clothes, laptop, and toiletries with him. Nothing about a binder filled with sketches, which, I'm sure, would have been mentioned, right? So I assumed he left it behind, along with his ID. His folks would have mentioned it when you interviewed them, right? Showed you the things he left behind."

"No one has shown me anything, yet." *Including his ID*, I thought, making a mental note to ask Lorna if she still had it. "And, no, he didn't leave it behind." I filled Sam in on my conversation with Jeanine, careful not to leave anything out.

"Sheesh. Flesh art," Sam said, when I'd finished. "The poor kid, thinking that about her brother all these years."

Sheesh? Not the language, or the response, I'd been expecting from this heavily tattooed, combat-boot-wearing woman. I dialed back my preconceived notions yet again. No matter how hard you try, sometimes you take on a bit of your parents, in this case, my father, who had a tendency to judge on appearance. I smiled at the thought. Was he, a year plus after his death, finally becoming less "perfect" and more "mere mortal"?

"The point is," I said, getting my thoughts back on track, "Brandon must have taken the sketches with him. If we can post something about them, it might resonate with him or with someone who knew or knows him. Can you remember anything about the ones he purchased?"

Sam nodded, albeit with reluctance. "I have some of the artist's vintage flash. He specialized in tarot and astronomy, but his main focus was tarot. Dave purchased a couple dozen sketches to help the guy out, and when Brandon expressed an interest in some of them, he was only too happy to recoup his investment and make a small profit. If I remember correctly, Brandon paid a hundred dollars for eight designs."

I did some mental math. Twelve-fifty a piece. It didn't seem like much. "What would they be worth today?"

"Hard to say, values vary on how well the artist is known and the complexity of the art, but they'd be still worth considerably more than what Dave or Brandon paid. Vintage flash is collectible, especially since Jonathan Shaw's book, *Vintage Tattoo Flash*, came out in 2016. It represents roughly seventy-five years of American tattooing from the Bowery to Texas to Los Angeles. His collection is quite remarkable."

"Jonathan Shaw. I'm not familiar with the name."

"Shaw was a renegade with a history of heroin addiction. In 1987, he cleaned up his act and opened the first storefront tattoo parlor in New York City, back when tattooing was illegal. He'd be in his sixties now. Last I read he split his time between New York, Los Angeles, and Rio de Janeiro, with Brazil being his residence of choice."

"Tattoos were illegal?"

"Having a tattoo wasn't illegal, but in 1961, after a Hepatitis B outbreak, New York's five boroughs banned tattooing. It wasn't legalized until 1997. I have Shaw's book at home, if you'd like me to bring it in sometime."

"Thanks for the offer, but I think it would be more helpful to see the vintage flash from the artist that Brandon liked. Do you mind if I take a look at it?"

"I suppose that would be okay." Sam slipped a key

from her back pocket and unlocked a drawer in a steel cabinet, pulling out a black binder with a cardboard compass pasted on the cover. She handed it to me, the gesture tentative, and I thought about my journal books, and how reluctant I would be to share them.

"Thank you." I opened the binder carefully and slowly thumbed my way through a dozen pages, each one filled with vibrantly colored designs and stylized elements from tarot's Minor Arcana, with multiple swords, wands, pentacles, and cups in various sizes, and three sketches from the Major Arcana: The Magician, The Hanged Man, and The World.

"I'm no expert, but to my eye, these are really exceptional," I said. "When would they have been drawn?"

"The artist was active from the mid 1950s, though I believe his fascination with tarot intensified with age."

"Do you mind if I take some photos with my phone? One of our team members is quite knowledgeable about tarot. I'd like her to see these."

"You can take the binder with you, if you think it will help. Just return it when it's told you all it can."

It was a generous offer, and not one that I might have made in the same circumstance. "Thank you for trusting me with it."

Sam shrugged. "I figure I owe you for holding out the first time."

"You had your reasons," I said. "The artist, who was he?"

"Nestor Sanchez. No relation to the famous salsa musician, Argentinian actor, or author. On the off-chance you made that connection."

I hadn't, mostly because I'd never heard of any of

them. I was about to ask if she and Nestor were related when Sam continued.

"He was an itinerant tattoo artist with a snot-nosed grandkid he dragged along on his travels after the snot-nosed grandkid's parents were killed in a car accident when she was five."

"And you are…?" I asked, suspecting the answer.

"The snot-nosed grandkid, all grown up," Sam said, smiling wide enough to reveal a glint of diamond sparkle. She brushed her hand against the tat on her scalp, the one that spelled Sanchez, and for the first time I took a moment to read the name written on the side of her left palm: Nestor.

"Is your grandfather still alive?"

"He'd be ninety if he was. When we arrived in Marketville, I wanted to set down roots. We'd been traveling from town to town for the better part of twelve years, a different school every semester, sometimes more than one. Nestor tried to settle down, he really did, but it just couldn't stick. He left right after New Year's Day 2000, knowing Dave would look after me. There were postcards once in a while, for the first few years."

"Do you have the postcards?"

"Of course. Why? Isn't the flash art enough?"

"To help with Brandon's disappearance? Yes. To help with your grandfather's…" I allowed the words trail off.

"Are you saying you can find out if Nestor is dead or alive?"

"I'm saying that I'm willing to try."

Sam shook her head. "Thanks for the offer, but sometimes it's better not to know."

I thought back to my own experience of looking for my mother. The woman had a point.

TWENTY-ONE

DESPITE SAM'S RELUCTANCE to share the postcards, I emailed Shirley as soon as I got home asking her to add the name Nestor Sanchez to her search for obituaries. I then took photos of each individual tattoo in the binder, cropped them to uniform size, and created a digital photo album on my computer. It was slow, tedious work, but I knew I couldn't keep the binder indefinitely. Finally, I composed an email to Misty, copying Chantelle and Shirley, and attached the photos.

Misty, these sketches are tattoo flash, which is the term used for the art form. Brandon Colbeck purchased six originals the week before he left home. All evidence points to him taking them with him. Can you go through these and tell me what, if anything, you make of them, and how we might be able to use them on the website? Thanks, Callie

I read it over, hit send, and called Arabella Carpenter. The call was picked up on the first ring.

"Glass Dolphin, Emily speaking. How may I help you?"

Emily Garland was Arabella's business partner. "Emily, it's Callie Barnstable. Is Arabella available?"

"She's with a customer right now, Callie. Is it urgent?"

"No, nothing that can't wait. Have her call me when she gets a minute."

I hung up, feeling frustrated. Patience may be a virtue, but it wasn't one of mine. I whiled away the time adding notes of today's meetings with Jeanine and Sam into my journal, then set about trying to decide what to eat. I was still debating my options when the phone rang. I positively leapt at it.

"Callie, what's up?" Arabella sounded concerned. "Emily said to call you as soon as possible."

I laughed. "Actually I said when you get a minute, but now's good. It's about a case I'm working on."

"You have another case already? Wow, that's great. Where do I fit in?"

"I have a sketchbook of tattoo flash drawn by an itinerant artist by the name of Nestor Sanchez. Some of the drawings date back to the 1950s. I was hoping you'd take a look at it."

"Vintage tattoo flash isn't exactly a specialty of mine. I've heard of Norman Collins, a.k.a. Sailor Jerry, but that's pretty much where my knowledge ends."

"Thanks, anyway." I tried to keep the disappointment out of my voice and knew I wasn't entirely successful.

"There is a short video clip on the PBS *Antiques Roadshow* website from 2016, give me a sec." I could hear the sound of her fingers clicking on the keyboard. "Found it. It's with appraiser Bruce Shackelford in Corpus Christi, Texas. He even shows some of Sailor Jerry's work. I'll send you the link. It's not much, but it might help."

"I'd love to see the video. Unfortunately, I don't think it will shed any light on Nestor Sanchez or his sketchbook."

"But Levon has, or had, a modest collection," Arabella said, and my spirits lifted. "Why don't you bring the sketchbook by tomorrow afternoon? The shop closes at three on Sundays and I'll ask Levon to join us if he's available. We can grab dinner at The Hanged Man's Noose afterwards."

Levon was Levon Larroquette, Arabella's exhusband, an antiques picker who still held the key to Arabella's heart, and I was pretty sure the reverse was true. In fact, I suspected they would eventually reconcile. Some people are just meant to be together. The Hanged Man's Noose was a pub with decent food and reasonable prices, owned by Arabella's friend, Betsy Ehrlich. If nothing else, it would be nice to see them again.

"That sounds great. See you tomorrow at three."

I hung up, feeling the first surge of optimism. Then I changed into my running gear and hit the trail behind Edward Street. It had been too long.

TWENTY-TWO

I SKIPPED COFFEE after Sunday morning run club, eager to transcribe my journal notes on my computer. I thought of the journal entries in the same way an author might think about writing a novel: the handwritten notes were the first draft, the transcription the second draft, with the third and final draft edited for clarity and ready to be attached to the final report.

Satisfied with the job done, I checked to find a "Will add Nestor Sanchez" email from Shirley and a "Working on the flash," text from Misty. I'd start the family tree this week. A light lunch of poached eggs on toast to save room and calories for a meal at The Hanged Man's Noose later, and I was ready to make the thirty-minute drive to Lount's Landing.

I took the scenic route, or at least the route that had once been scenic. Since my last visit to the Glass Dolphin, an entire forest had been razed to the ground, leaving nothing but dirt and a few rocks yet to be removed. An enormous billboard announced "Woodland Meadows Phase I: Coming Soon," the developer clearly missing the irony of the bulldozed trees. Another sign boasted, "Towns, semis, and detached family homes on 30-foot and extra wide 40-foot lots" and I had to laugh. At what point did forty-foot lots become extra wide?

The subdivision was less than ten minutes from Lount's Landing, and I was reminded of the developer who'd come to the small, historic town in 2015 with plans to build a mega box store. Arabella's business partner, Emily, then a reporter, had come to town at the same time, and soon found plenty to report on. I wondered how long it would be before Lount's Landing could no longer stave off development and suspected the time was coming sooner rather than later. Hopefully this time the outcome wouldn't result in murder.

I arrived at the parking lot behind the shop at the same time as a large black pickup truck. Levon hopped out, a lopsided smile lighting up eyes the color of denim. It wasn't difficult to imagine the attraction Arabella felt for her ex, though I couldn't help but notice the first strands of gray weaving their way through his signature shaggy brown hair. We were definitely all getting older. Wiser, maybe not so much. I grabbed my briefcase from the trunk of my car and sidled up alongside him.

"Hey, Callie. It's been too long," Levon said, giving me a quick one-armed hug.

"It has indeed. Thanks for making the time."

"Arabella was vague about what you were looking for. She mentioned tattoo flash, but nothing specific. I hope I can help."

We made our way to the shop, Arabella waiting by the door to let us in. Walking into the Glass Dolphin was like stepping back in time, It should have looked cluttered, but it looked cozy, wide pine plank floors, wooden desks, chairs, and bookcases, walls lined with antique clocks, vintage posters, embroidered samplers, and old maps; every shelf, nook, and cranny crammed full of dishes, duck decoys, and decorative objects, everything from paperweights to perfume bottles.

"This is new," I said, pointing to a rack of quilts and

a corner hutch filled with contemporary pottery, burl fruit bowls, silk scarves, and silver jewelry.

"New since the last time you were here. I never dreamed I'd sell anything that didn't have age to it, but after meeting an antiques dealer in Thornbury, I decided to promote local artisans. With the exception of the quilts, everything in that corner is on consignment. Emily handles all the details and it's been well enough received that we're considering taking on another couple of vendors. But you're not here to talk about our attempts to keep the lights on. Let's grab a seat at the appraisal table at the back of the shop."

The appraisal table reminded me a lot of my own multipurpose table. In addition to a computer and printer, there was a mason jar filled with various writing implements, a magnifying glass, and a jeweler's loupe. Behind the table, a bookshelf was filled with old auction catalogues and reference books of every conceivable size and color, filed not by author name, but by type: Clocks, Depression Glass, Paperweights, and so on.

"I see you still have your reference books. Google not good enough for you?" Levon knew I was teasing and grinned, but when it came to antiques, Arabella could be short on humor. She turned around and selected a thin paperback titled the *Bulletin*, 1978.

"This was published by the National Association of Watch and Clock Collectors. When I first opened the store, a man came in with a Sessions Regulator 'E' clock made in Forestville, Connecticut, what collectors would call a square regulator. They aren't particularly rare, or valuable, but what made my appraisal special is that the clock is pictured in this issue of the *Bulle-*

tin. So I was able to provide him with the exact cost of his clock when it was made." She flipped to the page. "See? The article says these clocks were produced between 1903 and 1908, with a retail price of $7.35 as a timepiece and $8.30 as a striker in 1915. A calendar attachment was forty-five cents extra for either model. That's the sort of thing you don't find on the internet."

"Point made and taken," I said. "I don't suppose you have anything on tattoo flash?"

"Sadly, I don't. Until you called, I hadn't even considered selling flash, but Levon tells me it's the kind of thing that attracts younger buyers."

Levon nodded. "I've built up a small personal collection, mostly vintage stuff, but a few by contemporary artists. When I started collecting I was in a small minority. But flash art now gets top dollar. At the July 2018 Ripley Auctions in Indianapolis there were six original tattoo flash art sheets attributed to Charlie Wagner and Sam O'Reilly which sold for more than forty-thousand dollars."

"I have no idea who they are," I admitted, "but that's a lot of money."

Levon warmed to his subject. "Sam O'Reilly learned tattooing in the Navy, patented the first tattooing machine in 1891, practiced in the Bowery in New York City. Charlie Wagner apprenticed with O'Reilly, patented his own tattoo machine in 1904, sold his machines and his own brand of ink. He died in 1953, but was a tattoo artist for fifty years. But it's the backstory that's a picker's dream."

"Do tell," I said, leaning forward. The man could spin a story.

"The sheets were found by an antiques collector in

the bottom of a trunk in the attic of an eighty-four-year-old career Marine Corps officer. The collector paid $10 for it."

"Wow, ten dollars for forty-thousand plus. Not a bad return on investment. I don't think what I've brought has anywhere near that value, but..." I opened my briefcase, handed over the sketchbook, and watched silently as Arabella and Levon carefully studied each page. Levon kept going back to a page filled with images from the Pentacles.

"I have this one in my collection, although mine is slightly larger," he finally said. He pointed to Sanchez's drawing of a man with curly dark brown hair wearing a bright red conical hat, shirt and leggings, a yellow tunic, and green shoes. He was juggling two yellow pentagrams on either side of a green ribbon shaped like a figure eight. "I never realized it was a tarot card. I always thought it was a circus tat, because of the vivid colors and the fanciful pose."

I felt a stir of excitement. "Do you remember where you bought it?"

"I'd have to check my records at home to be absolutely sure, but I'm almost certain that it was at a tattoo parlor in Marketville. Had a funny name..." Levon tilted his head back, thinking, then shook his head. "Nope, it's not coming to me, but I can get them to you. I recall the guy was going out of business and he was selling everything in the shop. By the time I got there, most of it had already been sold. This would have been maybe 2002 or 2003? I always thought he was the artist, but his name wasn't Nestor Sanchez. I'm pretty sure it was Dave something."

"Dave Samuels, 2003, and the tattoo parlor was

called Such & Such." I gave Levon and Arabella a brief recap of the case, finishing with Brandon's partially finished tattoo of The Fool, and his purchase of Sanchez's flash.

"Only a few of them are signed, and I'm no expert, but I think they show real talent," Arabella said, going through the sketchbook again. "He was really into tarot, wasn't he?"

"That he was—or possibly is, should he still be alive," I said. "So is his granddaughter, Sam Sanchez. She started her own tattoo parlor in Marketville after Samuels went out of business, a place called Trust Few on Poplar Street. But my hope was that one of you might tell me more about Nestor Sanchez. My gut tells me he holds, or at least held, a key to this investigation."

A glance passed between Levon and Arabella, but I could read between the lines. They had nothing more to tell me, at least not right now, though I knew both of them would leave here today and research Nestor Sanchez on my behalf. For now, that would have to be enough.

TWENTY-THREE

WALKING INTO THE Glass Dolphin was like stepping back in time, and walking into The Hanged Man's Noose was the same. It was like entering an old-time saloon, the sort of place you'd expect to see in a John Wayne western. The owner, Betsy Ehrlich, was a local history buff, and I'd learned the hard way about asking about the inspiration for the pub's name, and the town's namesake, Samuel Lount. Get Betsy talking about Lount, a nineteenth-century politician hanged for treason, and you were almost certain to learn more than you ever needed—or wanted—to know.

The Noose was filled to capacity, with a group of twenty-something men and women watching football on a big screen, sipping drinks, and munching on peanuts and nachos at the bar, and a mix of young, old, and every age in between filling up the booths. Betsy was deftly pouring draft beers, whiskey shots, and wine, a wide smile on her gamin-like face. She gave us a quick wave and motioned to a corner booth with a "Reserved" sign.

"I thought it might be busy today, so I made reservations," Arabella said. "Nice of Betsy to tuck us away from the betting crowd."

Our server came by with menus. Based on their casual banter, Arabella and Levon seemed to know her, and while I didn't, she looked vaguely familiar. I tried to put a finger on where I'd seen her before. Not here, I'd only been at The Hanged Man's Noose twice before, and both times it had been on a much quieter weekday, with Betsy serving us.

"The specials today are the Full Noose Nachos, Caesar salad with or without grilled chicken, and veggie sliders," the server said, introducing herself to me as Kavya. "We also have a two-for-one Treasontini deal."

The Treasontini was Betsy's signature drink, a blueberry martini that packed a punch. Given that I had a thirty-minute drive home, I opted for a club soda with lime. Levon ordered a Sleeman Honey Brown, and Arabella asked for a five-ounce house white and a glass of water.

"What's a veggie slider?" I asked. I made Caesar salads at home, didn't want to order one when I was out, and I wasn't big on nachos in general, though I knew the Full Noose Nachos were a favorite of Arabella's.

"They're incredible," Kavya said. "Roasted red, yellow, and orange bell peppers, sautéed onion, goat cheese spread, and balsamic reduction. Your choice of sourdough or pretzel bun. Comes with regular or sweet potato fries."

"That's what I'll have. Sourdough and sweet potato fries."

"Make that two," Levon said.

"Three," Arabella said. "Much as I love them, if I eat any more, I'll turn into one giant nacho."

"Kavya," I said to Arabella and Levon, after she'd left with our orders. "I'm sure I know her from somewhere, but she didn't seem to know me. Has she worked here long?"

"Three or four months, maybe," Arabella said, "and

just on Sunday afternoons to help Betsy out with the lunch to early dinner crowd. Monday to Friday she works at the Cedar County Retirement Residence as a PSW."

A personal support worker. That was it. She was the woman who'd been attending to Eleanor Colbeck. Funny how seeing someone out of context can block our minds from making a connection. There'd certainly been no spark of recognition in her eyes. Then again, I would have been anonymous to her, just another visitor.

I waited until Kavya had sorted our drinks to talk to her. "Kavya, Arabella tells me that you work at the Cedar County Retirement Residence."

Her amber eyes assessed me. "I remember you now. You had lunch with Eleanor Colbeck a few days ago."

"Mac and cheese and rice pudding," I said with a smile. "I'm hoping the food here is better."

Kavya laughed. "I can guarantee it. Say…didn't you visit Olivia Osgoode a couple of times?"

"She was my great-grandmother."

"I liked her. That would explain why you visited with Eleanor. The two of them were great friends. Ate breakfast, lunch, and dinner together every day for years."

"Actually, I was there to speak to Eleanor about her grandson, Brandon."

"Callie's an investigator," Arabella said. "She owns a company called Past & Present Investigations in Marketville."

"Terrible thing, that telephone scam."

"Actually, I've been hired to find Brandon." I didn't tell her that it was Olivia who had done the hiring. It didn't matter, and I wasn't sure how discreet Kavya would be. The last thing I needed was to get banned again by Platinum Blonde.

"Sorry for jumping to conclusions," Kavya said. "The stuff I see, it would turn your stomach. Family members waiting for their inheritance, the ones who only show up when the stench of death is in the air." A bell dinged at the bar. "That'll be your veggie sliders. I'm officially off shift in thirty. Hang tight. I might know something to help you."

THE SWEET POTATO fries were crisped to perfection, the veggie sliders every bit as delicious as Kavya had implied, and Levon was his usual charming self, entertaining Arabella and me with stories from the road, but all I could think of was what Kavya had to tell me. "Sorry I'm a few minutes late," she said slipping into the seat next to me. "I had to cash out and there was a situation with a declined credit card. I'm also second-guessing whether I should be telling you. Depending on where you're going with it, this could land me in some hot water. Then again, I'd like to see Eleanor Colbeck get some peace of mind."

"Levon and I should probably leave, regardless," Arabella said. "This is Callie's case, not ours, and I should really get back to the shop to do some much needed paperwork."

"I might be more comfortable just confiding in Callie," Kavya said, though her tone suggested she was still on the fence.

"In that case, we're out of here," Levon said. "We'll settle the tab with Betsy." I started to protest and he shook his head. "No discussion. And don't worry. Arabella and I will both see what else we can find out about Nestor Sanchez."

"I appreciate that." I got up to give him and Arabella a hug. They were good people, meant for each other. Maybe one day they'd admit it to themselves.

Kavya listened with interest and waited until Arabella and Levon were out the door before she spoke. "My brother was in community college with Brandon," she said. "They had classes together, he was one of the people the reporter interviewed after Brandon disappeared. I remember Raj saying Brandon was the last person he'd think would up and leave. I forgot about him until I started working at Cedar County and met Eleanor. She talks a lot about Brandon, especially after that scam phone call." Kavya frowned, and continued, "I looked Brandon up in that missing person's registry. There was a photo of his unfinished tattoo."

I wondered where Kavya's story was going, and nodded at her by way of encouragement.

"Okay, so this is a pretty small town," she said. "And there are only so many places where you'd get a tattoo—then and now. Sam Sanchez is one person with a tattoo parlor...and you were just talking about Nestor Sanchez."

I couldn't hide my surprise. "Nestor? Do you know him?"

"I met him at the retirement residence...but not in the way you might think."

TWENTY-FOUR

I STARED AT KAVYA. "What do you mean, not in the way I might think? Was he a resident at Cedar County? A visitor? How well do you know him?"

"I don't exactly know him…" Kavya paused. "Maybe you should tell me what you know about him first."

"Not much. He was an itinerant tattoo artist with a fascination in tarot. His granddaughter last saw him in 2000, right after New Year's. He sent an occasional postcard, but after a while those stopped."

"A granddaughter," Kavya said. "Is that Sam?"

"Yes. I interviewed Sam in relation to my investigation into the disappearance of Brandon Colbeck. She remembered Brandon buying some tattoo flash drawn by Nestor."

"Interesting, but where do Arabella and Levon fit in?"

Kavya would make a good investigator. "I called Arabella to find out if she knew anything about Nestor Sanchez's flash art. She didn't, but thought Levon might. He has a small collection of flash and it turns out that Levon owns one of Nestor's sketches. But neither Arabella nor Levon had much else, though they've both promised to do some digging." I smiled. "Your turn."

"I didn't know who he was, at first," Kavya began. "It was 2016. I'm sure of the year because I quit smoking for good on my thirtieth birthday, which was in

April, and off topic, let me tell you it was far from my first attempt. I can't remember the exact date, but I do remember it was during an extended cold spell, the temperatures well below freezing. The town issued an extreme cold weather alert, but the shelters were so overcrowded they had to turn people away."

I nodded politely, wishing that Kavya would get to the point. She seemed to sense my impatience, because she continued on.

"I went out behind the dumpster for a quick puff, there's a strict no-smoking policy inside the residence, and anywhere on the grounds, but the powers that be turn a blind eye at the dumpster, at least in the cruel depths of winter. I guess they figure if you're willing to freeze your arse off to get a nicotine fix while standing next to smelly trash, you can have at it. That day, there was an elderly man carrying a threadbare backpack by the dumpster. He could have been sixty, could have been ninety, it's difficult to judge someone's age if they live on the street. I suspected that he'd been rummaging through the garbage. He started to scamper off when he saw me, but I told him I could get him a hot meal and a warm place to sleep, if only for one night. He hesitated, but the cold and hunger got the better of him."

I thought of the snobbishness displayed by Platinum Blonde on my visits. "I'm surprised that Cedar County Retirement Residence would welcome someone like that."

"Welcome? Hardly. I was taking a huge risk bringing him into the building, but it was just so damned cold, and, I don't know, there was something about him that resonated with me. I took him to the furnace room. It's not exactly the Ritz, but I figured it was better than being outside. There's no shower down there, but there is a sink and toilet. I told him that I'd be back with food and a blanket as soon as my shift was over. All that time, he hadn't said a single word. I figured he'd be long gone by the time I returned."

"Let me guess. He was still there when you got back."

Kavya nodded. "When my shift ended, I grabbed a couple of juice boxes, leftover green beans, meat loaf, mashed potatoes, and two chocolate brownies. I told the kitchen staff it was for residents who hadn't made it to dinner."

"You still remember the food you brought him?"

"Like I said, I was taking a huge risk. I could have lost my job. So yeah, I remember. Anyway, I took the elevator up two flights to make it look good, waited to be sure the coast was clear, then took the stairs to the storage room, where I grabbed a pillow and a couple of blankets, one for him to lie on and one to cover him. By this time my heart was pounding. I sprinted down the last set of steps to the furnace room, and lo and behold, he was still there. He'd even made an effort to clean himself up, and I can still remember how that small detail tugged at my heart. He was sketching something inside a tattered notebook, but he slipped it inside his backpack as soon as he saw me. I remember that each of his fingers had circular symbols tattooed on them and wondered if he'd been in prison. That should have made me nervous, but he emanated kindness. I can't explain it."

"The circular symbols, they're called finger-bangers." *Which, when you thought about it, sounded like something you might get in prison.* "What happened next?"

"Nothing, really. I told him to enjoy the meal and

get a good night's sleep, and promised to come down with breakfast in the morning. Except the next morning he was gone."

I mulled over what Kavya had told me. "Did you ask him what his name was?"

Kavya blushed. "No. At the time I convinced myself that if he remained anonymous I could distance myself from any fallout. Now, I'm not sure. I don't like to think that because he was homeless, his name didn't matter."

"Don't beat yourself up. You did far more than most people would have. Which brings me to my next question. Did anyone else see him, before that day?"

"Uh-uh. I asked around after he left, not that I offered any reason for my curiosity. No one had, or at least, no one admitted to it. As the weeks went by, I was inclined to think it was a one-off. At least I did, back then."

"Back then?"

"The day before the crank call to Eleanor I was sitting in the lobby with one of the residents. We do that sometimes if there's a lull in the schedule—gets them out of their room for a bit, and they can watch who's coming and going in the reception area. Doesn't sound that exciting, I know, but the days can be long and dark, and small things like that can brighten it. Anyway, an elderly man came in holding a brown envelope. He was clean-cut with military short hair, wearing jeans and one of those puffy ski jackets. He shuffled his way over to Stephanie's station and I remember thinking he looked vaguely familiar. That's not so unusual. There's no shortage of elderly men visiting Cedar County. I left to take Eleanor back to her room. Stephanie pinged me a couple minutes later."

"Stephanie?"

"The platinum blonde on guard duty."

Stephanie. At least now I had a name. "Go on."

"She said there was a man waiting in the lobby who wanted to see me. She sounded suspicious, but Stephanie is hyper-vigilant."

Having been on the receiving end of Stephanie's vigilance, I could only imagine how she would have reacted to a stranger asking to see one of the personal support workers. "Did she give you a name?"

"Nestor Sanchez. The name meant nothing to me. Then she whispered that the guy had tattoos on each of his fingers. That's when I knew he was my homeless guy. I told Stephanie that he was an old family friend and that I'd talk to him in about twenty minutes, that I had to get my resident settled."

Nestor Sanchez. I thought back to Sam's response when I asked if her grandfather was still alive. She'd replied with something along the lines of "He'd be ninety if he was," and a comment about receiving sporadic postcards the first few years. No wonder she didn't want me to find out about Nestor. She knew full well how he was living. But why not tell me so? Why not share the postcards? My list of questions for Sam kept getting longer. I brought myself back to the present and Kavya.

"Was he still in the lobby when you got back?"

Kavya shook her head. "I asked Stephanie where he went and she shrugged and said he'd left me an envelope."

"What was inside it?"

"A sketch of a winged angel wearing a long, flowing white gown, standing barefoot in shallow water, and pouring liquid from one long-stemmed cup to another.

Later on, I learned it was the tarot card, Temperance, and that it represented commitment to a new life and sobriety, but at the time I had no idea what it meant, other than a gesture of thanks. He'd signed it—Nestor Sanchez. I liked the sketch enough to have it framed. It's still hanging on my wall at home. We could arrange to meet for coffee, if you'd like to see it."

It would serve as a fine piece of "show and tell" when I paid Sam another visit. "Do you think I could borrow it for a short time? I promise to return it."

"Sure, if you think it would help. I'll leave it at reception tomorrow and let Stephanie know you'll be coming by to pick it up one day through the week."

"That's perfect, thanks." A thought occurred to me, as we got ready to leave. "You said, later on you found out it was the tarot card, Temperance. It may not be important but how did you find out?"

"The guy I took it to for framing," Kavya said. "In fact, now that I think about it, he seemed to be familiar with the artist's work."

"Where did you take it?"

"A place called Frame-Up. It's on Poplar Street."

Poplar Street. The same street Trust Few was on. My list for Sam may have been getting bigger, but the circle around her was definitely getting smaller.

TWENTY-FIVE

I ARRIVED HOME just before dark, jotted down some quick notes, then spent the balance of Sunday reading the latest John Sandford *Prey* novel. There would be time enough for the case of Brandon Colbeck in the week ahead, and I needed a break before my mind imploded. By the time I went to bed, well past the hour I'd planned—just one more page, one more chapter—I was more than ready for a good night's sleep.

I woke up at seven a.m. Monday, my inner alarm clock kicking into gear, and dragged myself into the shower, the hot water washing over me until I was suitably bright-eyed and bushy-tailed.

I turned on my tablet and surfed past the latest news, sports, and entertainment headlines over a large mug of cinnamon rooibos tea and two slices of pumpernickel toast with peanut butter and wild blueberry jam, then settled in on Christie Blatchford's latest column in the *National Post*. I've followed Blatchford since 1995, after reading her daily coverage of the infamous Paul Bernardo trial in the *Toronto Sun*. I can still recall the way she described him as an oxygen thief, an appropriate term if there ever was one.

Breakfast finished, I went into work mode, first checking the day's calendar, which was a good thing, because somehow I'd almost forgotten about my noon meeting with Gloria Grace. It also served as a reminder that I had yet to meet with Michael Westlake, and I wanted to do that before I approached Sam Sanchez for a third time. I was at the point where I wasn't sure what she was hiding, it could be anything, right down to knowing Brandon's stepfather. I checked the time. Nine a.m. Not too early to make a telephone call. If I waited for him to call me, I might be waiting a very long time. I wasn't even sure if Lorna or Jeanine had passed on my request.

I lucked out on my first try to his mobile and started to introduce myself when he interrupted.

"I know who you are," he said. "You're the investigator who's been hired to look into my stepson's disappearance. Jeanine asked me to call you but it's…it's been a rough few days. At any rate, I'm not sure what I can tell you that you don't already know."

By rough, I assumed he meant Lorna filing for divorce. "I was hoping we could set up a time to meet in person. I pride myself on exploring every option."

There was a lengthy silence, then, "Very well. I can squeeze you in today at noon. Other than that, I'm booked solid for the foreseeable future."

It meant postponing my visit with Gloria, but she *had* recommended that I interview all of the family members first.

"I have a conflict, but I should be able to reschedule. Can I call you back in ten?"

"I'll be here," he said, and hung up. Not much on pleasantries, Michael Westlake.

I dialed Gloria Grace and filled her in.

"You absolutely must see Michael Westlake first," she said when I'd finished. "I can do Wednesday morning, say eleven? Will that work?"

"It will, and thanks. I owe you one." I hung up and redialed Westlake.

"We're on for noon today. Where shall we meet?"

"In my office. It's on the main floor of the old Office Works building at Edward and Water. Michael Westlake & Associates."

I knew the building, and was once again grateful for choosing Edward Street as my home base. I could walk there in ten minutes, fifteen if I wanted to take my time. I did some of my best thinking when I walked. "I'll be there."

The appointment confirmed, and with time to spare, I checked my messages to find a brief email from Shirley.

Hi Callie, as per your request, I did some digging into Dave Samuels, Such & Such tattoo parlor, Nestor Sanchez, Sam Sanchez, and Trust Few tattoo parlor. I made copies of everything and uploaded them to Dropbox, so all you have to do is download and print, vs. having to check a bunch of individual links. Hopefully some of this helps. Unfortunately, my search didn't reveal anything on Nestor Sanchez, outside of a brief mention in an advertisement for Trust Few. Seems he's Sam Sanchez's grandfather, though I expect you knew that already.

Let me know if you need me to look into anyone or anything else.

Thanks,

Shirley

I wasn't entirely surprised at the lack of information on Nestor Sanchez, though it was disappointing nonetheless. I clicked on the Dropbox link, thankful Shirley had taken the time to arrange them in a printable format. Each attachment had been carefully labeled, Dave-1, Sam-1, etc. She got bonus points for organization. I downloaded the files into my Brandon Colbeck folder, creating a sub-folder titled "Shirley Research," then printed each one, arranging them in order on the tabletop. As curious as I was to the contents, they would have to wait until after my interview with Michael Westlake. Right now, I had to pick an outfit. First impressions always mattered, but I had a feeling they mattered all the more to a man like the one Lorna and Jeanine had described.

I FLICKED ON a layer of mascara and burgundy lip gloss, slipped into a pair of black dress slacks, a white jersey knit camisole, and a black quilted blazer embellished with four geometric buttons shaped like a square, a diamond, a circle, and a rectangle. The sales associate had called them a whimsical touch. I studied myself in the mirror, satisfied with what I saw.

The Office Works building was located on prime Marketville real estate with the Dutch River on the left hand side of the property, and the town's multi-purpose trail system to the right. Built in the late nineteenth century, it was home to a prominent manufacturer of filing cabinets until the company, and the building, was sold in the early 1960s. A few incarnations and owners later, Office Works was now a mix of condominium housing on the three upper levels, and professional offices on the main floor. Despite all of that, and the carefully restored six-pane windows, it still looked like an old factory. There was, however, a side lot for visitors and reserved parking for the businesses and residents. I located four spaces with a neatly lettered sign: Reserved for Michael Westlake & Associates. Two spots, VISITOR painted in white on the pavement, were empty. The paint looked new, or at least new enough that it had yet to weather a Canadian winter. A white Hyundai Accent and a black Mercedes SUV filled the other two.

A brass plaque inside the entrance indicated that Michael Westlake & Associates was located in Suite 104. I made my way down a narrow, wainscoted hall, opened the door, and was greeted by a well-preserved, silver-streaked brunette. I pegged her as the owner of the Accent. Someone like Westlake would be the Mercedes-Benz type. Still, it never pays to make assumptions.

"Can I help you?" she asked, with a casual glance at my buttons. I wanted to tell her the mismatch was intentional, but bit my tongue. Too bad if she didn't appreciate whimsy.

"I have an appointment with Michael Westlake at noon. I'm a few minutes early."

"Have a seat. I'll let him know you're here." She picked up the phone, spoke quietly, and then turned to her computer, fingers flying across the keyboard as she worked her way through a massive pile of paperwork stacked next to her. Not only a receptionist, then.

"Is that your Accent?"

She looked up and nodded. "Why?"

"I'm thinking of getting one."

"It's very reliable."

"Good to know, thanks." I looked around the room. Tired was the best way to describe it. I settled into a well-worn tweed loveseat, mostly taupe with some twists of brown and caramel, and waited.

After everything I'd heard about Michael Westlake, I expected a large man, imposing in height and weight. The man before me stood no taller than five-foot-ten, with a slender build, steel gray hair, pale blue eyes, and a warm smile.

"Callie Barnstable," he said, holding out his hand. "Michael Westlake. Follow me. My office is at the end."

I did as instructed, taking note of two empty offices along the way. Either everyone was at lunch, or Westlake's associates were no longer employed with the firm. Was the Mercedes the last vestige of affluent appearances? For the first time I wondered just how much the family had invested, financially, to find Brandon Colbeck.

I was about to find out.

TWENTY-SIX

MICHAEL WESTLAKE'S OFFICE had a corner view that took in the trail, the river, and Edward Street. I could spot the spinning studio in the distance, and it dawned on me that New Beginnings Center for Life was a stone's throw away. Interesting that Jeanine had set up shop so close to her father. Some might even say Freudian.

Like the reception area, the furnishings were spartan, if slightly more high-end. A marble-topped mahogany desk with a telephone, desktop computer, a sleek black pen and pencil set in a Lucite block, and two clear plastic paper trays, one marked "Out," the other, "In." Both were empty. I wondered, briefly, if Westlake had emptied them before admitting me, and figured it was likely. Despite the warm smile, I suspected this was a man who didn't give up secrets willingly.

"Have a seat," Westlake said, pointing to one of two black leather armchairs across from his desk. It should have been nothing more than a friendly gesture, but somehow he made it seem like a command. Or was I allowing preconceived notions of who he was to influence my perception? I took a seat.

"Thank you for seeing me on such short notice. As you know, my firm, Past & Present Investigations, has been commissioned to find your stepson."

Westlake's lips twisted into a grimace. "You make it sound as if Brandon might still be alive. I find the prospect highly unlikely. Brandon may have been a confused young man, misguided, even, but he wasn't cruel. Surely he would have contacted Lorna or Jeanine at some point."

"There was the recent call to his grandmother."

"Which, I remind you, the police dismissed as a scam."

"That's certainly one possibility, but I've learned to explore every option, however remote." I made it sound as if I'd had years of experience, versus two cases. "At any rate, my purpose today isn't to debate the validity of the telephone call, but to find out about your relationship with Brandon as it might pertain to his leaving home, as well as what you remember about the days leading up to that decision."

"Fair enough, although I'm sure much of what I have to tell you will be repetitive," Westlake said. "I'd also like to go on record as saying that I'm unwilling to invest any more money to find him. That may sound heartless, but I've been down this road too many times, with nothing to show but a declining bank balance and the necessity to downsize."

My observation of the empty offices had been correct. "I can assure you that our bill will be paid by the individual who hired our firm. As for being repetitive, all I'm asking for is your honest recollection."

Westlake studied me for a moment. I kept my head high and my shoulders back, hoping I'd pass whatever test he was putting me through. After what seemed like forever, but was likely less than a minute, he began.

"Brandon and I had what might best be described as a complicated relationship. I entered Lorna's life when Brandon was seven. From the beginning, he resisted any parenting efforts on my part. Contrary to what Jeanine may have told you, I tried everything from being his friend to being his father. Nothing worked. As the years went on, Brandon became increasingly antagonistic towards me. He adored Jeanine, and he was always respectful to Lorna, though never submissive. Submissiveness was never part of his nature." He smiled. "Nor mine, truth be told."

"You say you tried to be his father, and yet you never adopted Brandon." I saw the dark flush spread across Westlake's face, and knew I should have been more diplomatic. "I'm sorry if that crossed a personal line, but I need to know everything that might provide insight into Brandon's state of mind."

The flush receded. "I planned to adopt him, but then Lorna got pregnant almost right away, and then Jeanine came along, and I was building up the firm, and…well, life got busy. A poor excuse, I know, but by the time Lorna and I sat down to discuss adoption with Brandon, he was ten. He told me in no uncertain terms that he didn't want to be adopted because one day his father would come for him. I blame his grandparents for filling his head with fairy tales and nonsense. Eleanor and Tom spoiled that boy to the point where he was virtually unmanageable, and Lorna did nothing to stop it. I put an end to those visits at their cottage."

For the first time, I had a sense of the real man behind the warm smile. Michael Westlake was someone used to getting his way, no matter the cost to anyone else. He was also used to being right, or at least being told he was right. I decided to play into that.

"It must have difficult for you, hearing that from a

boy you'd taken into your home and treated with love and respect."

Michael's pale blue eyes viewed me with suspicion. I managed to keep a poker face, easier said than done, given my growing dislike of the man before me, but I must have succeeded. He acknowledged the statement with a brief nod before continuing.

"It altered our relationship from that day forward. It was about that time I realized that tough love would be the only way to get through to Brandon."

Except you didn't get through to him, I thought. *You drove him further and further away, until he felt his only recourse was to leave home.* "Tell me about the days leading up to his departure."

"Brandon had always been a straight-A student, despite his best efforts not to be, but he flunked out of his first term in his second year of college. It surprised Lorna, but I'd seen it coming. He'd become increasingly detached. At first I suspected drugs or alcohol abuse, but there were none of the obvious signs. Then I thought it might be an addiction to online gaming, gambling, or porn…but it wasn't that, either."

"How can you be sure?"

"I monitored his internet browsing with tracking software."

Tracking software? Not only was that morally and ethically wrong on every possible level, I was pretty sure it was illegal. I refrained from offering my opinion of his actions, knowing that to do so would terminate our meeting immediately. "Was there anything he seemed obsessed with?"

"Tattoos and tarot. Brandon knew I wouldn't abide either, certainly not while he lived under my roof, and yet he had an online reading done every day, some-times more. As I recall, he was especially enamored with something called 'The Fool's Journey.'"

"What did the police make of that?"

For the first time since we'd sat across from each other, Westlake wasn't able to make eye contact. He shifted in his seat and that's when I knew. This was his secret. The secret Gloria Grace insisted they all had.

"You never told them," I said.

The flush deepened, spreading down his neck. "The keylogger software I used wasn't exactly legit. And I couldn't see how telling the cops about Brandon's fasci-nation with tattoos and tarot could help them find him. I never told anyone. Until now. And the only reason I'm telling you is because this is the absolutely last time I go down the 'Find Brandon' rabbit hole."

"You say you never told anyone. Not even your wife?"

"Especially not my wife. Lorna would never have approved." He pursed his lips. "She always took Bran-don's side."

Brandon's side? Who were the adults in this rela-tionship, and who was the child? The longer I sat in Westlake's office, the more I wanted to take a long, hot shower. I forced myself to stay calm. "Does the name Nestor Sanchez mean anything to you?"

Westlake frowned. "No, should it? Who is he? What does he have to do with Brandon?"

"I don't know, at least not yet. I do know Brandon had purchased some of his artwork, and I believe Bran-don took it with him when he left. Whether that's mean-ingful to his disappearance remains to be seen."

"Artwork?" Westlake seemed genuinely perplexed.

"Where would Brandon get the money for art? He wasn't employed, didn't even bother with a summer job before the fall semester."

"I don't have an answer for that."

Westlake shook his head. "Lorna. She must have been giving him an allowance. I should have known. The harder I worked, the more she spent. I blame Eleanor. Her mother never taught Lorna the value of a dollar. Then again, maybe it was Eleanor. She could never refuse Brandon anything—"

I stopped him before he went off on a tangent about his mother-in-law and his soon-to-be ex-wife. "Is there anything else you can think of, anything at all?"

"Nothing." His pale blue eyes locked into mine. Sincerity personified.

He was lying, I knew it and so did he. Proving it, and finding out what he was lying about, that would be another matter.

TWENTY-SEVEN

I MULLED OVER my meeting with Michael Westlake on the walk back. I was convinced he was holding something back. But what? I was no closer to an answer when I arrived home. Frustrated, I changed into my running gear and hit the trail. Sometimes the best thinking comes when you're not trying to think.

I was about five miles into the run when a thought struck me. Brandon took his laptop with him. And Westlake had been monitoring him remotely using keylogger software. Could he have traced Brandon's movements, at least initially? Is that why Westlake had taken four months before filing a missing person report? Because he knew his stepson was okay? Or because he knew he wasn't?

Whatever the answer, I couldn't confront Michael Westlake, at least not until I understood how keylogger software worked. That meant talking to a computer geek, someone who could tell me what was, or wasn't, possible in 2000. I didn't know anyone who fit the bill. I got back home, took a quick shower, and then googled keylogger. There were a multitude of generic articles about it online, all interesting, but not specific enough to be helpful. I waffled between asking the rest of the team. It was doubtful that Chantelle, Shirley, or Misty would know someone, and I didn't want our collective investigative efforts to be biased for or against Westlake.

But I needed a name. In the end, I emailed Chantelle, asking if she could provide me with the name of an IT expert, someone who'd been in the field at least twenty years. I didn't elaborate, but I knew Chantelle would trust that I'd tell her more when I was ready. That accomplished, I made myself a cup of tea and settled in to tackle the documents from Shirley.

I looked at the four piles: Dave Samuels, Such & Such, Sam Sanchez, and Trust Few. It made sense to work through them chronologically, which meant starting with Such & Such tattoo.

There were only two articles, both brief, both in the *Marketville Post*, both written by G.G. Pietrangelo. The first one, dated July 17, 1997, was a typical business announcement:

Such & Such Tattoo Opens Doors

Folks looking to get inked no longer have to trek to the city, now that Toronto tattoo artist Dave Samuels has opened his own shop in Marketville. Located at the back of Nature's Way, Samuels will specialize in custom tattoos, which he designs himself.

When asked how he came up with the unusual name of Such & Such, he admitted it wasn't part of the original plan. "When I was setting up everything, I'd tell myself, I just need to buy such and such, or as soon as I do such and such, I'll be ready to go. Somehow it just stuck."

In addition to designing and giving tattoos, Samuels has a solid collection of original and vintage artwork for sale. "It's called tattoo flash," Samuels explained. "Most traditional flash was designed for rapid tattooing to be used in 'street shops'—tattoo shops that handle a large volume of generic tattoos for walk-in customers."

The shop's address, hours, and telephone number were listed at the end. There were no photographs.

The second article was dated August 14, 2003, and announced the shop's closing:

Such & Such Shutters Doors:
New Shop Set to Open

After nearly six years in business, Dave Samuels has closed Such & Such tattoo parlor, which had been located at the back of Nature's Way. "We just weren't getting the traffic to justify keeping the lights on," Samuels said, clearly emotional about the decision. His remaining collection of vintage and original tattoo flash—the term used for the artwork—has been sold to a private buyer who prefers to remain anonymous. Asked about his future plans, Samuels said he was uncertain.

According to the lessor, the premises will be renovated to accommodate Sun, Moon & Stars, a new-age shop that will offer a variety of gifts, services, and handcrafted goods from local artisans.

I wondered who the private buyer was, and suspected it was Sam Sanchez. I opened my notebook and jotted down a reminder to ask her.

The only other mention of Dave Samuels was in his obituary, again in the *Marketville Post*. Whoever wrote it had kept it simple:

David Alexander Samuels 1950-2003
Passed away peacefully on November 14, 2003 at the Marketville Regional Hospital after a brief but courageous battle with pancreatic cancer. Born in Toronto, Dave was a talented tattoo artist who will be missed by his many friends and clients. If desired, a donation in Dave's name can be made to the charity of your choice.

The obituary might have been brief, but it was the photograph of Dave Samuels that told the story. He might have been fifty-three when he died, but the resemblance to the age-progressed sketches of a late-thirties Brandon Colbeck was undeniable. The ages also worked. Samuels was born in 1950, making him thirty when Brandon was born. Add to the mix that the man who impregnated Lorna told her his name was Alexander—Dave's middle name—and I was almost certain that Dave Samuels was Brandon Colbeck's father.

Which meant that Brandon's visit to Such & Such couldn't have been a coincidence. But how would he have figured out the connection? Lorna had told Brandon about his father in the weeks leading up to his leaving home, but she claimed all she knew was that his name might have been Alexander and that he had a large eagle tattoo across the top of his back.

Unless she'd lied to me.

And what about Sam Sanchez? I remembered her

slight hesitation when she first saw the age-progressed sketches. I referred back to my handwritten notes.

Me: "Do you recognize him?"

Sam: "If you're asking if these sketches remind me of the guy who walked in here on an icy March day looking for his first tattoo, I'd have to say, no."

Me: "What I meant is, have you seen him? The man in these sketches?"

Sam: "That would be another no."

I'd known, at the time, that Sam had been evasive, but I'd accepted her responses without pushing it one step further. What I should have asked was if the sketches reminded her of anyone else.

Well, I'd be asking her that, and more, but first I'd see what else Shirley had uncovered. I turned my attention back to the clippings. There were a handful of quarter-page ads in the *Marketville Post* advertising Trust Few as "a tattoo parlor you could trust," all placed within the first year of business. Sam had either decided that traditional advertising wasn't a worthwhile investment, or she'd developed enough of a clientele to discontinue the practice.

As with Such & Such, there was a brief announcement.

Trust Few Tattoo Parlor Opens on Poplar Street

When Such & Such Tattoo closed its doors in August of this year, tattoo artist Samantha (Sam) Sanchez found herself out of a job. Rather than seek employment elsewhere, she decided to open her own tattoo parlor on Poplar Street, renovating the recently vacated Handyman's Haven Hardware Store.

"The name Trust Few comes from a nineteenth-century proverb," Sanchez told us. "Love many, trust few, and always paddle your own canoe. It means act independently and decide your own fate. That resonated with me. I was raised by my grandfather, Nestor Sanchez, and we moved around quite a lot during my formative years."

Sanchez plans to specialize in custom designs, though she encourages her clientele to "think long term," noting that, "Tattoos are a commitment, and they should be something meaningful to you and your life."

There was a photograph of a young Sam Sanchez looking markedly different than her current incarnation, her dark hair bleached blonde and cut in a style vaguely reminiscent of Jennifer Aniston's infamous "Rachel" cut. She was smiling for the camera and I noticed the absence of the diamond chip in her front tooth. But it was more than the hair and the teeth—it was the way she carried herself, then and now, that was the key differentiator. The girl in this picture had an air of innocence about her. Somewhere along the way, the Sam I'd met had lost that. I suppose we all do as the years go by.

Shirley's search for Samantha and/or Sam Sanchez had yielded no more than a single entry in the *Marketville Post*, as reported by Jenny Lynn Simcoe.

Marketville Tattoo Artist Comes First in 50K Run For the Homeless

A longtime runner, Trust Few tattoo parlor owner Sam Sanchez exceeded her own expectations by entering—and winning—the 50K Run for the

Homeless. Sanchez took on the challenge of the 31-mile race to raise awareness and funds to the growing homeless population in Cedar County.

I could understand Sam's commitment to the cause but as someone training for their first 30K and deliberating the sanity—or insanity—of that decision, I had to wonder what sort of person put themselves through a fifty-kilometer run. I read on, considering Sam Sanchez in a different light than before. A woman who would do whatever it took to achieve an end goal.

"My grandfather was an itinerant tattoo artist, and while we were never homeless, we came very close," Sanchez said, when asked for her motivation. "As the population of Cedar County grows, we absolutely need more shelter spaces, especially during the coldest days of winter."

When asked for training tips to complete an ultra-marathon, Sanchez suggested following a program that includes back-to-back long runs once a week, for example, three hours on Saturday and three hours on Sunday, planned recovery days, as well as one 10k tempo run midweek, and another day practicing hill repeats for about an hour.

"It's also important to train on the terrain the race will be held on, and practicing nutrition and hydration during training runs," said Sanchez. "You're going to be out there for several hours. You can't do it on an energy bar and a couple of bottles of water. Find out what fuels your body without causing gastric issues, every runner is different. What works for your buddy may not work for you. Experiment before race day, not on it."

Sanchez also stresses the importance of having a mantra, a short phrase that you can repeat to yourself when the going gets tough. So what's Sanchez's mantra?

"The same as it's been my entire life," she said. "Stay strong and carry on."

Stay strong and carry on. I'd have to remember that, the next time I visited Sam Sanchez.

TWENTY-EIGHT

TUESDAY MORNING HAD me trying to define my priorities. I needed to see Sam, but instinct told me that there was more to find out before I contacted her again. It might not have been scientific, but my gut had never let me down. That left calling Jenny Lynn Simcoe, the journalist who'd reported on Brandon's disappearance in the *Marketville Post*, picking up Kavya's sketch by Nestor Sanchez at the Cedar County Retirement Residence, and paying a visit to Frame Up once I had it in hand. I also needed to set up another meeting with Eleanor Colbeck with the faint hope she'd known about Dave Samuels, and furthermore, remembered him. I thought back to her rigid demeanor when I'd asked why Michael hadn't adopted Brandon, and referred back to my notes.

E.C.: I can't tell you why Michael didn't adopt Brandon because I don't know the reason. Lorna never discussed the matter, and it wasn't my place to ask. It was a topic relegated to 'need to know' status and apparently I didn't need to know.

Nothing about Brandon's biological father being the reason, not that I'd thought to ask her if she knew who he was, or where he might be. I wanted to kick myself. It was such an obvious question. I checked the time. Eight thirty. Reception didn't open until nine and I wasn't willing to leave a voice mail asking for a call back. I wouldn't be Platinum Blonde's top priority.

I spent the next half hour trying to find Jenny Lynn Simcoe, and coming up empty. Nothing in the way of a social media presence, she wasn't listed in the online staff directory of the *Marketville Post*, and she hadn't contributed anything to the newspaper beyond the two articles relating to Brandon's disappearance. Interesting, but not helpful. Hopefully Gloria Grace would know something about the mysterious Jenny Lynn. In the meantime, it was finally nine o'clock.

Platinum Blonde—I couldn't think of her as Stephanie—answered the phone on the first ring, answering with an upbeat, "Cedar County Retirement Residence, how can I help you?"

"Hello, this is Callie Barnstable, Eleanor Colbeck's friend?"

"Yes, Ms. Barnstable, I remember you," she said, the frost firmly back in her tone.

I wondered if she treated all the callers like that or whether her disdain was reserved for me. I suspected the latter, thanks to my grandfather's herculean efforts to stop me from visiting Olivia. I tried to keep my tone light and bright. "I'm wondering if Eleanor is free for lunch today. If so, I'd love to take her out for a nice meal. I thought she might enjoy a change of scenery."

There was a loud *tsk* on the other end of the phone. "Oh, I'm afraid that's not a good idea. Mrs. Colbeck gets confused easily. It's far better if she remains in familiar surroundings. Now, if there's nothing else, I have another call waiting."

I wasn't about to be so easily dismissed. "Is it possible to join her for lunch in the dining room?"

"Thursday at one o'clock would be acceptable for that."

I wondered why I had to wait until Thursday. "I was hoping to dine with her today. Kavya is leaving something for me at reception."

"I'm well aware."

Meaning it is already there for me to pick up, and that she doesn't approve. "So today would be acceptable?"

"To pick up the envelope Kavya has left with me, yes. To have lunch with Eleanor, no. You may wish to do both on the same day. Which, as I said before, would be Thursday."

I decided not to push my luck. Thursday was only two days away. "Thursday will be fine."

"Very well. Let me put you on a brief hold while I consult the menu."

I waited on hold, the musical interludes interrupted by a message thanking me for my patience every thirty seconds. I was debating which was more annoying when Platinum Blonde came back on the line.

"Sorry for the delay," she said, not sounding in the least bit contrite. "The special on Thursday is tomato soup and grilled cheese. Shall I order for you?"

I envisioned a single slice of processed cheese in between two slices of over-buttered junk white bread. "Sounds great."

"If you can, please arrive five minutes ahead of time to arrange payment." She ended the call without any further pleasantries, but at least I'd gotten a "please" out of her.

I was debating the best way to approach Eleanor about Nestor Sanchez and Dave Samuels when *By the Light of the Silvery Moon* played on my phone. I checked the call display. Levon Larroquette.

"Levon, to what do I owe the pleasure?"

"Hi, Callie. I've been making calls to all the auction houses and galleries I know of who specialize in tattoo flash. I'd just about given up finding someone who'd heard of Nestor Sanchez, let alone sold his work, when one of my contacts mentioned a place called Light Box Auction Gallery. I'd never heard of them, but I called and spoke to the owner, a pleasant woman by the name of Nicolette Baxter, and here's the good news. She recently came into possession of some flash signed by Nestor Sanchez, though she didn't provide any details. She is, however, willing to meet with you." He rattled off the phone number.

"You're the best," I said, writing down the number. "I owe you one."

"You don't owe me a thing. Oh, and Callie?"

"Yes?"

"I didn't tell Baxter why you wanted to see the flash, just that you were interested in his work. I wasn't sure how much you wanted her to know about the investigation."

"Good thinking. Thanks again. I'll call her as soon as we hang up."

"In that case, I'll leave you to it. Don't be a stranger."

I googled Light Box Auction Gallery before calling Nicolette Baxter, and found the company's website. I clicked on the "About Us" tab, and began reading.

Started in January 2019, Light Box Auction Gallery is an e-commerce venture specializing in vintage and original tattoo flash. Our company name was derived from a tool used by tattoo artists to create custom tattoo stencils. Laying images on a light box makes them easier to trace and modify, allowing the artist to create a tattoo design that is an appropriate size for the body part to be tattooed while meeting the client's expectations. Whether you're thinking of consigning or buying, your satisfaction is always guaranteed. Online auctions held twice a year; check back for updates and sign up to receive our latest catalog when available. Gallery is open by chance or appointment.

The recent opening would explain why Levon hadn't heard of them before now. I entered "Sanchez" into the Search bar, which took me to a page, titled *Nestor Sanchez*. Pictured were a half dozen colorful tarot-inspired flash, priced between $350 and $1,500. The page included an all-too-brief bio that raised more questions than it answered.

Nestor Sanchez was a Toronto-born tattoo artist who lived his life without borders. His work was heavily influenced by his fascination with tarot. Additional examples are available on request.

Three sentences that yielded two important pieces of information: Nicolette Baxter referred to Nestor Sanchez in the past tense *and* her gallery had been commissioned to sell his flash art. The question was, when had it been commissioned and who had commissioned it? Could Brandon Colbeck be selling his collection? Or was Sam behind this yet again?

I picked up the phone and dialed.

A woman answered the phone on the second ring. "Light Box Auction Gallery, Nicolette speaking."

"Hi, Nicolette. My name's Callie Barnstable. I understand you were speaking to my friend, Levon Larroquette."

"Right, Levon. I've heard a lot about him from some of my colleagues—all good, I assure you—but we've never met. Levon tells me you're interested in purchasing flash by Nestor Sanchez. We have a few other examples in stock, beyond what you see online. It's quite an interesting collection if you're into tarot. I acquired it two days ago."

Did I tell Nicolette my interest wasn't in purchasing it but rather finding out who the consignor was? I'd have to, of course, but not yet. Not before I'd had an opportunity to view the art and meet Nicolette in person. "I'd certainly like to see, it," I said, purposely noncommittal.

"Would you like to make an appointment? I'm in Burlington."

Burlington was a picturesque city on Lake Ontario, located midway between Toronto and Niagara Falls. The thought of Niagara Falls reminded me of Royce and our unfulfilled plans to visit there. I pushed the thought aside.

"Yes, I would. I'm in Marketville, so an appointment outside of rush hour to and from Toronto would be much appreciated."

That elicited a dry chuckle. "I hear you. How's Friday at noon? I can't guarantee a traffic-free drive, but I can text you the address and the fastest route to get here."

"Sounds perfect. Is it okay if I bring a friend?"

"Absolutely. I'll look forward to meeting you both."

I called Chantelle next. The ninety-minute drive there and back would be a lot more pleasurable with some company, and I could catch her up on the case. I hoped she'd be available, she'd been spending most of her free time with Lance.

I was in luck. Not only was it Chantelle's day off at the gym, she was keen to tag along, offering apologies for being somewhat absent, and promising to get me up-to-date on the drive.

"I do have the name of an IT guy, though. I was just about to text you. Benjamin Benedetti."

"That's terrific. Where did you find him?"

"I didn't. I asked Lance. He used to work with Benedetti, called him a white hat hacker, whatever the heck that means. Lance assures me the guy can answer your questions. I'll text you the info."

Lance, and once again, not Lance the Loser. "That's great, thank Lance for me. By the way, have you had a chance to work on the Ancestry.ca side of things for our case?"

"I have, though I'm afraid the results are disappointing, which is why I haven't sent an update yet. There are more than one hundred and thirty entries for family trees, last name Colbeck, but no matches for Eleanor, Brandon, or Lorna Colbeck. I also checked the member list, again, no luck. I tried Michael Westlake on the off-chance he'd have started a family tree and included Brandon."

"Let me guess, there were no Michael Westlakes."

"Actually, there are four members listed, but none of them are our Michael Westlake. However, there are over four *hundred* records under that name. That includes everything from birth, marriage, and death certificates to voting lists and immigration documents. I'm still culling through that, but I'm not optimistic I'll find anything to help us in the search for Brandon."

"I have to agree, but thanks for being thorough. Can you add another name to the search?"

"Of course. Who is it?"

"David Alexander Samuels."

"David Alexander Samuels," Chantelle repeated. "Got it. Who is he?"

"I think he may be Brandon's biological father."

"Wow, talk about burying the lead."

"I hope to have more than that to tell you about on Friday."

"Can't wait. In the meantime if anything pops up on Samuels, I'll let you know right away."

I hung up, thinking that Chantelle sounded even more upbeat than usual. It had to be Lance. I knew he'd broken her heart once before, but Chantelle was a big girl, and if her world came crumbling down around her, I'd be there to help her pick up the pieces.

I just hoped it wouldn't come to that.

TWENTY-NINE

I GOOGLED "WHITE HAT HACKER" before calling Benjamin Benedetti. According to Wikipedia, "white hat" referred to an ethical computer hacker, or a computer security expert. Fair enough. I punched in the phone number Chantelle had given me and waited.

Not only did Benedetti answer on the first ring, Lance had apparently told him to expect my call. He suggested meeting for coffee at Debbie's Downhome Diner in the north end of town. I hesitated briefly, not because Debbie's was a bit of a greasy spoon—she made a terrific cup of coffee, and the food was good and reasonably priced—but because it had been one of Royce's favorite places to grab a quick bite. We'd met there on a few occasions, always enjoying the meal.

And each other's company, I thought, my stomach doing a quick flip. I pushed aside my reluctance. Marketville wasn't Toronto, I was bound to run into Royce eventually, and I couldn't spend the rest of my life trying to avoid him. Besides, it was coming up on suppertime and I was getting hungry.

"Debbie's sounds great. Can I buy you dinner?"

"I can definitely be talked into having dinner," Benedetti said, "but I insist on paying my own way. Lance tells me this involved a keylogger case dating back to 2000. It piqued my interest."

We agreed to meet in an hour, and I bustled upstairs to freshen up, apply a bit of make-up, and pick an outfit—I was thinking my moss green thigh-length sweater, black denim skinny jeans, and maybe the black suede ankle boots that Royce had always admired. I know, pathetic, right? It was my lack of commitment that led to our breakup in the first place. And in the second place, Royce wasn't about to see my feet under the table, even if he just so happened to be there.

I slipped the boots on anyway. When you're going for pathetic, you may as well go all the way.

THE INSIDE OF Debbie's Downhome Diner had walls lined with sponsorship plaques for local sports teams, bench seats upholstered in red leatherette, and red and white checked tablecloths topped with the obligatory stainless steel napkin holder, salt and pepper shakers, and vinegar bottle. I wrinkled my nose at the vinegar bottle. Why would anyone want to sprinkle vinegar on their fries?

I stood at the entrance and looked around the diner, and wondered what Benjamin Benedetti looked like. My money was on a dark-haired man mesmerized by whatever was on his phone.

I was about to walk over and introduce myself when the door opened behind me. I turned around to come face to face with a forty-something guy who could have been Matt Czuchry's double. I've been a fan of Czuchry's since his days as Logan Huntzberger in the *Gilmore Girls*. I hoped this was my white hat hacker.

"Callie?" the man asked.

I nodded, ridiculously pleased that I'd worn my black suede ankle boots. "You must be Benjamin Benedetti."

He smiled, revealing a row of straight white teeth.

"Guilty as charged, though I go by Ben. Let's grab a seat, shall we?"

We found a vacant booth at the back of the restaurant. We had no sooner taken our seats when our server came over with laminated menus and two glasses of water.

"The dinner special is meat loaf, mashed potatoes, and mushy peas," she said, removing an order pad from her pocket. "Soup of the day is split pea with ham or minestrone. Sandwich is roast turkey with cranberry chutney, served with a side of fries or garden salad. Or you can have a half sandwich and soup."

"Thanks," Ben said. "We'll just take a minute to look at the menu, though the dinner special sounds good. Is it possible to get coffee now?"

"Milk or cream?"

"Milk for me. Callie?"

"Coffee now would be great. Milk for me, too."

We took the next few minutes looking over the menu, a companionable silence settling over us.

"I think I'm going to go with the meat loaf," Ben said, closing his menu.

"I'm going with the soup and sandwich combo."

That decided, and our orders placed, we got to the purpose of the meeting.

"Chantelle tells me you were a white hat hacker. I googled it, though I'm not sure I should trust Wiki as my source."

"What would we do without Wikipedia?" Ben asked, smiling. "The term 'white hat' is from old Western movies where the good guys wore white cowboy hats, and the bad guys wore black cowboy hats, or at least that's the cliché. A white hat hacker is an ethical hacker, a computer security specialist employed to break into protected systems and networks to test and assess their security. Their job is to expose vulnerabilities before malicious hackers, known as black hat hackers, can detect and exploit them."

"It sounds interesting."

"It was, but not as interesting as your line of work. Lance tells me you and his ex-wife are private eyes."

"Not exactly. We aren't licensed investigators and we don't do typical PI stuff, like spying on a cheating spouse or what have you. I like to think we're hired to find out the truth about the past, and bring it into the present."

"What about the case you're working on?"

I was about to tell him when our food arrived. "Let's eat. Then we'll talk."

THE MEAL FINISHED, dessert declined, bills on the table to be paid "whenever we were ready," and a fresh cup of coffee poured, I gave Ben a quick recap. "Brandon Colbeck was at a low point in his life. He'd dropped out of school, didn't have a job, and lived with a stepfather who pushed all his buttons. He left home in March 2000, leaving a note saying he was going to find himself. He took some personal belongings and his laptop, but no ID. No one has heard from him since."

"Brandon Colbeck," Ben mused, when I was finished. "Why does that name seem familiar?"

"There was an article about him in the *Marketville Post* three years ago," I said. "Maybe you remember reading it?"

Ben frowned. "I don't think that's it, the story doesn't ring any bells, and I seldom read the *Post*. Maybe it'll come to me later. Now, satisfy my curiosity and tell me how a keylogger in 2000 impacts your case."

"Brandon's stepfather, Michael Westlake, admitted to me that he had installed keylogger software onto Brandon's laptop. Even though Brandon left in March, the Colbecks didn't file a missing person report until August."

"You're thinking Michael Westlake was following Brandon's journey via the laptop during those four months, and that's why they didn't file a missing person report."

"Yes."

Ben shook his head. "It wouldn't have been possible. Not in 2000."

I felt a crush of disappointment. I'd been so sure this is what Westlake had been hiding. "You're absolutely sure it wouldn't have been possible?"

"One hundred percent. In 2000, a lot of people that had computers were still using dial-up to connect to the web. Broadband and such was just starting to make inroads. To this day most laptops do not have GPS, and it wasn't until 2004 or 2005 that cell phones had GPS installed. As far as tracking the location of a laptop, the first widely available software started appearing in 2005. This coincides with things moving away from dial-up and going to broadband or cable modems, or more rarely back then, wireless."

I pushed aside my disappointment. There had to be another way. Maybe if I understood the technical side of it better…it wasn't a perfect strategy, but at least I'd have a solid reason to visit Westlake again, to challenge him with what I'd learned.

I pulled a pen and a small gray notebook out of my

purse, the cover embossed with the words, "BE BOLD." Despite my ability to recall most conversations verbatim, my technical brain can be woefully inadequate.

"What can you tell me about the keylogger process?"

THIRTY

BEN COLLECTED HIS THOUGHTS. "Okay, back in 2000, Brandon was probably using a PC, running Windows 98, maybe Windows 2000. Westlake would have had two options. Either download the software himself from his own computer or have a geek friend get it for him, though if he was trying to keep things on the down low, my guess is the former."

"I don't understand. If he downloaded the software to his PC, how does it get onto Brandon's laptop?"

"There are a couple of options. In 2000, assuming they had a home computer network, Brandon's laptop would have been hardwired in via an Ethernet cable. Computers on networks can see each other, Westlake or his tech buddy could hack Brandon's laptop from Westlake's computer and download the software."

"What if his laptop was turned off? Or it was password protected?"

"If the computer was connected to the home network and plugged in, it would be easy for someone with expertise to access the hard drive. There was also a low-tech option where the keylogger software would be written onto a 3.5 inch floppy disk."

I'd all but forgotten about floppy disks. It was another reminder of how quickly technology continued to evolve. "Go on."

"Westlake would have needed access to Brandon's

laptop for long enough to plug in the floppy disk and run the installation program for the keylogger software. Then he'd eject the disk and dispose of it. That's what I would have done in his place."

"The man I met wouldn't be sloppy with the floppy."

"Good one," Ben said, laughing. "Anyway, once installed, the software would launch itself each time Brandon turned on the machine. Once running, it would write every keystroke into a text file. It would not alert the user, Brandon in this case, to the fact that it was running in the background."

"When you say everything Brandon typed on his laptop would have been written into a text file, what does that mean exactly?"

"When Brandon opened a web browser, any web address he entered into the browser would be recorded. If he went to a website that had a login page which required him to type in a name and password, that would also be recorded by the software."

"How would Michael Westlake gain access to the text file?"

"He would once again need access to Brandon's laptop to copy the text files to another floppy disk. Once he had the files, he could open it at his leisure on another computer and review the file to see everything Brandon had been typing since the software had been installed."

I thought about that for a moment. If the files were in his browser history or his documents, Brandon would assuredly have discovered it almost immediately. "Where would the text files be stored?"

"Excellent question," Ben said. "When the software was installed on Brandon's laptop, Westlake decides where to put the files created. The default location could be in a folder called 'Logs' on the hard drive. This would be indicated as 'c colon backslash Logs.' Each day a file would be created in this folder with the date as the name. When Westlake plugged in his floppy disk, he could copy all the files in the Logs folder to his floppy, or just specific ones based on the date. After he copied them, he would then be able to delete them, leaving behind no trace."

I wrote "floppy disks" and "c:/Logs" in my notebook, pondering the ramifications of what Ben had told me. "If Brandon discovered this invasion of his privacy, that could have provided the impetus for him leaving home. But, if the files were hidden away where no one would think to look, or they were deleted without leaving any trace, then that theory is quashed."

"Unless Brandon discovered it before the files were deleted," Ben said.

I considered that for a moment, a nugget of an idea forming. "Let's say Brandon discovered the keylogger software, how would he have done it?"

"It could be as simple as Brandon thinking that this laptop wasn't running as fast as it used to. If defragging the hard drive didn't speed things up, he'd run antivirus software. The software would alert him that keylogger software had been installed on his laptop."

The nugget was getting bigger. "Could he tie it back to his stepfather?"

"There would be no direct link, no signature, if that's what you're asking."

I slumped back into my chair. For a moment I…

"There's always Occam's Razor," Ben said, interrupting my thoughts.

I leaned forward. "Occam's Razor? Is that some sort of spyware?"

"Nothing so sophisticated. It's a problem-solving principle where the simplest solution tends to be the correct one. In other words, consider the options and select the solution with the fewest assumptions. Scenario one, Westlake or a tech friend hacked Brandon's laptop via the home computer system. Scenario two, Westlake asked Brandon to borrow his laptop."

Select the solution with the fewest assumptions. "I think that's unlikely. Brandon despised his stepfather. I can't imagine Westlake asking to borrow Brandon's laptop. He would immediately have raised Brandon's suspicions."

"In that case, scenario three, Westlake waited until Brandon was out of the house and left his laptop in his bedroom. If Brandon had his laptop password-protected, he'd have to guess at the password. That's easier to do than you might think."

I tapped my fingertips on the table. "I'm going to have to think on it. In the meantime, thank you. This information will really help."

"There's something else you may not have considered," Ben said. "If Brandon discovered the keylogger software, he may well have led his stepfather on a wild goose chase."

"In other words, he deliberately planted false clues by visiting websites he had no interest in."

I was mulling that over when I noticed our server bustling around, manning multiple tables. There wasn't an empty booth in sight. "We should probably pay up and get going."

"You're right." Ben shifted in his seat. "I know we've

just met, but I wondered. Would you…would you like to get a drink sometime?"

I could do a lot worse than have a drink with a Matt Czuchry lookalike, but I wasn't quite ready to go down the dating road again. Or was I?

I was still debating the answer when the door opened and Royce Ashford walked in, Mercy Dellacorte by his side.

THIRTY-ONE

I TRIED TO slink further into the booth, hoping Royce wouldn't notice me. Notice us. No such luck. The pair sauntered over, a fake smile plastered on Mercy's face.

"Hello, Royce," I said, forcing my own fake smile. "And you must be Mercy Dellacorte. Lovely to finally meet you."

"Lovely to meet you as well," Mercy said, her tone suggesting it was anything but.

Royce was assessing Ben, his gaze unabashedly curious. "I'm afraid we haven't met. Royce Ashford. I'm an old friend of Callie's."

Ben, bless his bleeding heart, took me by the hand, the gesture gentle and possessive, as he helped me up from the table. "Benjamin Benedetti. It's so nice to meet you both, though I'm afraid we can't stay and chat."

I murmured a quick goodbye and allowed Ben to usher me out onto the street, his arm wrapped possessively around my waist.

"Thank you," I said, untangling myself when we were out of sight.

"An ex-boyfriend, I assume."

"You read people well."

Ben chuckled. "Mercy didn't seem overly enthused to meet you and I got the distinct impression the feeling was mutual. And the way Royce looked at you, and then at me…it was pretty easy to put two and two together. I gather it's a recent breakup?"

"Fairly recent, but it was more of a petering out than an actual breakup. We just never seemed to find time for one another."

"She looked familiar."

"She's an actress. Mostly theater."

"I've seen her in something, not that I go to a lot of plays."

"She's in the new Icelandic yogurt commercials."

"That's it. Well, if it's any comfort, her real name probably isn't Mercy Dellacorte. My money's on something like Mary Dell."

Mary Dell. The same name that I'd thought of. I might be a skeptic when it comes to psychics, but I do believe in signs. This *seemed* like a sign, like I should consider dating again after all. "Tell me something. Do you like vinegar on your fries?"

Ben laughed, a warm, earthy sound. "That's an odd question, but no. I think it's a custom that should have stayed in England. I'm strictly a salt and pepper guy, no gravy, no vinegar, and definitely no poutine."

A man after my own heart. "In that case, I'd like to go out for a drink sometime."

"How about now?"

WE ENDED UP at UnWired, a recently opened pub on Edward Street that strongly discouraged the use of mobile phones, tablets, and other electronic devices in favor of conversing with the ones you were with. It was not an establishment where you took a quick pic of your BFF drinking a beer to post on Instagram. Based on the effusive greetings as we walked in, everyone knowing

Ben, he was a regular. Was my loser radar back after all? The last thing I needed, or wanted, was to date a guy who spent the bulk of his spare time at a bar.

I handed my jacket and phone to an apple-cheeked brunette at the coat check by the front door, received a numbered ticket for each in return, then scoped out the interior. It was Mid-century modern with a distinctly Scandinavian flair, round glass-topped coffee tables and slung-back swivel lounge chairs in vibrant shades of teal, emerald green, and violet. A brass starburst clock was the focal point behind a well-stocked teak bar, tended by a clean-shaven thirty-something man wearing a uniform of black pants, white dress shirt with silver cufflinks, and red bowtie.

"Interesting décor," I said. "It definitely fits the tech-free directive."

"Do you think a place like this can succeed?" Ben asked.

I thought about it for a moment. "I don't know. It's an interesting concept, but we're all connected to our phones these days. I have to admit it was difficult for me to hand mine over. It just seemed weird, you know? But I hope so. I hate to see any business fail, and Edward Street has seen its share of restaurants and bars come and go."

Ben smiled. "I hope so, too, albeit for entirely different reasons. I own this place."

"An IT guy who doesn't want technology in his bar? Seems like an oxymoron."

"I said I used to be an IT guy. Now, I'm not, a long story for another day. Let's just say that sometimes I go for hours, even a day or two, without turning on my cell, and I avoid social media like the plague." Ben smiled.

"Now that you know I'm a slightly neurotic, fledgling pub owner, are you still interested in that drink?"

I smiled back. "Can you recommend the house white?"

"We have a nice Italian Pinot Grigio."

"Sounds perfect."

WE SWITCHED FROM wine to club soda after the first glass, and talked about everything from starting a business to being raised by a single parent, in Ben's case, by his mother. Neither of us volunteered any details on the parent who hadn't been around. There are some things you don't discuss on a first date, or even a second. Despite that, the evening ended far too soon, at least from my perspective.

I was back home, polar fleece PJ's on, sipping on hot cocoa in a mug, when my cellphone buzzed. I checked the caller ID. Ben.

"Hello."

"So you do leave your phone on," Ben said, a chuckle in his voice.

"Guilty as charged, though true confession. I checked the caller ID."

"I'm flattered to have gotten through your rigid security."

"As you should be," I said. "It's not everyone who gets a free pass at…" I checked my watch. "Midnight. Seriously, what's up? Beyond the fact that you can't wait to see me again." *OMG, did I actually say that out loud?*

"I've been thinking about Brandon Colbeck, though I'll admit in large part it was because any information I might have would provide an excuse to see you again."

"And the smaller part?"

"As I said earlier, I'm sure I know the name Brandon Colbeck from somewhere. I thought if you had any photos of him, it might refresh my memory. Do you have any?"

"As a matter of fact, I do. I can email them to you now if you'd like. My computer is shut down, but it will only take a couple of minutes to boot up. Of course, you probably want to wait until the morning."

"Now's good. I won't sleep until I know, or at least try to know," Ben said, giving me his email address.

I turned on my computer, chatting as I did so. "There will be one jpeg and two PDFs. The photograph of him smiling was taken the summer before he left home, in 1999. He would have been nineteen at the time. The other two are age-progressed sketches drawn by a police artist." I navigated through the various windows that popped open, found the Brandon Colbeck folder, selected the files, and hit send. "They're on their way."

"Got them. Give me a minute, don't hang up, okay?"

"Okay."

"I recognize him," Ben said, after a lengthy pause. "Not the older version of him, but the one taken in the summer of 1999. I taught a Dreamweaver course at Cedar County College, and Brandon was one of my students. It would have been the last semester of 1998, September to December. I don't recall him being a problem. The opposite, really, most of the other students were interested in e-commerce, launching a website, or getting rich quick. Brandon was quiet, studious."

"He'd been a straight A student until the fall of 1999, when his personality changed and his grades began to fail. You didn't have him in any other semesters?"

"I only taught that one semester, and only that one

class. I was trying to get my foot in the door, you know? Then in December 1998, I was offered a full-time job as an ethical hacker for a company that shall remain nameless, thanks to a non-disclosure agreement. Remember the Y2K bug, we thought a virus would wreak havoc on computers everywhere? It was a very lucrative time if you were in IT, everyone wanted to make sure their networks were safe. Being a white hat paid a lot more than part-time college professor."

The new millennium. A memory of sitting around a makeshift campfire in my father's Scarborough backyard flooded over me. The air had been cold and crisp, with the sort of clean scent that only seemed possible on a cloudless winter night. We were sipping on cocoa fortified with generous dollops of Bailey's Irish Cream, wondering if the world as we knew it would be forever altered, the flames flickering in the darkness, warming our hearts and bodies. It had been just him and me, and I could no more imagine walking out of his life than I could imagine walking on the moon. I wondered how the Westlakes had spent New Year's Eve that year, together or apart, and whether Brandon had been part of their celebration.

"Do you remember anything else, even things that would seem insignificant?"

"It was a long time ago, and there were fifty-plus students in that class. I don't have any of the paperwork, not after all this time." There was a long pause and then, "As I recall, he used to hang out with a girl, attractive, long dark hair, though I don't think they were an item. There was never any sense of intimacy between them."

"Do you remember her name?"

"I don't think I ever knew it. She wasn't in my class.

The only reason I remember her is because she had a large tattoo on her left calf. Unusual for 1999."

"Do you remember what the tattoo looked like?"

"A pistol with four aces, and some words."

"Did it say, *Smith and Wesson Beats 4 Aces*?"

"I'm not sure, but it's possible."

"I'm going to send you another photo, okay?"

"Sure."

I found the *Marketville Post* promotional piece for the opening of Trust Few in 2003, the one with the photograph of a young Sam Sanchez. I was once again struck by the difference of her then, and now, her dark hair bleached blonde.

There was another long pause and then, "It *might* be her but like I said, the girl with Brandon had long dark hair, almost to her waist, and she was more of an adolescent than the young woman in this picture. I'm sorry, I wish I could be more help."

"You've been far more help than you know."

"Anything you want to share?"

"The girl in the photo, her name is Samantha Sanchez, Sam for short. She has a tattoo like you described, owns Trust Few Tattoo on Poplar Street. I've interviewed her a couple of times."

"Let me guess," Ben said. "She didn't mention that she knew Brandon."

"She admitted knowing Brandon as a client in March 2000, but I was left with the impression that he'd been a stranger before then. It would appear she deliberately led me to a false conclusion. The question is, why?"

"A valid question. I suppose you could come out and ask her."

"I'm not sure that's my best approach, but it's late,

and I'm tired. Too tired to think about it and sort through the possibilities."

"In that case, I bid you good night and sweet dreams. I'm heading out of town for a few days, but I'd like to call you on Sunday, set up a time to go out. If that's okay with you."

"More than okay," I said, and found myself looking forward to Sunday.

THIRTY-TWO

I EXPECTED A sleepless night but exhaustion quickly took over. I woke up feeling refreshed and ready for my meeting with Gloria Grace Pietrangelo. The drive to Barrie was uneventful, traffic on Highway 400 unusually light, and I arrived at her studio promptly at eleven o'clock. It was tucked inside the middle unit of a small strip plaza that included a pizza place, sub shop, chiropractic clinic, combination laundromat/dry cleaner, and convenience store, an unlikely location for a nature photographer.

Inside, the studio was plastered with stunning photographs. I paused to admire *Birds of Prey*, remembering it from my last visit. Gloria Grace had captured a blue jay fighting off a hawk, claws against talons, the abject fear in the jay's eyes as palpable as the merciless will to kill in the eyes of the hawk. How long had she waited to get this particular shot? Definitely a woman of infinite patience, far more than I had.

I was about to ring the silver bell on the counter when Gloria Grace sauntered into the reception area. She was a woman of generous proportions in her early sixties, gray hair pulled into a ponytail, with a ruddy complexion that spoke of decades in the great outdoors. There were new lines around pale brown eyes that might have been amber in another light, and the creases around her nose and mouth were more deeply entrenched.

"Callie, it's so good to see you again," she said, giving me a quick hug. "It's too early for lunch, but come on back and I'll get us some tea and a snack. I have scones. I remember you enjoyed them the last time you were here."

I followed her down the hall, passing a closed door labeled Office, one marked Washroom, and a stark white room with baskets of dog and cat toys, which I knew she used in her pet photography.

Unlike the front of the studio, the kitchenette's soft green walls were devoid of any photographs or other ornamentation. A small, rectangular wooden table, painted white, was tucked against one wall. Gloria Grace gestured for me to sit in one of the two chairs, plugged in the kettle, and uncovered a plate with lemon cranberry and blueberry scones.

"I recall that your preference was blueberry," she said, "and that you liked Earl Grey tea, just the tea, no milk or sugar."

"You have a good memory."

"You need a good memory to be a journalist." She slid a manila folder off the counter and placed it in front of me. "I made photocopies of my notes, along with the articles I wrote for the *Marketville Post* about Brandon's disappearance. No need to return them, I have the originals. I'll warn you, there isn't much there that isn't in the paper, but call or email with any questions once you've gone through them."

"Thank you." I skimmed through the file as she bustled about getting the scones heated and the tea poured into oversized ceramic mugs, coming up with my first surprise. "You're Jenny Lynn Simcoe."

"Guilty as charged. The *Post* approached me when

Jeanine Westlake requested a follow-up piece. I agreed as long as the byline wasn't under my name, though the editor added the 'with files from G.G. Pietrangelo' on the first one. Being a journalist is in my past. I don't want it to be identified with my present."

"And yet, not only did you agree to meet with the family four years ago, you exposed the grandparent scam."

Gloria placed plates, scones, butter, and mugs of tea on the table before slipping into her seat. "Jeanine can be very persuasive. Besides, the case has haunted me for years, and the thought of someone trying to scam Eleanor Colbeck based on information gleaned from my article infuriated me. I felt I had an obligation to try to make it right."

Jeanine can be very persuasive. Not Lorna. Not Michael. *Jeanine.* Of course, it was possible that she'd merely agreed to be the family spokesperson, but what if both her parents had been less than willing participants? Not just Michael, but Lorna as well? I set the thought aside for later consideration and buttered my scone.

"I tried to find Jenny Lynn Simcoe," I said, taking a bite and savoring the delicate blend of blueberry and sugar. "No luck, which is unusual for a journalist. In retrospect, I should have recognized your writing style. It makes me wonder what else I've missed."

"Don't be so hard on yourself. You had no reason to think I was Jenny Lynn Simcoe, though I'm grateful to learn that my cover hasn't been blown by one of the family. Then again, they're a secretive lot. I reread my notes after you called, and the thing that struck me, again, was that everyone in that family seemed to be holding something back, even Jeanine. Have you learned their secrets yet?"

"Some of them." I gave Gloria Grace a quick recap of everything I'd found out about the Colbeck-Westlake family so far—Jeanine's misunderstanding of flash art, Michael's use of keylogger software, Eleanor's reminisces of a young Brandon, pre-Michael, Lorna's admission that she'd told Brandon about his father shortly before he left home. "Lorna claims not to know the father's true identity, but I think she's lying, and I also think she told Brandon his name."

"I always had the same feeling," Gloria Grace said, "but what brings you to that conclusion?"

"Nothing scientific, I'm afraid. I just sense that she hasn't told me everything. It could be she was aware of the keylogger business. I've yet to ask her. It's better to have as much information as I can gather before going down that road. Besides, it may not even be necessary if..." I let the words dangle.

"If?" A gentle prompt, ever the journalist for all her talk about leaving the life behind.

Not "if," I thought, *but "what if?"*

"Did you consider the telephone call might not have been a scam? That the man calling Eleanor might have been Brandon Colbeck?"

Gloria Grace studied me through narrowed eyes. "Do *you* believe it was Brandon?"

"I haven't uncovered any evidence to lead to that conclusion," I said, knowing that I sounded evasive. But I was unwilling, and perhaps more than a little embarrassed, to admit that I'd been considering the possibility since seeing Nestor Sanchez's flash on the Light Box website. "Unless Brandon's remains are found or he resurfaces there's no way to know for sure. And I'm being paid to find the 'for sure.' Or at least try to."

"Have you thought about asking the family to offer a reward? They could place an ad in all the major city and national newspapers. It would be an expense but it might lead to something."

"I thought of that but I think a reward would only encourage more scammers to come forward." I didn't tell Gloria Grace I'd just come up with another idea. One that almost certainly wouldn't meet with police approval, let alone trying to persuade the family. I decided to keep my latest brainstorm to myself for the time being. It might not even be necessary to go down that path. I had more leads to follow up, more interviews to hold. But at least now I had a Plan B.

THIRTY-THREE

I LEFT GLORIA Grace's studio with a promise to keep her posted, mulling over my plans for the rest of the afternoon and Thursday. Reading over the files she'd provided would take the rest of my day. Rather than anticipation, the thought of reading them—much of it bound to be repetitive—exhausted me. I was more interested in a long, leisurely soak in a lavender-scented bathtub with a good book and a glass of white wine.

I bribed myself for the task with a treat and stopped at my favorite Thai takeout on the way home, ordering *Som Tum*, a spicy green papaya salad that was to die-for, and *Kai Med Ma Muang*, a delicious concoction of chicken with cashews, carrots, chilies, pepper, and mushrooms.

MY BELLY FULL of Thai and a glass of wine by my side, I settled in to read the files. I started with an article dated September 21, 2000. This, then, was the first media report of Brandon's disappearance. The family hadn't filed a missing person report until early August that year. Was waiting another six or seven weeks to get it in the local paper meaningful? I hoped that Gloria's notes would offer some insight. I turned my attention to the article.

It was the same one I'd read when I started the investigation, but I reread it, noting that there were no quotes from Jeanine or Michael Westlake. Jeanine made sense given she was only twelve at the time. It was interesting, however, that Michael hadn't been quoted. I hadn't picked up on that before.

I flipped past the newspaper clippings until I found Gloria Grace's original notes. As expected, she'd accumulated background information not in the article: Lorna's place of work—an insurance brokerage—Michael's business, the name of Jeanine's school. She'd taken the time to call upon the couple's co-workers and neighbors, as well as Brandon's teachers and fellow students.

I scanned the list of names, and found Raj Bhardwaj—that must be Kavya's older brother. I didn't see Ben's name, nor had I expected to, as he would have started his new job. No Sam Sanchez either, not surprising given her reluctance to talk even now. But it was interesting that no one remembered Brandon hanging out with a girl with long black hair and a tattoo. Ben remembered and he'd known Brandon for only a few weeks.

No one could shed light on why Brandon had left, or where he'd gone, though she was left with the impression that Michael Westlake was more humiliated than upset by his stepson's disappearance.

I flipped to Gloria Grace's notes relating to the 2015 article. There was virtually nothing there that differed from the original article, though this time she'd jotted down that everyone in the family, with the exception of Eleanor Colbeck, seemed to be hiding something. "Find their secrets, Callie, and you'll find out the truth," she'd told me when I'd first called her. Well, I was finding them out, but I was still no closer to finding out what happened to Brandon.

The final article addressed the grandparent scam, prompted by the telephone call to Eleanor Colbeck. Here, again, the notes revealed little that wasn't in the paper, though I finally remembered where I knew the name Detective Aaron Beecham. Arabella had dated him for about five minutes a couple of years ago after he'd given her a speeding ticket near Miakoda Falls. It was one more thing to cross off my "don't know or remember" list, but it was hardly helpful to the case at hand.

I closed the folder and put it with the rest of my "Find Brandon Colbeck" material. Rifled through my To Be Read pile and selected *A Hole In One*, the mystery I'd picked up at the used bookstore on Poplar. Then into the kitchen, where I poured myself a glass of wine in a plastic tumbler. It was time for a bubble bath.

THIRTY-FOUR

I SLEPT IN Thursday morning, desperately needing a break after days of setting an early alarm. A light, if late, breakfast of peanut butter on toast and a cup of tea, and I was headed over to the Cedar County Retirement Residence for arrival by twelve thirty.

Platinum Blonde was at her station. She gave me a frosty smile and handed me a thin, brown box, "For Callie Barnstable" written across the front in aquamarine ink.

"Thank you, Stephanie," I said, handing her a ten-dollar bill for lunch. I could tell she was trying to sort out how I knew her name. It wouldn't be long before she connected the dots to Kavya.

"Here's your lunch ticket," she said. Was there warmth to her tone that hadn't existed before? Had I been too harsh in my judgement of her? Perhaps Stephanie's only crime was she'd tired of being the invisible receptionist. And then she spoke. Staccato sentences punctuated with a hint of derision masked by a polite veneer.

"Please wait in the lobby. A PCW will take you to Mrs. Colbeck at one o'clock. Unfortunately, you won't be able to visit with her after lunch. Dental checkup."

I suspected Eleanor's dental checkup was the reason Stephanie had insisted on Thursday lunch versus any other day of the week. I forced a wide smile. "Thank you for the information." At least one of us could be congenial. I made my way to the seating area, anxious to look at Sanchez's artwork before I sat down with Eleanor. I had about ten minutes.

As Kavya had told me, the sketch depicted a winged angel in a long, flowing gown, standing in shallow water, pouring liquid from one gold cup into another. It was devoid of background, no fields or sky, elements I knew were often important messages in tarot. Had Sanchez simplified his drawing because it was meant to be a tattoo? Or was there a hidden meaning? I snapped a couple of photos with my phone before putting the sketch back in the box, then emailed them to Misty with a quick note.

Misty, investigation into Brandon Colbeck continues. Need you to compare this drawing with the tarot card, Temperance. What elements are missing? Could the exclusions be meaningful? Thanks as always for your help. Callie
PS Don't post on website or social media.

I'd no sooner hit send when Kavya stood before me. "I see you got the sketch."

"Yes, thanks again for that. I should be able to return it later today. Just want to show it to the person at Frame Up, take a few photos of it."

"Whenever, seriously, no rush. Now off we go to the dining room. Stephanie's giving us the evil eye and Eleanor's waiting. By the way, you got lucky. Eleanor's having one of her good days."

TABLE SEVEN WAS once again set for two, with cutlery, white china cups, cloth napkins, and a glass vase, this time sporting a single pink carnation.

Eleanor Colbeck was already seated, the oxygen tank strapped to the back of her wheelchair, the plastic tubing inserted in her nose, but her blue eyes looked brighter today, and there was a smile on her face that hadn't been there on my last visit. I hoped the good day would last.

"Callie, how nice to see you again. Olivia would be pleased to know you've come round. Do you have an update on Brandon?"

The anticipation on her face broke my heart. What could I tell her? That her son-in-law had planted key-logger software on his stepson's laptop a few days before he left? That her daughter had recently filed for divorce, and her granddaughter was still trying to come to terms with being the family favorite. Or that I'd come to think of this investigation as a fool's journey, in more ways than one. I reminded myself the sole purpose of my visit was to find out if Eleanor knew or remembered Dave Samuels.

"The investigation is starting to take shape, but my team and I are still piecing together all the bits and bytes."

I was saved from having to expand on that by the arrival of our lunch. I'd been right about the grilled cheese. One thin slice of processed cheese between two slices of crustless white bread, over-buttered and barely browned. The mixed greens resembled wilting dandelion leaves and an unidentifiable substance that might have been shredded cabbage, a drizzle of balsamic dressing barely visible. Thankfully the tomato soup, while a tad on the watery side, wasn't bad. Then again, you'd be hard pressed to screw up canned tomato soup, and if this were made from scratch, I'd be looking for a new cook.

Despite the meal's many shortcomings, we ate in companionable silence, Eleanor adding my four-pack of saltines to her already cracker-filled bowl of tomato soup mush, her face lighting up as she stirred her spoon around the bowl. It's the little things in life that keep us going.

Dessert was lime gelatin or vanilla pudding. "The pudding tends to be lumpy," Eleanor had whispered loudly, thinking no one else could hear her. We both asked for the gelatin and I got to the point. We had fifteen minutes to talk before Eleanor would be taken to her dental checkup.

"I came here to show you something," I began.

"I thought so." Eleanor seemed pleased with herself for figuring that out. I gave her an encouraging smile and pulled out a copy of the photograph included in the obituary for David Alexander Samuels. I'd blown it up as much as I could without getting excessive granulation, and cut out the actual notice. I didn't need Eleanor to get fixated on another death.

"Do you recognize this man? I'm sorry the photo quality isn't as sharp as I'd like."

Eleanor took the photograph with trembling hands, studying it from every angle. For a moment I was hopeful.

"He looks a bit like the sketches the police made of Brandon, the way he's supposed to look now." She peered up at me, hopeful, a tremble in her reed-thin voice. "Is it Brandon?"

I shook my head, wishing now that I hadn't come. Did I really think this memory-addled old woman might have an epiphany, despite her earlier assurances that she'd never been told the name of Brandon's biological father?

"It's a man by the name of David Alexander Samuels."

"David Alexander Samuels. I'm sorry, I've never heard of him." I watched as the brightness faded from her pale blue eyes, replaced by the blank, rheumy look of our first meeting.

Well done, Calamity. You've just managed to re-break this old woman's heart.

THIRTY-FIVE

I LEFT ELEANOR and the Cedar County Retirement Residence feeling contrite. My purpose was to bring some measure of peace, or at the very least, answers, to Eleanor. I'd just done the opposite. I made my way to Frame Up, hoping to redeem myself.

Frame Up might have been on Poplar—the same street as Trust Few—but it was several blocks south, a somewhat more desirable location, though still far from upmarket. There was ample parking at the back of the store, shared with other businesses. Most spots were empty, which didn't bode well for the success of the local shops, but it made my life a whole lot easier. I really hate street parking.

Frame Up was a small space, every wall filled; I could barely see the paint behind the displays. There were multiple examples of frames in every shape, size, material, and color imaginable, as well as a selection of laminated, poster board, and plaque options.

One wall had works by local and regional artists for sale: pen and ink, oil, acrylic on canvas, watercolors, and what could best be described as experimental paintings. There was a small selection of flash art, and though none were by Nestor Sanchez, there were two that had been signed by "Samantha S." One had an astrological theme, filled with the twelve symbols of the zodiac, the other a large sketch of Sagittarius.

The proprietor was a thin, middle-aged man with ice-gray eyes, silver wire-frame glasses, a pallid complexion, and a prominent Adam's apple. An embroidered patch on his denim shirt pocket told me his name was Dan. He smiled, revealing a row of semi-crooked teeth yellowed by time. "Are you interested in flash?"

"These two, the ones signed by Samantha S. Are they by Sam Sanchez?"

Dan nodded. "I take it you've been to Trust Few. Yes, they are. Sam signs them that way because she doesn't want to trade on her grandfather's name." Dan gave a hollow laugh. "Far be it for me to tell her hardly anyone has heard of him, despite his talent."

"Actually, that's why I'm here." I rested the box on top of the counter, opened it, and carefully removed the artwork. "The woman who owns this brought it here for framing. She said you told her it was 'Temperance' from the Rider-Waite tarot deck."

Dan regarded me with a hint of suspicion. "I remember this. What exactly is your interest?"

I handed him a business card. "I'm investigating a missing person case."

"If Sanchez is missing, it's intentional. He's a nomad. Always has been, always will be."

It always amazed me when a simple inquiry could lead to an unexpected outcome. I'd never considered that the owner of Frame Up might actually know Nestor Sanchez. "How well did you know him?"

"As well as anyone except Sam. Your classic loner, first drifted into town in the late nineties with his granddaughter in tow. They popped in, hoping to sell some of his flash. I thought they could stand up on their own as works of art, and I've always had a fascination with

tarot. I purchased a few for ten bucks apiece. I do remember feeling sorry for the girl. Teenagers need sta-
bility and Nestor was anything but. I was glad when
Dave offered her the apprentice gig after Nestor beat
the streets."

"Dave?" I knew who he was referring to, but wondered what Dan might say.

"Dave Samuels. He owned Such & Such Tattoo in
the Nature's Way plaza. Died a few years back. Pancreatic cancer. Sam ended up starting Trust Few on her
own, and she managed to make a go of it. Of course, it
helps that tattoos exploded in popularity, but she's also
a smart businesswoman. But I'm guessing you already
knew all of this."

I didn't answer directly. Instead I drew his attention
to the art that had brought me here. "Kavya, the woman
who owns this, tells me it was a gift from Nestor Sanchez. Have you seen him recently?"

"I haven't seen him in a dog's age. Sam might have,
though. You'd have to ask her."

I intended to do just that. But, I had one more question to ask. "I assume you sold the flash you'd purchased
from Nestor. Do you remember who might have purchased them?"

"It was a long time ago. I do remember that I gave
one of them to a woman who read tarot cards, but which
one it was, that I can't tell you." A faint flush spread
across his pale face. "As I recall, she rented a basement
apartment on Trillium Way."

The flush made me think Dan had been a client,
almost certainly more than once. "Do you remember
her name?"

"Something like Stormy? Rainy?"

Rainy? "Could it have been Misty?"

"Misty. You know, come to think of it, Misty sounds right."

Misty Rivers. And now we'd come full circle. At least I knew where to find her.

THIRTY-SIX

QUESTIONS SWIRLED INSIDE my mind as I drove home from Frame Up. Had Misty returned my email? Did the Temperance drawing remind her of the flash Dan had sold her, and if so, did she still own it? Lastly, I wondered why she hadn't mentioned any of this when we first started talking about Brandon's tattoo. I sighed. It was tough enough wading through everyone's secrets without a member of my team keeping them. I decided to call Misty and ask her to come over to deal with this face to face.

I slipped into a parking spot behind a row of shops on Poplar and walked around to Triple P Pizza, Pasta & Panzerotti. The woman behind the counter recognized me and smiled. "Back for the chicken lasagna?" she asked.

"Takeout pizza today. I just need to make a quick call."

"Take your time."

Misty answered on the first ring. "Great minds think alike. I was just about to call you. We need to meet."

"I'm just about to order a pizza. Care to join me for dinner?"

"I'd like that."

"Any favorite toppings?"

"I love a good Hawaiian."

Ham and pineapple were not my idea of proper pizza

toppings, but I could live with it. "Consider it done. Come by in forty-five?"

"See you then."

MISTY ARRIVED FORTY-FIVE minutes later to the minute, making me wonder if she'd been circling the block. I welcomed her in, poured her a glass of Merlot, then placed plates, napkins, and the pizza on the table.

"First we eat, then we talk," I said, ushering Misty to her seat. She nodded, her silver-tipped, midnight blue manicured fingernails reaching for a slice, then another.

The pizza finished—I wrapped the remaining slices for Misty to take home with her—and we were ready to get down to business. I slid the Temperance flash in front of her.

Misty studied it carefully, murmuring to herself as she did so, nodding as though bringing back a long ago past. After what seemed like an eternity she spoke.

"I used to do tarot readings in my home. Tea leaves, too, though only if a client wanted it as an add-on to the tarot. Sort of like, 'Do you want fries with that?' you know?"

I nodded, hoping she'd get to the point before my body was covered in blue mold.

"I was living in a basement apartment on Trillium Way, damp and dingy, but the rent was cheap. I had a steady clientele—at least I did until my landlord threatened to turf me out. One of my regulars was a guy named Dan, and I never did get a last name. He'd come around once a month or so for a reading. One day he offered me a trade—a tarot reading in exchange for a tattoo design. I liked him, and it, enough to take him up on the offer."

Misty reached into a purse the size of a duffel bag and placed her drawing adjacent to Temperance. "Mine is signed with the initials, NS, rather than a full name. There are similarities that lead me to believe they were drawn by the same artist, for instance the overall stylization, and the absence of some of the elements on the card."

As someone without an expertise in tarot or tattoos, I wouldn't have known which cards these were meant to represent. I said as much to Misty.

"Right, well, mine with the orange wheel and the mysterious symbols represents the Wheel of Fortune, card number ten in the Major Arcana—not the TV show with Vanna White and Pat Sajak," Misty said, with a smile. She pulled a tarot deck from her bag and flipped through it, pulling out Temperance and Wheel of Fortune.

"Notice the symbolism in Wheel of Fortune, each corner with a winged image resting in clouds. These represent the four fixed signs, or seasons, of the zodiac, as well as the elements of the Minor Arcana. The angel represents Aquarius or air, the eagle for Scorpio or water, the lion for Leo or fire, and the bull for Taurus or earth. As the wheel turns around and around, so too does the year."

Misty took a sip of her wine. "Notice that none of these elements appear on the artwork, though Nestor Sanchez has included the snake, sphinx, and the Egyptian god of tombs, Anubis, that surround the wheel. With card number fourteen, Temperance, the angel is depicted standing in a river while pouring water from one cup to another, but there is no evidence of the path behind him leading to the mountains and sun, nor has

Sanchez incorporated the daffodils on the right. My assumption is that the designs were modified for a tattoo. Sanchez wanted to capture the main message from each card, but was willing to let go of the more subliminal ones. He's actually created a perfect blend of simplicity and intricacy."

"Thank you. I'm not quite sure what to do with all this information, but you've been a huge help."

Misty beamed. "Any time, but I'm afraid I have to go. Shirley's set me up on a blind date. It's just for a drink but…"

I smiled at the thought of sexagenarian Shirley setting up tarot-card-reading, fifty-something Misty, but it was nice to think that they'd become friends. "Scoot, and don't forget to take the leftover pizza with you. It's cold enough outside that it'll stay refrigerated in your car."

I made myself another cup of tea after Misty left, considering everything she'd told me, my mind eventually drifting back to Brandon's partially completed tattoo of The Fool. Had Sam Sanchez planned to include all the elements of a tarot card, or did she, like her grandfather, plan to exclude some? I didn't know if it mattered, but it was one more thing to ask her when I paid her another visit.

THIRTY-SEVEN

I PICKED UP Chantelle at nine a.m. sharp Friday morning, allowing us ample time to make the trek to Burlington. As usual, she looked drop-dead gorgeous, her blonde hair worn casually loose, black jeggings accentuating toned legs, and a gray sweater that would have looked drab on most, but only served to intensify the smoky charcoal of her eyes. Even so, I couldn't help but notice the blue smudges beneath them.

"Are you okay?" I asked as she settled into the passenger seat and buckled up.

"Yeah, why?"

"I don't know. You look…tired."

"If you must know, I had a late night." She pressed her lips together in a thin line, then turned her focus to the passenger side window.

"Whatever you say." I put the car in gear and hit the road, determined to ignore both Chantelle and her snippy response. We'd been driving in silence for a few minutes when she spoke again.

"It's Lance."

"What's Lance?"

Chantelle exhaled the exaggerated sigh a teenager might bestow upon a particularly clueless parent. "The reason I'm not sleeping is because of Lance and trust me, no one is more surprised about it than I am." She squirmed in her seat, fidgeting with her seatbelt.

"I know you've been helping him with his family tree. Has something…" I searched for the right words, "…worrisome come out of that?"

"Worrisome. I suppose that depends on your point of view. We discovered a few matches, mostly fourth to sixth cousins, meaning they share a great-great-great grandparent plus another one or two greats, and most of those didn't have family trees. But one match was encouraging—a female second cousin that's willing to meet with him."

I wasn't seeing the connection. "That's good news, right? That he's found someone who might be able to help him trace his roots."

"Yes, it's good news, except now Lance doesn't want my help going forward. He says he can do it without me, and that it's better that he take this journey with Sienna."

"Sienna?"

"Cleopatra's real name."

"Ah." *Sienna, Mercy. Why couldn't they have regular names like Kathy or Vicki?*

"I know what you're thinking," Chantelle said. "It's been over between us for ages. I mean, we're divorced, right? But these past few weeks, I don't know. It just felt like it used to, before the bitching and the bickering and the oh-too-inevitable—and if I'm being honest— welcome breakup. It felt comfortable, like coming home after an extended time away. Part of me thought we might try again. As if. I should have known he'd break my heart all over again."

The bitterness in Chantelle's voice concerned me. "A wise woman once told me that we shouldn't be afraid to get our hearts broken."

Chantelle laughed. "Touché, my friend. Way to throw it back at me. Speaking of broken hearts, how is Royce?"

I told her about running into him with Mercy at the diner, then filled her in on my meeting with Ben Benedetti. I decided to skip the part about our mutual attraction. For one, it was early days and for the other, she was already feeling fragile enough. She didn't need her best friend getting all gloaty.

"What are you going to do with the information?" Chantelle asked when I'd finished.

"My plan is to confront Michael Westlake with it in the hopes that he'll come clean with me. My guess is Brandon discovered the keylogger software and that triggered him to leave home."

"Still doesn't change the outcome though, does it?"

I admitted it didn't. "What about David Alexander Samuels? Find anything in the DNA databank?"

"I'm sorry, I should have told you about that right away instead of blathering on about Lance. There are close to a thousand entries under that name. It's going to take some time to weed through them, but I've scheduled a few days off from the gym. I should have an answer sooner rather than later."

A few days off from the gym? That was a first. I decided to withhold comment.

LIGHT BOX AUCTION GALLERY was on Burlington's main downtown strip. Brant Street had colorful awnings and varied facades—everything from brightly painted stucco to brick and barn board—lending an eclectic vibe to the upscale shops, galleries, and restaurants vying for business. Most stores had apartments above them, seamlessly blending commercial, retail, and residential space.

"There it is," Chantelle said, pointing to a narrow, stone-fronted building with a magenta door and a matching awning lettered "Light Box Auction Gallery."

I found a spot on the street just up from the gallery and took a deep breath. "Parallel parking. Not my strong suit." An understatement. Have I mentioned that I hate street parking? It's actually more like fear. I haven't parallel parked since the day I got my driver's license. I kept driving.

"Seriously?" Chantelle said. "That spot was prime."

"Maybe there's a Green P lot somewhere."

"Oh, for heaven's sake, circle the block and I'll guide you in step-by-step."

I circled the block, wondering what made Chantelle an expert and deciding that the wisest course of action was to hold my tongue. I slowed down on Brant, saw the coveted spot had been taken and drove down a few spaces. "There's one up ahead."

"That will do," Chantelle said. "The first step is to line up the back of the car with the back of the front car, then stop."

I lined up and stopped.

"Now, then turn the wheel all the way to the right. All the way." Chantelle's voice brooked no argument. I did as instructed.

"Perfect, now turn around and look out the back of the car, then slowly begin backing up until the right-front corner of the rear car is in the exact middle of the rear windshield. When you get there, stop again."

"Done," I said, stopping again.

"Okay, now while stopped, turn the wheel back to

the middle position. I repeat, while stopped, turn the wheel back to the middle position."

"I heard you the first time."

"Fine. Now, back up slowly until your car barely clears the front car, then stop again."

"I don't want to hit—"

"You won't."

I backed up slowly into position. "Got it."

"Perfect. Turn the wheel all the way to the left, and begin backing in again, keeping the wheel to the left until the car is parallel to the curb."

OMG, it worked. But apparently I wasn't done yet.

"Final step. Turn the wheel to face forward. That way you're ready to drive off at a moment's notice. You know, just in case you're a bandito or something."

I turned the wheel, shut the car off, took the keys out of the ignition, and wiped a bead of perspiration off my forehead.

"Piece of cake," Chantelle said, hopping out of the car.

I waited until a lengthy procession of vehicles passed by, grateful for the opportunity to steady my breathing. *Seriously,* I thought, giving myself a mental slap upside the head. *You go around digging into death, deception, and desperation, but parallel parking freaks you out?* I opened the driver's door and slipped out quickly to join Chantelle on the sidewalk.

"Thanks."

Chantelle waved me off. "Rented a basement apartment at Main and Danforth when I first moved from Ottawa to Toronto with Lance. You either learned to park on the street or you gave up your car."

A small sign in the front window of Light Box Auction Gallery posted the hours as "By chance or appointment." It had been flipped over from Open to Closed.

"I hope we didn't come all this way for nothing," I said, battling between panic and annoyance. Surely I hadn't just taken Parallel Parking 101 for naught.

Chantelle, ever the optimist, tried the door. "Chill out. It's open."

We walked in, a bell tinkling above us to announce our presence. Dark hardwood floors, color-blocked walls in varying shades of plum and purple, and recessed lighting highlighted the tattoo flash on display. In addition, there were vintage Disney cels and original comic book art. At least I assumed they were vintage and original. A statuesque woman emerged from double doors at the rear of the shop, her slender physique made taller by six-inch stilettos. "Right on time," she said, by way of introduction. "Nicolette Baxter."

Nicolette Baxter was a study in scarlet, with flaming, waist length red hair, thinly penciled eyebrows, perfectly manicured fingernails, pinstriped palazzo pants, and a matching crop top that revealed sculpted abs and a ruby-studded belly button. She was striking, rather than beautiful, with impossibly high cheekbones, jet black eyes, and a smattering of freckles on porcelain skin. Everything about Nicolette Baxter was riveting. I expected she worked hard to maintain that image with regular visits to the gym, spa, and assorted stylists and salons that offered treatments I'd never heard of and probably couldn't afford.

"Callie Barnstable. This is my friend and colleague, Chantelle Marchand. Thanks for seeing us."

"I'd be hard-pressed to sell anything if I didn't," Baxter said with a grin. "Levon tells me that you're interested in the Nestor Sanchez flash."

"Yes, that's why we're here," I said, wondering how I was going to tell her the real reason for our visit.

"I have to be honest. I met with another potential buyer yesterday. She's interested in purchasing the entire lot. I told her that I'd already set up this meeting, and it would be unfair to sell it before you had the opportunity to view them." Baxter gave us the once over, a frown creasing her flawless brow. "Maybe I should have taken her up on the offer. Something tells me you're not here as collectors."

It wasn't the way I wanted to start the conversation, but at least it opened the door to full disclosure. "We're not. I apologize if I gave you that impression on the phone. We're actually co-owners of Past & Present Investigations."

"Private investigators?" Baxter's posture stiffened, the taut muscles in her bejeweled abdomen getting tauter. "I can assure you that I came by the Sanchez collection honestly. In fact, the consignor sought me out, not the other way around."

"Apologies again," I said. "We're not here to accuse you of anything. We're here because Nestor Sanchez's name came up in a missing person investigation we're working on."

"A missing person case?"

"Yes," I said, hoping to avoid the specifics, at least for the moment. "Can we ask who the potential buyer is? The information may be helpful."

"You can ask, but I'm afraid she didn't offer her name."

"You let a potential buyer leave without getting her contact information?"

"I gather the investigator in you doesn't approve. What can I say? The lady promised to call me on Monday. If she's still interested, she'll call. If not, my barraging her with phone calls, texts, and emails won't change her mind. I like to think I'm above that, you know?"

"Can you describe her?"

"That I can do," Baxter said. "Attractive. Hispanic. Mid-thirties. Wore a black turtleneck, ripped jeans, a fleece-lined denim jacket, black combat boots, gray dollar store gloves, and a Detroit Red Wings baseball cap."

Which meant the tattoos and shaved head would have been fully covered. "You'd make a good investigator," I said, "remembering all those details."

"It *was* only yesterday," Baxter said, but I could tell that the compliment pleased her.

"Was there anything noticeable about her?"

"Yeah. She had a diamond chip in her front tooth. Looked good. Made me think of getting one."

The potential buyer was definitely Sam Sanchez. "Do you know how this woman came upon your gallery?"

"She claimed to have seen the pix on Instagram. I had no reason to doubt her. Why? Is it important?"

"Probably not," I said, thinking just the opposite. It was one more thing to add to the list of secrets being stockpiled by the mysterious Sam Sanchez.

I also wanted to know who consigned the flash, but I sensed Nicolette Baxter was tiring of my questions. I'd ask later, after Chantelle and I saw the Nestor Sanchez inventory. "Do you mind if we take a look at the flash by Sanchez now? Even though we aren't planning to buy anything?"

"I don't see why not. Follow me. The collection is near the back of the gallery, right side. There are fourteen in all. Most show some wear, though thankfully there's no water damage or foxing. Foxing, that's the worst, brown spots eating through the paper. I've taken the step of employing archival picture framing techniques to preserve them going forward. His art deserves no less."

With one exception, the sketches were all tarot-related, with the twenty-two cards in the Major Arcana captured on five pages: numbers one through twenty-one on four pages, and The Fool and The World, the first and last cards, on the fifth. My first thought was that each of these drawings appeared to have the same balance of simplicity and intricacy Misty had pointed out to me in the Temperance and Wheel of Fortune designs. My second thought was that she would love to own the one with The Fool and The World. I checked the price: $1,500. Sorry, Misty.

The rest of the flash depicted the fifty-six cards in the Minor Arcana. Four pages were devoted to the four court cards in each suit, Cups, Pentacles, Swords, and Wands, Page, Knight, Queen, and King. That left four pages for the rest of the Minor Arcana. I did a quick count, finding ten sketches per sheet, one for every card numbered in Roman numerals, I through X. One thing stood out. Whether the sketches were large or small, in full color or black ink, they were meticulous in their detail.

I turned my attention to the only flash that didn't cover tarot. It was a portrait, more complex than some-

thing you'd ink on your body. A portrait of a young Hispanic woman. No shaved head, no diamond chip, but a
young Sam Sanchez nonetheless.

"The woman who came here. Did she look like this?"

Baxter surveyed the sketch. "Now that you mention
it, yeah, maybe a little, although she was a lot older than
this, you know?" She shook her head. "I don't know
how I didn't see it. I've usually got a good eye."

"It's easy to miss things when you aren't looking
for them."

"I guess," Baxter said, sounding unconvinced. "He
was very talented, wasn't he? Nestor Sanchez. I wonder why he never got more recognition."

Was? "Probably because he didn't want it. Not everyone aspires to fame and fortune." I waited a beat
then, "You said Nestor 'was' very talented. How do
you know he's dead?"

"I haven't seen his death certificate, if that's what
you're asking."

"Tell me about the person who sold these to you.
Young? Old? Did he say he knew Nestor Sanchez?"

"Middle-ish aged man. Old enough to have a little
gray in his hair. Frankly, he didn't know much about
the flash or Sanchez."

"You said you bought Nestor's art. Isn't it more common for an auction gallery to work on consignment?"

"Yes, and it's my preference, but I wouldn't have
gotten these otherwise. I told him he might do better at
auction, but he said he needed the cash now, not later."

The website had listed pricing from $350 to $1,500
per. Using an average of $850, and allowing for some
good old-fashioned bartering, Baxter stood to make a
little over $11,000. My guess was she'd paid less than

half of that. I wanted to ask out of curiosity, but couldn't justify the question. It did make me wonder why someone would give up a collection like this for $5,000 and change. I was mulling that over when Chantelle spoke up. Until now, she'd been a silent observer.

"Can you tell us when you bought the collection? And who sold it to you?"

"It was three weeks ago Sunday. I remember the date because it was my birthday. He said his name was Brian Cole, that he was in between places." Baxter laughed. "He called it the Imposer's World Tour. I got a kick out of that."

Brian Cole. Brandon Colbeck.

Chantelle already had her phone out, scrolling through her photos. "Does this guy look familiar? Or this one?"

Baxter took the phone and flipped back and forth between the photograph from 1999, clean-shaven Brandon, and scruffy Brandon before handing it back to Chantelle. "The man in the photograph by the water, no. He doesn't look older than twenty, and he has this innocent look about him Brian Cole might have had once but lost a decade plus ago. The bearded guy in the sketches, however, definitely bears a strong resemblance to the guy who called himself Brian Cole. Who is he? The guy in the sketch?"

"Brandon Colbeck."

"Your missing man? The one you've been hired to find?"

"Yes."

"He's been gone since he looked like the young man in the photograph?"

I nodded. "Nineteen years and counting."

"Wow." Baxter rocked back on her stiletto heels, and I marveled at her ability to stay upright.

"His family...they just want to know he's okay."

"Sometimes my family drives me crazy, but I can't imagine disappearing from their lives without a trace. Do you have a business card? I can't think of anything else right now, but there's something niggling on the edge of my brain. I just can't bring it into focus."

I handed over my card. "Call anytime." I just hoped she would.

THIRTY-EIGHT

SUNDAY MORNING RUN club was a welcome respite from the ongoing investigation and I savored every mile of the two-plus hours it took me to complete our assigned route, my cell phone turned off to keep the world out. I kept it off once we returned to the club's weekly meeting location—a local running store that actually encouraged the crowd of post-run sweaty bodies and their gym bags filled with a change of clothes, water, energy bars, and other magic potions and lotions each runner swore by. I found a vacant spot on the laminate floor and concentrated on my cool-down stretches: calf, hamstrings, quads, glutes, IT band, piriformis, back, spine, groin, and psoas. It was a ritual I found mind-numbingly boring, but I'd learned the hard way it was necessary if I wanted to remain injury-free.

Most of the other runners were heading to the nearby coffee shop by the time I was finished. I promised to meet them, popped into the washroom to do a quick change, tugging off my sweaty sports bra, spandex tights, and long-sleeved tee in exchange for clean sweats. Only then did I turn my phone back on.

There were three missed calls: Royce Ashford, Ben Benedetti, and Nicolette Baxter. I checked voice mail, prepared to listen to the messages in order.

"Hi, Callie, Royce here. I wanted to apologize if there was any awkwardness when we ran into each other last week. I'll admit that I was surprised to see you with a date. Sorry, that came out wrong. Of course you're free to date anyone you wish, and Ben seems like a nice guy. Anyway, I'd like to stay friends if that's at all possible. Call me back when you get a chance." There was a long pause, and then, said so softly that I had to strain to hear it, "I miss you, Callie."

Miss me? Friends? Really? Why not suggest a double date? I deleted the message, went to the next one.

Ben's voice was as warm as the cup of hot chocolate I'd been planning to order. "Hi, Callie, sorry I missed you. I wanted to let you know that I'm still out of town until Wednesday. It's nothing serious, just some old business to take care of. Let's do dinner when I'm back. I'll call you then."

Some old business. What did I expect, a true confession from a guy I'd met exactly once? Still, I'd been looking forward to seeing Ben again and finding out where that might take us. Besides, it was for the best. I had a case to solve and needed my head in the game. I saved the message without having any good reason to do so, and went on to the voice mail from Nicolette Baxter.

"Hello, Callie, Nicolette Baxter here, the owner of Light Box Auction Gallery? I promised to call if I remembered anything else, and in fact I have. Ring me when you get this."

I took a minute to decide between calling Nicolette and heading for hot chocolate. I wasn't quite ready to shed my post-run glow, and I enjoyed the after-run camaraderie our group shared, but I was curious.

Baxter won.

She answered on the first ring, as if sitting on her phone, waiting for me to call back. "I remembered the thing that was niggling at me," she said, an undercurrent of excitement in her voice. "It's about Brian Cole."

"Go on."

"He came in on his own, but he got into the passenger side of a black SUV parked outside the gallery when he left. I didn't get a good look at the person driving, but it was a man."

"Did you get a license plate number?"

"Didn't occur to me to look."

A man wasn't much to go on. "Can you describe the man at all?"

"Not really. The door was only open for a minute and the vehicle had tinted windows. He might have had gray hair."

"Okay, thanks." I tried to keep the disappointment out of my voice.

"Before you go there's one more thing I haven't told you. I'm ninety-five percent sure the SUV was a Mercedes. My ex-husband drives one, the lying, cheating bastard that he is." She exhaled loudly, as if trying to exorcise the memory of her ex.

A black Mercedes. Just like the one that Michael Westlake drives.

"Does that help?" Baxter asked. "The information about the SUV?"

"More than you can imagine. Thank you."

I hung up, assessing the implications. Was the man who called himself Brian Cole actually Brandon Colbeck, as I suspected? If so, why was he hanging around with the stepfather he supposedly hated? More importantly, why was Michael Westlake keeping silent about it?

THIRTY-NINE

WHO TO CONTACT FIRST, Samantha Sanchez or Michael Westlake? Unsure of what to do, and in desperate need of something to eat and drink, I made my way to my car, tossed in my bag of sweat-soaked clothes, and headed to the coffee shop to join the group. One of the rocket-fast runners, Howard Portland, had saved a seat for me, and I knew he was curious about my delayed arrival. Portland, a retired criminal prosecutor, had been helpful in Past & Present's last case, but I couldn't see how he could help me with this one. I gave him a bright-eyed smile, and joined the queue to order.

Restored by an extra-large hot chocolate and a toasted twelve-grain bagel with peanut butter, I spent the next half hour enjoying the runners' mindless banter on blisters, tensor bandages, and the prideful admissions of blackened and missing toenails.

Back home, I paced. And paced. And paced some more. When I'd left Michael Westlake's office, I knew he'd been hiding something. I hadn't expected that something to be Brandon Colbeck.

But what about Sam Sanchez? I had so many unanswered questions to ask her, not the least of which involved her possibly deceased, possibly alive grandfather, Nestor.

I considered asking Chantelle for her opinion, but I didn't want to distract her from the Ancestry research on Michael Westlake. Royce was out, though I'll admit I briefly considered confiding in him. And I could hardly call out-of-town-on-business-barely-know-him Ben. Could I?

No, I couldn't.

After more pacing I decided to call Sam Sanchez. She'd been keeping secrets from the beginning, and something told me she held the key to everything.

IT TURNED OUT Trust Few was closed on Sundays, but I left a voice mail on the off-chance Sam would check her messages, then went and took a much-needed shower.

I was getting dressed when my phone rang. Sam Sanchez.

"Hi, Sam, thanks for calling back."

"I take it the investigation continues."

"It does. I've learned some things, but there are still plenty of gaps. I'm hoping maybe we could get together and you could fill some of them in."

"You're one determined lady."

"I've been hired to find out the truth. I take that responsibility very seriously. When can we get together?"

There was a long pause, then, "Oh, what the hell. Today, tomorrow, Tuesday, it doesn't really matter, does it? You're not going to leave me alone until I answer all of your questions, are you?"

"Probably not."

"Then it might as well be today. Except this time, I'll come to you."

SAM ARRIVED THIRTY minutes later, turned down my offer of coffee or water, and sank into one of the Mission oak recliners. Her Sunday look—black yoga pants and an above-the-knee waffle knit sweater—was markedly different from the one she sported at Trust Few. Even the plum lipstick and combat boots were missing, replaced with clear lip gloss and white sneakers.

"Thanks for coming."

Sam shrugged. "No biggie. What do you want to know?"

I grabbed my notebook and slipped into the chair next to her. "Some of these might seem random, but I've been writing down questions since the last time we spoke."

"Ask away."

"Let's start with Dave Samuels. One of my team members, Shirley Harrington, is a retired research librarian. She's good at digging through old newspaper archives, tracking down stuff that's pre-digital era. She found an article in the *Marketville Post* dated August 14, 2003."

I referred to my notes and began reading. "After nearly six years in business, Dave Samuels has closed Such & Such tattoo parlor, which had been located at the back of Nature's Way. His remaining collection of vintage and original tattoo flash—the term used for the artwork—has been sold to a private buyer who prefers to remain anonymous." I glanced at Sam. "Were you the private buyer?"

"Sorry to disappoint, but no. I would have loved to but didn't have the money to buy his collection and open Trust Few."

"Do you know who did?"

"A woman named Nicolette Baxter. She was a bigtime collector back then."

I wrote down "Nicolette Baxter" in my notebook, as if it were a new lead, then resumed my questioning.

"Did Dave Samuels have a tattoo of an eagle on his back, stretching between his shoulder blades?"

Sam's eyebrows shot up. "Yeah, how'd you know?"

I ignored the question. "The other thing we found in the *Marketville Post* was Dave's obituary. With his photograph. Tell me, Sam, when did you realize Brandon Colbeck was Dave's son? Was it the day he walked into Such & Such, or when you befriended him in college?"

The color drained from Sam's face. Whatever she'd been expecting, it hadn't been that.

"How do you know we were friends in college?"

"How I know doesn't matter. Brandon wasn't a stranger that day in March when he walked into Such & Such. What matters is that you lied."

"It wasn't a complete lie. Dave hadn't met Brandon yet. He didn't even know he had a son."

"You thought if Brandon came in for a tattoo, they could get to know each other?"

Sam nodded. "Brandon was obsessed with meeting his real father. He loathed Michael Westlake. From what he told me, the feeling was mutual. The first time I saw Brandon on campus, I was struck by how much he reminded me of Dave, small things, like how they'd line up their plastic takeout cutlery in a neat parallel line."

"When was that?"

"We were both in first year at Cedar County College. Brandon was taking business admin and computer sciences, and I was taking graphic arts. When Nestor left, Dave offered me the apprentice job. Money was tight and I figured I'd learn more from him than any college professor. After I dropped out, Brandon and I stayed in touch, though there was never any more to it than friendship and a shared interest in tarot."

"When did his interest in tarot begin?"

"With me. Though he wasn't particularly interested until I told him many followers of tarot believed the Major Arcana represented The Fool's Journey. That's when he started to really confide in me, told me his stepfather often called him a fool. Somewhere along the line, he became obsessed with taking his own journey." Sam paused. "It sounds disloyal to say this, but Brandon was like that. He'd get fixated on something, whether it was his hatred for his stepfather, finding his biological father, or tarot, and it would become all-consuming. Dave was like that, too."

"You knew he planned to leave home."

"I did, though I expected him to get the tattoo finished first. He'd talked about heading out when the weather got better. Something must have triggered him to leave early."

Something like Michael Westlake's keylogger software, I thought. "When did you learn that he'd left home?"

"He called me, would have been mid-March, maybe a bit later. He said he was fine, that he was hitching rides, taking buses, making his way out west to Vancouver." Sam chewed on her lower lip. "I never heard from him again. Even so, I didn't think of him as missing, you know? At least not until I read the article in the *Marketville Post* that summer."

"Why didn't you call the police?"

Sam shrugged. "My experience with Nestor. I assumed Brandon didn't want to be found. After a while,

I tucked my memories of him in a storage compartment at the back of my brain."

"And when you read the *Marketville Post* article in 2015, the family still searching, did you still believe he didn't want to be found?"

"I didn't know what to believe. Part of me thought he might be dead. The other part hoped he'd started a new life. Either way, I wasn't going to the police." Sam paused. "You know, as much as Brandon was like Dave, I was never sure. Except one day Brandon told me his mother had finally relented, given him a tiny nugget of information."

"The eagle tattoo."

Sam nodded. "That's when I knew. Maybe if I hadn't figured it out, hadn't told Brandon about Dave. Maybe if Dave hadn't disappointed him, hadn't joked about getting all his tats in a single day. Maybe if I hadn't filled his head full of The Fool's Journey. Maybe, then…" Sam's voice trailed off, her blue eyes glistening with unshed tears.

At long last, I thought, *the real reason behind Sam's secrets*. "You blame yourself for Brandon leaving."

"Yeah. I guess I do."

FORTY

I POURED US each a drink, a double shot of dark rum on ice with a splash of cola for Sam, white wine for me. Put together a plate of cheese and crackers, raw veggies, scooped out the last of a container of red pepper hummus. I needed to talk to her about Light Box Auction Gallery, but that could wait ten minutes.

The rum seemed to restore her spirits, with the added bonus of loosening her tongue.

"There's something else I haven't told you," she said.

"I'm listening."

"It's about Nicolette Baxter, the woman who purchased Dave's flash. She recently opened an auction gallery in Burlington. On Brant Street. Light Box Auction Galleries. She specializes in vintage flash, Disney cels, original comic art, that sort of thing. I went to see her on Thursday."

I could have played true confessions in return but I didn't. "What prompted you to go there?"

"Google Alerts."

Google Alerts? My confusion was apparent, because Sam explained, "I have Google Alerts set up to ping me if Nestor Sanchez's name pops up on the internet. Last week, I got an alert with a link to Light Box Auction Gallery. They wrote about him in the past tense, as if he were dead, claimed to have some of his vintage flash."

A dark flush spread across Sam's face. "I lied to you

before, when I said I hadn't heard from my grandfather in years. Truth is, he stops by Trust Few every now and again. Never stays more than a week or two, then he's back on the road, but he needs a permanent address to collect his government pensions. The last time I saw him was a month ago. He looked good, better than he had in a long time. I'm not saying he's immortal, and he's barely on the green side of ninety, but he wears a Road ID bracelet—the kind runners and cyclists wear—and my contact information is on it. If he'd died, someone would have called me. They haven't."

Unless he lost the bracelet, I thought, but didn't say. I needed to get Sam back on track. "You said you went to Light Box Auction Gallery."

"My first thought was that my grandfather had sold some of his vintage flash because he needed the cash. I'd give him money if he asked, but he's stubborn like that. It could have been his idea of a joke, telling Nicolette that Nestor Sanchez had died. He does value his anonymity. But then I looked at the flash that she'd posted on the website. I couldn't be sure, not until I saw it in person, but it reminded me of the flash that Brandon had purchased back in 2000."

I felt my pulse quicken. "What did you think when you saw it?"

"I can't be positive after all these years, at least not about the ones focused on tarot, though if I was a betting woman, I'd go all in."

"Why is that?"

"There was one sketch of me. I didn't want Dave to sell it, but he said Nestor could always do another one." Sam gave a rueful smile. "I didn't realize it at the time, but my guess is Brandon wanted something to remember me by after he left."

Now was the time for true confessions. I admitted to Sam that Chantelle and I had visited the gallery the day after her visit. I wasn't sure how she would react to the admission, but I wasn't expecting the wide smile that lit up her face.

"I thought the person who'd expressed interest might be you," she said. "Kudos. Then I gather she told you the name of the seller was Brian Cole."

I nodded. "I suspect Brian Cole may be Brandon Colbeck."

"I'd say it's more like a sure thing. He tried out new names for himself before he started his fool's journey. Brian Cole was his favorite. He did his research, read it was easier to remember a fake name if you kept the same initials. He left his ID behind. He said he was wiping the hard drive on his laptop and selling it, too much personal information there."

"His family thought he'd taken it with him."

"Maybe he did, all I know is he wanted to stop being Brandon Colbeck the day he left home."

And there you had it. All this time, Sam had information that could have helped the police, the family. Not closure, perhaps, but something tangible to grab onto.

I had one more question to ask her.

"Nicolette Baxter said she saw Brian Cole get into a black Mercedes SUV." I studied Sam's face for any sign of recognition, found none. "She didn't get a good look at the driver, beyond it being a man with short gray hair."

"And that's important, how?"

"Michael Westlake has short gray hair and he drives a black Mercedes SUV."

Sam shook her head. "No way. I told you, Brandon loathed his stepfather, and the feeling was mutual."

"And yet, all roads lead to Westlake being the driver."

"Okay, let's say you're right, that the driver was Michael Westlake. What are you going to do next?"

"The only thing I can do. Confront Michael Westlake."

"I'd pay admission for that," Sam said, "but something tells me you're not going to be selling tickets."

FORTY-ONE

I SPENT A sleepless night waiting for Monday morning. My plan was to call Michael Westlake as soon as his office opened at nine a.m. It was time for the moment of truth.

The moment came sooner than anticipated, albeit not in the way I'd envisioned, when Leith Hampton called at precisely 7:37 a.m. I don't get a lot of phone calls at that time of the morning, especially from Leith. I prepared myself for his latest news blast, thinking back to the deaths of my father, my great-grandmother. Who would it be now? My grandfather, Corbin Osgoode? My grandmother, Yvette? A long-lost Barnstable? I picked up the call.

"You're officially off the Brandon Colbeck case," Leith said brusquely.

"Off the case? I don't understand. You told me I had three months. It's been less than a month, and I've made a lot of progress."

"I'm sure you have, but your services are no longer required. Don't worry about the money. You still stand to inherit under the terms of Olivia Osgoode's last will and testament."

The money? That's what Leith thought concerned me? This wasn't about the inheritance. Brandon Colbeck's disappearance consumed every waking hour, haunted my every night, maybe even messed up whatever relationship I'd had with Royce. And now Leith was telling me that I'd been fired.

"It's not about the money," I said. "It's about finishing what I started."

Leith let out one of his practiced, theatrical sighs. "There's nothing to finish. Brandon Colbeck returned home Wednesday. He initially made contact with his stepfather, Michael Westlake. In turn, Westlake took what he assures me were the necessary steps to authenticate the man's identity before contacting me, and before informing the rest of the family."

"They've done DNA testing? I thought that process took longer than a few days." Admittedly my knowledge was based on television crime shows, but still…

"No DNA test. Westlake wanted to bring his family together without unnecessary delays, said they'd waited long enough. A rigorous questioning by the officer in charge and Westlake himself erased any doubt that the man who now calls himself Brian Cole is Brandon Colbeck."

"Well, I guess that's that then," I said, feeling strangely hollow.

"If it's any consolation, you've been invited to Brandon's official welcome home lunch. The family thought it was the least they could do after all the work you've done on their behalf."

"When is it?"

"That's why I'm calling you this early. It's at noon today. Jeanine Westlake is hosting at her house," Leith said, rattling off the address. "In fact, it's Jeanine who insisted on your presence. With the exception of you, this is strictly a family affair."

In other words, no Chantelle, no Shirley, no Misty,

and by extension, no Sam Sanchez. It seemed to me that Brandon would want to see Sam, but perhaps he wanted to do that privately.

I wasn't sure what someone wore to a welcome home lunch for someone who'd been missing for years. I figured casual was best, black jeans and a jewel-toned sweater that brought out the green in my hazel eyes. Minimal makeup and I was ready to go.

JEANINE WESTLAKE LIVED in a two-story brick and stucco townhouse in a new subdivision on the southeast edge of town. The lot was barely wider than the length of my car. I parked and made my way to the door, suddenly apprehensive.

The door swung open before I had an opportunity to knock.

"Callie, thanks so much for coming." Jeanine ushered me past a gleaming hardwood staircase leading up to the second floor, and into a surprisingly spacious living room. The décor was what could best be described as urban contemporary with a touch of Ikea, neutral tones of tan and taupe accessorized with vivid punches of turquoise and teal. A grouping of silver "Welcome Home" helium balloons bobbed in one corner like a giant bouquet.

Lorna and Michael were already seated on the sofa, Eleanor in the middle, presumably acting as a buffer. There was no sign of the man of the hour.

"Brandon will be down momentarily," Lorna said, as if reading my mind. "Please, take a seat."

I gave Eleanor a brief hug, shook hands with Lorna and Michael, then sank into a butter-soft leather chair positioned near the balloon brigade. Lorna had significantly altered her appearance. With the exception of a beaded macramé bracelet, she'd traded in her bohemian hippie look for crisply pleated black dress slacks, brightly patterned paisley scarf, and long-sleeved black jersey tee. This version of Lorna was as buttoned-up as her ex-husband's blue button-down shirt. Eleanor appeared to be oblivious. Maybe she was, or maybe she'd learned that escaping into her own world could provide sanctuary.

A linen-covered folding table: champagne flutes and miniature bottles of sparkling wine, a platter of deli sandwiches, napkins, paper plates, and plastic utensils. It looked more like a corporate reception than a welcome home celebration, but what was I expecting? A church social?

Jeanine kept fluttering in and out of the room, reminding me of one of the origami birds at her office, their wings trembling in the harsh fluorescent light. An oven buzzer went off and I followed her into the kitchen, wondering what the heck was going on. This wasn't the calm, collected social worker I'd met on two previous occasions.

This woman was a nervous wreck.

JEANINE WAS ARRANGING an assortment of appetizers, the heat-and-serve kind you buy in the frozen food section of the grocery store: spring rolls, battered mozzarella sticks, jalapeño poppers, and spinach puffs.

"What's going on, Jeanine?" I asked.

She stared at me, wide-eyed and frightened. "Can I trust you, Callie? I mean really trust you."

"Of course. Why?"

"Because I think the man claiming to be my brother is an imposter."

FORTY-TWO

I STARED AT JEANINE. "An impostor? Are you sure?" I kept my voice low, so as not to be heard in the next room.

"No, I'm not positive," she whispered. "That's why I insisted on having you here. I thought you could find out."

Find out how? I'm an investigator, not a magician. "What about your parents? Your grandmother? What do they think?"

"They're convinced he's the real deal. He certainly seems to have most of the answers."

"Most of the answers?"

"He forgot about the teapot. I may be overanalyzing, but how could he forget a thing like that?" She was about to say more when Lorna flitted into the room; Brandon was waiting for us in the living room. I shot Jeanine a quick look, which I hope relayed that I was still on the case, all the while deliberating. Would a forty-year-old man remember covering up for his kid sister the time she broke a teapot in the kitchen?

Maybe, if he'd been beaten with a belt for taking the blame. But just because a memory had haunted Jeanine, didn't mean it had haunted him. I followed mother and daughter into the living room, wondering what I could find out without it coming across like an interrogation.

My first impression of Brandon Colbeck was that

he resembled the age-progressed sketches well enough. Unlike the clean-cut and scruffy versions of the man in the sketches, he fit somewhere in-between, with silver-streaked reddish-brown hair curling at his collar and the sort of perfectly trimmed five o'clock shadow that had become the fashion of late.

"Brandon, this is Calamity Barnstable," Jeanine said, guiding me toward him. "I've told you about her, the owner of Past & Present Investigations."

"It's Callie," I said, shaking Brandon's hand as he rose from his chair.

Brandon smiled warmly, though I noticed the smile didn't quite reach his eyes.

"You'll have to tell me where your investigation led, Callie," he said, the smile still in place. "I didn't think I'd left any bread crumbs behind."

"Everyone leaves a trail," I said. "Yours was just a bit more complicated." I took my position by the balloon bouquet. "What brought you back to Marketville?"

"I've been homesick for a very long time, but I was too proud, or too stubborn, to come back before now. I googled myself, found the article in the *Marketville Post,* and that led me to the Ontario Registry of Missing and Unidentified Adults website. I realized how selfish I'd been, how much pain I'd caused everyone. I was ashamed of myself, of my behavior. I finally summoned up the courage to call Nana Ellie." Brandon's expression was filled with remorse. "I botched it. I sounded like I was trying to scam her." His turned his attention to Eleanor. "I'm so sorry, Nana Ellie. I should have talked about how much I missed our days at the cottage with Grandpa Tom, or the time I tripped over my fishing rod and smashed my nose on the dock. Instead, I only upset you. I can never forgive myself for that.

"There's nothing to forgive," Eleanor said, misty-eyed. "We're all just happy you called Michael and asked to come home."

"Brandon called me a week ago," Michael explained. "I'm afraid I put my stepson through his paces, asked him a litany of questions about our past. He passed with flying colors, even recalled some of the not-so-pleasant memories every family has, no matter how close. Once I was satisfied, I had Lorna, Jeanine, and Eleanor ask their own questions, and they're satisfied."

Except Jeanine isn't entirely satisfied. And you alone made the decision to bypass a DNA test. Why?

"Michael is being kind," Brandon said. "I didn't comment on Mom's macramé bracelet until she asked me if I remembered making it. And I'd forgotten about taking the blame for Jeanine breaking a teapot when we were kids. But Jeanine doesn't remember the umpteen times I moved her bike out of the driveway because she always left it right behind the car."

"What color was the teapot?" I asked.

Brandon held his hands in the air, palms towards me in mock surrender. "Mea culpa. I can't remember. But Jeanine's bike was pink. Any other questions to try to trip me up, Callie?"

I blushed. "I'm sorry, I've overstepped. I'm afraid it's a hazard of the trade."

"Why don't we eat?" Lorna said, in an attempt to diffuse the tension. "Jeanine's put on a lovely spread and there's champagne to celebrate Brandon's return home."

We filled our plates while Jeanine poured the champagne.

"Time for a toast," Michael announced once we each had a glass. "To my stepson, Brandon. Welcome home."

We clinked glasses, Jeanine's eyes seeking mine, and I registered her silent plea. I took a deep breath and hoped my next idea would pay off.

"We're missing someone who would love to be here."

Five curious expressions stared back at me.

"Who'd we miss?" Michael asked, his tone tinged with annoyance.

"Sam Sanchez."

"Sam Sanchez?" Eleanor asked. "Who's he?"

Brandon set down his champagne flute and rolled up his sleeve to reveal a fully finished tattoo of The Fool. "Sam Sanchez started this tattoo nineteen years ago on a blustery March day. I had it finished in Sudbury. It's the first card in tarot, the beginning of what believers call The Fool's Journey. Back then, I thought of it as symbolic, the start of my own fool's journey." He produced a disarming grin. "What can I say? I was young and idealistic."

Now I really did wish Sam was here, because though the tattoo looked new to me—the lines not "blown out" the way she'd described—I wasn't sure.

Michael Westlake spoke, an undercurrent of warning in his voice. "The vintage tattoo art you sold to the gallery in Burlington last week, Brandon, that was by Nestor Sanchez, was it not? You said you didn't want any more reminders of the past, that it would be too painful. It's probably best if you don't see Sam Sanchez again."

"I appreciate your concern, Michael," Brandon said, "but Callie's absolutely right. Sam and I met in our first year of college and we became best friends, even confidantes. He should most definitely be here. Perhaps Callie can set something up."

"Yes, of course," I said. "There's just one small problem."

"What's that?" Brandon asked.

"Your good friend, Sam? Her name is Samantha, as in she versus he. But then again, you'd have known that if you really were Brandon Colbeck, wouldn't you?"

FORTY-THREE

THERE WERE AUDIBLE gasps in the room from everyone but Brandon and Michael, who were stone-faced and silent. Lorna and Eleanor appeared to be shell-shocked. I couldn't read the expression on Jeanine's face? Relief? Disappointment? A combination of the two?

"What's your real name?" I demanded of the man who had been posing as Brandon Colbeck.

"Adam," he said.

Michael looked surprised. "Adam? I thought your name was Brian Cole."

"Brian Cole is the name Brandon assumed after he left home," Adam said.

"Adam or Brian, the name doesn't matter. You still knew he was an imposter," I said to Michael, gesturing toward Adam. "Before you took him to Light Box Auction Gallery? After? What gave him away? Did you know all along? If so, why did you want to deceive your family?"

Michael's body sagged as if the air had been let out of him. In a way, I suppose it had, not that I felt any sympathy for him. What kind of person lied about something so important?

I focused my attention on Adam next. "And you, capitalizing on a family's grief. How could you?"

He flashed a sardonic smile. "How could I? Simple. I needed money. Michael Westlake was willing to supply it."

"But how did you find him? Find us?" Lorna speaking now, her face tear-stained, her voice barely audible. "How did you know about Brandon?"

"I really did google him, but I looked for Brian Cole. I eventually found him as a Missing Adult on the website for the Ontario Registry of Missing and Unidentified Adults. But trust me when I tell you that my initial intentions were pure."

"Pure? Is that the tale you're going to spin?" Michael hissed out the words. "The only reason you came to me was to demand money in exchange for what you knew."

Adam shrugged. "Admittedly, I'd hoped for a sizeable reward in exchange for the information, but the rest of this unfortunate charade was your idea, Michael."

It was the only plausible explanation, of course, the one I'd anticipated from the moment I'd heard that Brandon's first contact had been with the stepfather he hated.

Lorna stepped forward and slapped her ex-husband's face hard enough to leave an imprint of her hand across his cheek. I'm not an advocate of violence, but I couldn't help but think he deserved that, and more.

Lorna walked across the room, put her back against the wall, and clenched her fists. She glared at Michael with a mixture of loathing and disdain. "All these years," she said, "all these years I blamed you for Brandon leaving, your tough love, installing spyware on his computer, yammering at him night after night after night about finding a job. But I blamed myself, too, because I knew what you were doing, and I stood by and let it happen. Even with all of that, never in my wildest dreams could I have imagined you'd be evil enough to perpetrate this deception. How could you?"

"Yes, Father, how could you?" Jeanine asked. She crossed the room and put her arms around her grandmother. A spark of some emotion—sadness? Anger?—flitted across Eleanor's face before she retreated back into her fog, jaw slack, eyes unfocused. I wondered if she'd ever reenter reality. I didn't think so. Maybe it was better that way.

"I just wanted the constant searching for Brandon to be over," Michael said. "I thought it was, then Calamity Barnstable came knocking, and everyone started believing again. Worse than that, Callie kept digging, never satisfied until she'd found out every one of our secrets, secrets better left in the past. She was tearing this family apart all over again. Don't you see that? The same way Brandon tried to tear this family apart all those years ago. I had to find a way to end it. And then Bri... Adam called and I thought I'd found the answer."

"And Brandon?" Jeanine asked, her voice barely a whisper, a thread of hope running through it. "Is he alive, just not wanting to come home?"

Adam shook his head. "I'm sorry, Jeanine. I'm afraid your brother died many years ago."

FORTY-FOUR

THE ROOM FELL SILENT, each of us processing what Adam had revealed. Brandon was dead. It was one thing to suspect it, quite another to have your suspicions acknowledged.

Jeanine spoke first. "Will you tell us everything you know? We've waited so long to find out what happened to my brother."

Adam considered the request. "Perhaps I should retain a lawyer first."

Lorna shot Jeanine a quick look, and I could almost feel the mental telepathy between mother and daughter. Jeanine gave a barely perceptible nod, stood up, and requested my presence in the kitchen. I followed her, intrigued.

"We don't want to report Adam to the authorities," Jeanine said. "To do so would mean exposing my father's complicity in the matter. That, in turn, would bring unwelcome attention to the rest of our family."

"I understand. I will have to include everything I've learned in my final report, of course, but I have been retained on behalf of your family. Who you share that report with is entirely up to you."

"Thank you."

I followed her back to the living room, once again observing the exchanged glances between mother and daughter. For two women who claimed to have an uncommunicative relationship, they were communicating pretty well.

"Hiring a lawyer won't be necessary," Lorna said, once we'd taken our seats. "We have no intention of pressing charges, and Ms. Barnstable has assured my daughter of her firm's complete discretion. Your impersonation of my son will never leave the confines of this room. If you'd like us to sign something to that effect, it can be arranged."

"Your word is sufficient," Adam said.

"With that assurance, will you tell us what you know?"

"Yes, and not just because it's the right thing to do. Frankly, I'm tired of carrying Brandon on my shoulders. All I ask is that you allow me to tell this my way."

Lorna, Jeanine, and I nodded in unison. Michael slumped deeper into himself, defeated, humbled.

"I first met Brandon in May 2000 on a bus traveling from Winnipeg to Regina," Adam began. "Looking at him was like looking in the mirror, people on the bus thought we were brothers. The trip took the better part of a day, giving us plenty of time to talk. He said he was Brian Cole, from the Toronto area, on the road since March, taking odd jobs in Sudbury, Sault Ste. Marie, Thunder Bay, and Winnipeg. However, he struck me as someone unused to living rough. He was well-groomed, almost too careful with his appearance, even put a paper napkin across his knees before he ate."

"He was fastidious like that, even as a child," Lorna said. "Never could stand to have crumbs fall on his clothes."

"I had the impression he missed his family. He talked about his childhood at his Nana Ellie and Grandpa

Tom's cottage, the things he'd do when he was there. His face lit up when he spoke about his mother and sister. The only time his face clouded over was when I asked about his dad. He said his stepfather despised him and his real father didn't know he existed."

That brought a small gasp from Lorna, but she stayed silent.

"We were halfway to Regina when Brian showed me his tattoo of The Fool, which he'd had completed in Sudbury. He was so proud of that tattoo, and spoke about the artist who'd designed it, Sam Sanchez, and how the two of them had been friends since college." Adam gave a wry smile. "Unfortunately, Brian didn't mention that Sam was short for Samantha. If it hadn't been for that…"

"If it's any consolation, I suspected you were an imposter long before that," Jeanine said. "There were just too many things you didn't remember. I would have insisted on a DNA test eventually."

"It was just a matter of time, wasn't it? Anyway, we stayed together when we arrived in Regina and found ourselves a spot in a shelter. We were there about a week, running out of time for the maximum stay allowed, and Brian was depressed because he couldn't find work. One night he gave me his backpack. He said he'd never find a job lugging it around like a homeless guy. He made me promise to take care of it until he returned. Except he didn't return, not that day, and not the next."

Adam's face had lost all color, and I knew that we were finally arriving at the moment of truth. I leaned forward as his voice sank to a near whisper.

"Two days later, I read about an unidentified man

who had died after stepping into the path of an east-bound train. He died instantly, the death ruled accidental. The police sketch wasn't a particularly good likeness of Brian. There was also a vague description of what remained of a tattoo, but he'd been hit by a train, so…" Adam's voice trailed off, then, "I should have gone to the police, but I was on probation for shoplifting in Toronto and wasn't supposed to leave Ontario. Visions of incarceration stopped me."

I stared at Adam. If he'd come forward all those years ago, Brandon's family would have had a chance to move on with their lives. Instead, his selfishness had cost them the better part of two decades. "You could have phoned in an anonymous tip," I said. "Something that would have given the police something to go on."

"I could have. I didn't. Instead, I searched his backpack. I removed what little money there was, and a folder filled with sketches of tarot cards. I thought I might be able to sell those. I tossed his backpack, clothes and all, in a dumpster, and bought myself a bus ticket to Toronto. I've lived there ever since. I tried to look for Brian's family. I checked the Toronto phone book, but there were a lot of Coles, and I didn't know the name of his parents, or where they lived. I gave up and concentrated on building a proper life for myself. I found a job, an apartment, even a girlfriend for a while, not that we lasted."

"When did you learn that Brian Cole was Brandon Colbeck?" I asked.

"About three months ago there was a story in the *Toronto Sun* about the Ontario Registry of Missing and Unidentified Adults. It reminded me of Brian. Despite what you think about me, I wanted to know who he was. I entered 'Brian Cole' in the Search for Missing Adults database, but nothing came up. I left the name field blank and entered 2000 under 'Year Missing.' That brought up a dozen hits. And there, under the name of Brandon Colbeck, was a photo of Brian Cole. I clicked on the link, found the age-progressed sketches, and to my surprise, found I still looked like him. I read the articles in the *Marketville Post*. I had an idea, call Eleanor Colbeck, Brandon's Nana Ellie. Except the call went badly. I decided it wasn't worth the risk. I've been on the right side of the law for almost twenty years and things were going well. But the company I'd been working for filed for bankruptcy, which meant no severance pay. I had some savings, but Toronto is an expensive city. My girlfriend left. Nothing left to lose, right? I found the website for Westlake & Associates, called Michael and told him I had information about Brandon. I thought he'd offer me a reward. Instead he offered me a proposition."

FORTY-FIVE

Two weeks had passed since my final meeting with the Colbeck-Westlake family. I was sitting with Chantelle in a private room at UnWired, celebrating the end of the case. We were sipping on complimentary glasses of insanely expensive champagne. Apparently you needed to know the proprietor to be allowed access to both the room and the insanely expensive champagne, or that's what Ben Benedetti told me. I don't want to jinx things, but I have a good feeling about that guy.

"Okay, Callie, no more stringing me along," Chantelle said. "When are you going to fill me in on the Brandon Colbeck case?"

"I haven't been stringing you along. I promised Lorna and Jeanine my report would be kept confidential. I've spent the better part of the last few days trying to convince them that, as my business partner, you deserve to know what happened. They finally consented, or should I say relented, this morning. I've informed Levon and Arabella they can discontinue their research on Nestor Sanchez. As for Misty and Shirley, the official statement is the case has been solved, but due to legalities, details can't be released. That would have been my last word to you too, but you kept badgering me."

"I'm very good at badgering," Chantelle said, taking a generous swig of champagne. "Just ask Lance the

Loser or that size zero adolescent he's been dating. Apparently she doesn't care for me calling my ex."

So we were back to Lance the Loser. "She's probably just insecure," I said. "I would be too, if someone who looked like you was my boyfriend's ex."

"Fiancé, not boyfriend. And don't give me that look because I don't want to talk about it. What I want to talk about is how you closed the case."

It took me a good hour to fill her in and I didn't have all the answers. No one knew if Brandon's death had been an accident or suicide, or what had actually motivated Michael to ask Adam to impersonate Brandon. Why was he so concerned about someone digging around in his past? I suspected there were hidden skeletons that went far beyond Brandon's bones, but it wasn't our case any longer. I said as much to Chantelle.

"Michael Westlake *is* a mystery. I haven't been able to find a single trace of him prior to 1986 when he formed his business, but I plan to keep digging."

"No, don't do that. Leith made it very clear that I had to back off the case completely. The last thing we need is a claim of harassment, or worse, a lawsuit filed by Westlake."

"Point made and taken," Chantelle said. "What I don't understand is why Adam finally decided to sell the tattoo flash. I mean, he kept it for almost twenty years."

"Adam never wanted to sell it. It was Michael's idea. The plan was to tell Jeanine that Brandon had sold it to Light Box Auction Gallery, but that he regretted his decision. Michael thought Jeanine would go to the gallery, recognize the flash by Nestor Sanchez as the sketches Brandon had taken with him, and she would think it was really Brandon who had come back. Their plan backfired. What they didn't know was that Jeanine had never actually seen the flash, or that she'd thought that it was 'flesh art,' or porn. What she did know was that her brother treasured those sketches enough to take them with him when he was willing to leave the rest of his life behind. When the man claiming to be Brandon informed her he'd sold it, it made her all the more suspicious."

"Hmmm," Chantelle said. "That leaves one final question."

"Shoot."

"We're talking about two open cases, one person missing, and one unidentified. If the family doesn't want to report Adam's impersonation of Brandon, how will those cases get closed?"

"It took a bit of gentle persuasion, but Adam stepped up and did the right thing, albeit anonymously. He emailed Lucy Daneluk at the Ontario Registry of Missing and Unidentified Adults using something called a VPN—a virtual private network—to conceal his identity." I grinned. "I gather Lucy grilled him thoroughly, but he never wavered from his story, that he traveled and got to know Brandon a.k.a. Brian on the bus from Winnipeg to Regina, that they stayed in a shelter together, looked unsuccessfully for work, and that Brian had been killed by an eastbound train. When she was convinced that Adam was telling the truth, Lucy contacted Detective Aaron Beecham at the Cedar County Police Department."

"What finally convinced her?"

"The longer Adam talked, the more Lucy was reminded of a cold case listed on the Registry, an unidentified young man who died by walking into a train, and in Regina. The two sets of composite sketches and re-constructions only slightly resembled Brandon. Lucy said only once she thought the two cases were connected she could see some similarity."

"Wow. To think that the whole time the answer was on the Registry."

"I think Lucy's beating herself up about it, not that she should. That woman is tireless in her efforts and even the police didn't see the connection. Anyway, Beecham took over and immediately contacted the Regina Police Cold Case Unit."

"The wheels of justice aren't so slow after all."

"Yes and no. Luckily Brandon didn't die that long ago, and it's standard procedure to keep DNA records on file for John and Jane Doe cases. The police are running the necessary DNA tests. Later, Lorna and Jeanine can request the photos of the body taken by the Coroner's Office."

Chantelle shuddered. "Maybe they won't want to see those, but I get your point. Now that they know where and how Brandon died, they can get more information."

"Exactly. That process will take time, but no one doubts that the deceased man in Regina was Brandon, least of all the Colbeck-Westlakes. After the legalities are out of the way, they'll bring Brandon home."

"It's not closure," Chantelle said, "but at least those who loved him finally have some answers."

At least those who loved him finally have some answers. All but one person.

I looked at my phone. Not quite nine o'clock. Trust Few closed at 9:30. If I hurried, I could still make it. I would call Ben later, thank him for the exclusive use of the room, the champagne, explain why I had to leave in the middle of a supposed celebration.

"I'm sorry, Chantelle, I have to go."

"At this hour? Where to?"

"I've been thinking about getting a tattoo."

* * * * *

ACKNOWLEDGMENTS

I AM EXCEEDINGLY grateful for the support of family, friends, and fans as I immersed myself into Callie's world once again. While space precludes me from listing everyone, I would be remiss if I didn't recognize the following individuals:

My three beautiful nieces: Ashley Sametz for helping me create Sam Sanchez and her world of tattoos and tattoo artists; Rebecca Sheluk, MSW, for authenticating the voice and knowledge of Jeanine Westlake; and Leah Patrick for finding the perfect location in Burlington for Light Box Auction Gallery.

Author Cori Lynn Arnold, for her recommendation of keylogger software, and Michael Benedetti for his expertise in the IT world, circa 2000. Any mistakes in technology are mine alone.

Lusia Dion, founder and owner of Ontario's Missing Adults, and the inspiration behind Lucy Daneluk and the Ontario Registry of Missing and Unidentified Adults.

Ti Locke, every author's dream editor, and Victoria Gladwish for her hawk-eyed proofreading.

Last, but not least, my heartfelt thanks to my husband, Mike, for his unfailing love, faith, and encouragement on every step of this writer's journey.

AUTHOR NOTE

THE INSPIRATION FOR *A Fool's Journey* came to me after reading a newspaper article about a young man who had gone missing fifteen years earlier. Despite the family's constant search, no one—not family or friends—has seen or heard from him in the decade and a half since his disappearance.

The story haunted me. I carefully clipped out the article and went to the website referenced: Ontario's Missing Adults. Overwhelmed by the sheer number of unsolved cases featured, I contacted the site's founder and owner, Lusia Dion. Compassionate, completely invested in her mission, and unfailingly helpful in mine, Lusia helped me flesh out Callie's newest case, that of Brandon Colbeck, who disappeared in March 2000. Much later, John Doe of Regina was introduced to the novel.

While the character of Brandon Colbeck is a compilation of several missing persons, John Doe of Regina is based upon an actual case of an unidentified man. Despite this, *A Fool's Journey* is a work of fiction. It is, however, my hope that this novel leads to a positive outcome for locating any missing person, as well as the identification of John Doe of Regina. Visit missing-adults.ca and search for SK-UM-1995-07-00108 (John Doe, Regina) for additional information.